By Eliana West

A Paris Walk
Compass of the Heart
Dreidel Date

EMERALD HEARTS
Four Holly Dates
Summer of Noelle
Falling for Joy
Be the Match

MOCKINGBIRD BRIDGE
The Way Forward
The Way Home
The Way Beyond
A Hidden Heart

A HIDDEN *Heart*

ELIANA WEST

Published by
SECOND PRESS
info@secondpress.com

Second Edition
First Published as *The Way to Hope* by Tule Publishing, May 2022

Trade Paperback ISBN: 9781963011098
Digital ISBN 9781963011081
Digital eBook published August 2024
v. 2.0

For Geoff, and all the unsung heroes who work tirelessly in the fight against hate. Thank you for keeping us safe.

ACKNOWLEDGMENTS

A BIG thank you and congratulations to Lisa Dixon, who took time away studying for her veterinary boards to answer questions, read scenes and talk about her experiences. All creatures great and small will benefit from your kindness, compassion, and care.

To my sisters in words. Carmen Cook, Anne Turner, Aliyah Burke, and Dahlia Rose. You make me so proud to be a part of the writing community and I love you all.

Neva West, for always being an inspiration.

To my husband David, who put up with many tears and bouts of self-doubt. Thank you for always believing in me. To Jackie and Satchel, you inspire me every day, and it is a privilege to be your mom. Thank you.

Chapter One

Rhett Colton reached for the worn handle with every intention of opening the door. He gripped the black iron knob tightly, took one deep breath, and then another before letting go. The cabin that brought happy memories hadn't changed over the years. Large, peeled logs, turned dark golden brown with age, were still solid, holding the little cabin together precisely the way his grandfather had built it. The green metal roof had faded over time, along with the screen door painted to match. Rhett imagined restoring both to their original deep hunter green. The floorboards under his feet were solid, and the willow rocking chairs his grandpa built were still lined up on the porch in front of the large living room window.

Ten pristine acres surrounded the cabin. The centerpiece of the property was a large pond, ringed with cattails and a small cluster of indigo bush at one end. In the evening, the pond's occupants put on a show, leaping out of the water to catch the skeeter bugs and mosquitos that also called the body of water home. A bright blue kingfisher with a brown band across his belly usually joined the fray, swooping in, competing with the fish to fill its belly with insects for dinner. The evening activity assured Rhett that the pond was still fully stocked, and its occupants had been left to their own devices for far too long. He looked at the empty fishing pole rack and wondered if the vintage fishing reels his grandpa had prized were stored somewhere inside. Everything, the pond, the cabin, and its contents, were all his now. It would be up to Rhett to make sure the rods were put back in their proper place.

He bowed his head. This wasn't the reward he'd expected or wanted for what he did.

"You shouldn't have done it," Rhett muttered, backing away from the front door, fingering the hair tie he kept on his wrist, snapping it. The slight sting wasn't enough to distract him from the more significant pain he felt at the loss of his grandfather.

The agency had wanted him to cut his hair before he went on his assignment, but he'd refused. It was one piece of himself he wasn't willing to give up.

His best friend, the only loyal friend he'd had for the last couple of years, whined and pressed himself against Rhett's leg, bringing him out of his musings and back to the present.

He glanced down at his watch. Somehow he'd lost over an hour standing in front of his grandpa's cabin.

"Not today, Rebel," Rhett said.

He'd been saying that just about every day for months now. An invisible wall of regret and guilt kept Rhett from opening the door and claiming what was rightfully his. Rhett's grandpa left him everything he owned. He knew what his grandpa was trying to do with his gift. It was his way of saying he was sorry.

Pictures flashed through his mind like flipping through pages of a photo album while Rhett walked down to the pond. He sat down on the large cypress log at the water's edge. How many hours had he spent here sitting next to his grandpa with a pole in the water?

Rhett's father would comment on how he and his grandpa were like peas in a pod. Rhett had shared a bond with him that was unbreakable. They understood each other. Of all his cousins, he was the one his grandpa spent the most time with. He hadn't always led a good life, but when George Colton took his last breath, he left this earth having done everything he could to make amends and be worthy of his family and friends.

Rhett wanted to make sure his grandpa's legacy would be one of honor. But that meant destroying his reputation. His parents no longer looked at him with parental pride. Now his father looked at him with pity and sorrow in his eyes. It was almost worse than the anger and disappointment.

"I've got to go away for a while," Rhett said, digging his fingers into Rebel's soft fur. I've got a little more business to do, and then we can get back to normal, whatever that is." Now that his assignment with the FBI was over, all Rhett wanted was to rebuild the life he had before. Only that wasn't turning out to be as easy as he thought it would be. Rebel nudged his hand in a not-so-subtle reminder for Rhett to keep petting him. He knelt down and gently stroked the fur around the dog's muzzle. "You're going to stay with Jasmine Owens. Jacob says Dr. Owens is a good person, and she's a vet, so I know she'll take good care of you. We have to trust people again at some point, don't we? She's doing us a big favor, so be on your best behavior, okay?" Rebel gave him a wet kiss. "It's just a couple of weeks while I go to DC. We can do this."

Rebel rested his paw on Rhett's knee. He needed Rebel's reassurance more than the dog needed him. Rebel was the one thing that kept him from losing his humanity, his hope. He'd saved Rebel, but it turned out that Rebel had saved him too.

Remembering the first time he saw the scared German shepherd mix still made his stomach clench and his heart race. Rebel was just a puppy and about to be thrown into a dogfighting ring as bait. Rhett almost blew his cover before his assignment had gotten off the ground. He had to think quickly when he snatched the small ball of fur from his cousin's arms and yelled for him to stop. Thinking quickly, he came up with a story about how he needed a guard dog and threw in a hundred dollars. Money, he said. He was going to bet on the fight to keep him. He clutched the shivering body covered in tan and black fur close to his chest. The puppy looked up at him with enormous amber eyes and then peed all over him. Everyone in the room wanted to know what he was going to name him. He had to pick something suitable for the person he was pretending to be, so he chose Rebel.

"It's almost over. Two more weeks. We can do that, can't we, boy?" he asked, stroking Rebel's back.

He received a wet kiss for his reassurance.

Fourteen days would be easy compared to the two years he'd spent undercover with a White supremacist group. He'd be on leave when he came back from Washington. Three months, time to decide if he wanted to continue with the FBI or forge an alternative path. The only problem was, he couldn't figure out what that would be.

A flash of dark gray caught his eye, and he looked over at the pickup truck pulling up to the cabin with dread. He took in the scenery around him one more time before he slowly got up. His future looked like the murky blue waters of the pond when he turned and walked away.

Jacob Winters, the man who had been his handler while he was undercover, leaned against the hood of his truck, emblazoned with Winters Hardware on the driver's side door in cream against the gray paint.

Jacob had come to Colton for the assignment and stayed for love and the community that embraced him.

"Thanks for doing this," Rhett said, shaking Jacob's hand.

"It's the least I can do."

"Let me just grab my pack and Rebel's stuff from the porch, and we can go."

He held his hand up, and Rebel sat while he jogged back to the cabin and grabbed his stuff.

Jacob looked down at Rebel. "He could have served as an MPC with my unit with the Schutzhund training you've given him."

Rhett had used the training method for police dogs, emphasizing tracking, obedience, and protection skills. He'd done it in part to keep up the story that he wanted a guard dog and in part to protect both of them. Rebel would defend Rhett with his life, and Rhett would do the same for him. They were a team, and he wasn't sure if he could function without his best friend at his side.

"Thanks." He reached down and scratched Rebel between the ears. "I thought about going overseas when this was all over, but they wouldn't take Rebel as a multi-purpose canine since I'm not a certified trainer. He'd be fine if he was with me, but—" Rhett pressed his lips together, shaking his head.

"The Army won't guarantee that," Jacob finished.

Rebel had already given him so much comfort. He couldn't ask his best friend to risk his life as well.

With the truck loaded, Rhett took one last look at the cabin as they drove away. The closer he got to town, the more uncomfortable Rhett became. He was thankful Jacob didn't attempt too much small talk on the drive. Jacob Winters had served him well as his handler, and Rhett was grateful that he let him do his job without a lot of interference. They were alike in a lot of ways. They observed before they acted and didn't waste words. But Jacob had softened in the last year. He had a lightness… happiness around him that Rhett envied. His marriage and his son's birth transformed him. Rhett wondered what it would take for him to find the happiness Jacob had.

It had become a habit to hunch his shoulders and duck his head when he was in town. He bowed his head, letting his hair fall forward to hide his face. Even then, people stopped and some pointed when they drove by.

Rhett felt split in two. Half the folks in Colton saw him as a hero who helped save the mayor when the group he was embedded with hatched a plan to kidnap her. The other half had a hard time believing he wasn't really what he'd been pretending to be. It had been easier to avoid both groups and keep to himself since his real identity was revealed. In a strange way, it was fitting. Colton was a town of halves. Half White, half Black, the citizens that lived in the Mississippi Delta town reflected two sides of history, descendants of the enslaved and descendants of their owners. Rhett looked at the gazebo, the centerpiece of Colton's town square, a witness to history for over six generations, and wondered if he would ever find the peace and happiness that folklore promised would come to any couple that married under its canopy.

It had worked for Jacob. His former handler was happier than he'd ever known him to be.

Jacob pulled up to the new vet clinic that had just opened a few weeks ago. Originally built as a cigar factory in the early 1900s, the brick two-story building became a dental office and then was abandoned for many years. Now the building sat newly restored, with Colton Animal Clinic written on the window with vintage script in a bright emerald green outlined in white and silver.

He glanced at Rebel sitting next to him. "What do you think, boy, can you hang out here for a little while?"

"I've known Jasmine Owens since she was in high school," Jacob said. "The Owens family are good people. I promise Jasmine will take good care of Rebel."

Rhett dipped his head in agreement. Everyone in town was happy to welcome sheriff Isiah Owens's sister and another new business to the town's restoration efforts.

The new sheriff made a good impression, and Rhett liked and respected him. Sheriff Owens was doing a good job bringing order back to the area after years of the town being run by a corrupt sheriff and town council. Colton, Mississippi, had a brighter future now with new leadership, including the mayor, Jacob's wife, Mae. Rhett closed his eyes and tried to breathe in air that was suddenly difficult to find. His undercover work had ended the night the group he was with kidnapped Mae. Rhett had kept any harm from coming to her, but for those horrible hours on the Fourth of July, while everyone else was celebrating the nation's birthday, he was in the middle of a fight, trying to keep Colton's mayor from being killed.

"Rhett!" Jacob gave him a gentle shake. "You okay?"

He opened his eyes. How long had he had them closed?

"Yeah, I'm fine I was just—"

"Remembering?"

Rhett exhaled.

"That night haunts us all," Jacob said quietly.

"How is Mae doing? Is she still having nightmares?"

"She's doing well. She hasn't had a nightmare in a few weeks now."

Rhett shook his head. "She shouldn't have had them in the first place."

"It's not your fault, Rhett. You've got to lay that burden down."

"I could have stopped the kidnapping before it happened."

"You were trying to make sure you had a bulletproof case against those assholes. You wanted to have as much evidence as possible. I signed off on it too. This isn't all on you, Rhett."

It was easier to nod in agreement than keep arguing, even though Jacob was wrong. Rhett was the one undercover. It was his assignment and his fault things went too far. Rhett opened the door, and Rebel jumped out behind him.

"Come on, let me introduce you to Jasmine," Jacob said.

Rhett crouched down and held Rebel's face. "You be a good boy for Ms. Owens, ya hear? You show her you know how to mind your manners."

Rebel flicked his ears forward and cocked his head.

Rhett swallowed, trying to get past the lump that formed in his throat. Rebel was his best friend and confidant, and they hadn't spent time apart since the day he first held him.

He took a deep breath and walked into the clinic. Rhett almost tripped over his own feet when he laid eyes on Dr. Owens for the first time. Her dark, tightly curled hair was pulled up on top of her head in a twisty knot. She looked up at him with a wide-open smile that was reflected in her dark eyes. The oversized scrubs she wore must have been at least two sizes too big for her. They disguised her body, but he could see her well-toned warm brown arms under the short sleeves of her top. She had to be strong, working with animals all day.

She came toward him with her hand outstretched, and when it slid into his, it was a key that slid into a lock, opening his heart for the first time in a very long time. She must have felt the spark that arced between them too, because her eyes widened for a fraction of a second before he let her hand go.

He could see her lips moving, but he didn't register what she was saying right away. His breath caught. His first instinct was to turn around and leave, to get as far away from Dr. Owens's kind eyes and inviting smile as possible. She was the first person who didn't look at him with pity in their eyes since his assignment ended.

"Can you repeat that?" he murmured when he realized she was looking at him expectantly.

"I was asking how long you've had Rebel?"

"Two years, ma'am. I mean, Doctor."

She smiled. "Just call me Jasmine."

"I appreciate you doing this for me. I hope having Rebel won't be an added burden with your work."

Jasmine reached down and scratched Rebel between the ears. "Not at all. It will be nice to have a roommate for a while. I have an apartment above the clinic, so it will be easy to check on him throughout the day."

"I promise he won't chew up the furniture or anything like that."

"I'm sure he won't. We're going to get along just fine."

Rebel looked up at Jasmine, already smitten with his new friend. Rhett couldn't blame him. Jasmine Owens was someone he already knew he wanted to get to know better. Romance and a life undercover didn't mesh. The sudden desire to get to know this woman standing before him took him by surprise. If life were different, if he was any other man, he would have asked her out, but that wasn't possible. Rhett couldn't ask that from anyone, and especially not this woman. What woman would want him with his scars, especially a Black woman?

She was smiling at him. The light had shifted, and he noticed the flecks of green and gold in her brown eyes. They were kind eyes, but there was just a tinge of something in them that let him know that she'd experienced sorrow on some level. It made him want to miss his flight, stay, and talk to her. It had been a long time since he wanted to talk to anyone. He was wrong for her, but that didn't stop him from returning her smile and wondering, *What if?*

Chapter Two

Jasmine Owens eyed the man with long, blond, shaggy hair as he crouched down, talking to his dog next to Jacob's truck. It was sweet the way he held the dog's face in his hands while he talked to him. It was clear man and animal shared a close bond.

She knew who Rhett Colton was and had seen him from a distance a few times, always with his head down, folded in on himself, sending a clear signal he wanted to be left alone. Even though people in town knew Rhett had been undercover pretending to be a White supremacist, she'd seen more than one person move out of his way when he walked down the street, avoiding the man and his canine companion, who was always at his side.

Her brother had nothing but good things to say about Rhett. Isiah was an excellent judge of character. If he liked Rhett, Jasmine knew she would too.

Jacob Winters came into her clinic while Rhett was still outside with his dog. "I appreciate you doing this for me, Jasmine," he said. "Rhett's been worried about leaving Rebel. Having a veterinarian taking care of Rebel is a big relief for him. You came to Colton at just the right time."

Jasmine turned to her brother's best friend. Over the years, she'd seen rare glimpses of Jacob's warm, loving side. Coming to Colton had transformed him. Now he was a husband and father and settled into small-town life, happier than she'd ever seen him.

"You know I'd never turn you down. You've done so much to help me get settled in. I'm happy to return the favor."

Her brother's friends, Jacob Winters and Dax Ellis, and their wives had bent over backward to welcome her to Colton and help her get her clinic set up. Yes, they could be a little overprotective and overbearing sometimes, but they were like family and a big part of why Jasmine wanted to open her clinic in Colton. She would always have help and support if she needed it. All she had to do was ask.

Jacob looked at Rhett and back at Jasmine. "Listen, I know you already know this, but some folks have a hard time believing Rhett didn't buy into any of that crap he had to listen to and live with. He's not a racist. You should know...." Jacob's jaw ticked. "Rhett's had a rough couple of years, and it's taken a toll on him. He's not a warm and friendly guy, so don't take his gruffness personally. After what he's been through, he doesn't... he's not very trusting, but underneath his standoffish attitude is a good man."

Jasmine studied the man through the window. She couldn't imagine what Rhett had to endure, spending so much time undercover with a White supremacist group. Her brother had been part of the raid on the compound where they had taken Jacob's wife after group members kidnapped her. If it hadn't been for Rhett, they could have killed Mae. Jasmine shuddered, remembering her brother's account of what happened that night.

The door opened, and Rhett walked in with his dog at his side. He wasn't as tall as Jacob or her brother, just a few inches taller than her five foot seven inches. The jeans and sweater he wore hung off his lean frame. Jasmine suspected it wasn't because he purchased them too large, the way she preferred to wear her own clothes. The combination of his long blond hair and the angle of his head made it difficult to get a good look at his face.

She held her hand out to him, and when he grasped it, a bolt of electricity arced between them. He looked up, and his eyes met hers. They were bright blue and reminded her of the pretty little bird with blue feathers and a brown band around its neck that liked to dance on her windowsill.

The German shepherd mix waited at his owner's side, his large amber eyes watching her. There was no wariness, just an open curiosity. He was a beautiful animal with a healthy golden tan and black fur coat.

Rhett introduced himself. His voice settled over her with a slow, deep drawl that brought to mind an image of the wildflower honey she'd bought at the farmer's market.

Jasmine crouched down and held out her hand with her fingers curled under. "You must be Rebel."

The dog cocked his head and studied her for a moment before he lifted his paw. She turned her hand over and gave it a shake.

"You're a proper gentleman, aren't you?" she said. She asked Rhett how long he'd had Rebel, and he just stared at her.

He gave her a small smile when she asked again. The way he called her "ma'am" and then corrected himself was endearing. She didn't see the gruff man that Jacob described.

"Thank you for taking Rebel, ma'am."

"I'll take good care of him."

Rhett's head jerked up, and she saw his eyes for the first time. The sadness in his gaze made her breath catch. His eyes searched hers for a minute, and then he tipped his head, his expression morphing into something that looked like regret to her.

Jacob came forward and clapped Rhett on the shoulder. "I'll check in on him too."

"If anything comes up or if there's any problem, you have to let me know. I'll be away for two weeks unless something comes up."

The way he said it, almost pleading, Jasmine's heart went out to him. He didn't want to leave his best friend.

"It's Jasmine, remember? And I promise you, Rebel and I are going to get along just fine. I would never abandon an animal that needed help."

As if he understood what she said, Rebel left Rhett's side and came over to her, pressing his body against her legs. She reached down and patted the dog with a smile, appreciating the canine version of a hug.

Rhett watched them for a moment and then pulled out an envelope from his back pocket. "Here's all his papers. He's caught up on all his shots and stuff. I've got his food and water bowl and some other things in the truck." He pivoted on his heel and walked out.

"This isn't easy for him," Jacob said with a heavy sigh.

Jasmine watched Rhett's hunched figure. "I… he doesn't look good."

"No, he doesn't."

"Is there anything I can do for him?" she asked.

Jacob pointed to Rebel. "You're doing it."

Rhett came back in with a bag of dog food over one shoulder and a bowl and leash in his hand. Jasmine was pleased to see that Rebel was getting a high-quality kibble. Rhett took good care of his dog, and that said a lot about what kind of person he was.

"Rebel likes broccoli and carrots too," Rhett said.

Jasmine went over to the reception desk, pulled out a clipboard with a new patient intake form, and held it out to Rhett.

"You can put down anything you'd like me to know here along with his medical records."

He waved off the clipboard. "Everything's in the envelope I gave you."

"Oh, okay."

Jacob glanced at his watch. "We've got to get going, or you'll miss your flight."

"Yeah, I just need a minute with Rebel," he said.

Jasmine caught the gruff note in his voice.

"Jacob, why don't you and I wait outside while Rhett says goodbye?" she suggested.

Jacob nodded, and they left the two of them, heading outside to stand on the sidewalk.

"I don't know what I was expecting, but I didn't think he'd be so… hurt," Jasmine said, looking through the clinic window to where Rhett knelt inside on the floor with Rebel.

She recognized the look she'd seen in Rhett's eyes. It was the same one she'd seen on her boyfriend Darren's face. Jasmine blinked back a wave of tears that took her by surprise. That was something she was learning about grief. It had its own timeline. Instead of trying to control it, you needed to be open to accepting the moment for what it was. Jasmine let the memory wash over her of the morning she'd received the phone call telling her she wouldn't see Darren in class that day. She took a few breaths, allowing the moment to pass, and then put her heartache away when Rhett came out and jerked his head toward Jacob's truck.

"Let's go," he growled. He jumped into the truck without another word, his face pinched and drawn.

"I'll check in on you later," Jacob said with a worried look in Rhett's direction.

She waved as they pulled away, but Rhett didn't look up.

Rebel was lying on the floor, his head between his paws. His ears flicked forward, and he raised his head when she came in.

"Come on, Rebel. Let's look at what's in that envelope your dad left behind."

Rebel got up and trotted to her side. Jasmine pulled the envelope Rhett gave her out of her pocket and sat down on the bench Jacob had built for her along one wall in the waiting room. Everyone in town had pitched in one way or another to help get her place ready. Jacob built the cabinets and long countertop that served as the reception desk. He crafted the benches for the waiting room and the kitchen cabinets for her apartment upstairs. Taylor Colton and his team helped with the design details, using her project for an episode of his hit TV show *Colton Reborn.* With his help, the space combined the rustic vintage elements that already existed in the original building with modern touches Jasmine needed to make the space practical. There were two exam rooms, a surgical room, and another room for X-rays. Separate kennel space for dogs and cats were in the back. It wasn't a big clinic, but she had everything she needed for a small rural practice. Jasmine leaned against the reclaimed wood accent wall, admiring the way the blue and green accents in the upholstery on the cushions highlighted the warm tones in the wood. It was a perfect balance, a practical clinical office that still felt warm and inviting.

She patted the bench, inviting Rebel to come up and join her. He didn't hesitate. Jumping up, he lay down next to her side and rested his head on her thigh.

Pulling the sheafs of paper out of the envelope Rhett left behind, she gave Rebel's medical records a glance, noting that he'd received his shots and checkups by a vet in Memphis, a two-hour drive away. Hopefully, Rhett would transfer him into her care so he wouldn't have to make such a long trip in the future. Rebel was up-to-date on all his vaccinations, and he'd received his shots on time and was neutered. She set his medical records aside and unfolded a handwritten note paper-clipped to the top of the other paperwork.

Rhett's neat and even handwriting filled the page.

Dr. Owens,

Thank you for taking care of Rebel for me. Rebel came into my life when I didn't know how much I would need a friend. I owe him my life. This is the first time I've ever been away from him.

Rebel has mastered all the basic commands, as well as shake, crawl, and leap.

Jasmine stroked Rebel's head. "You're a very well-trained boy, aren't you?"

Rebel is not a barker and will not bite unless I order him to. He's good around other animals, he doesn't chase cats or anything like that. Some people are afraid when they see him, but he would never hurt anyone on purpose. He will always protect the people he loves.

"Of course you will," she said.

Knowing the sacrifice he'd made, Jasmine couldn't help wondering if Rhett realized he could have been writing about himself.

Dr. Owens, you are already kind enough to take in Rebel for me. I don't have the right to ask you for anything else, but if you can, will you send me a picture every once in a while? And, if you don't mind, maybe I can call or text and check in. It would help make the hard days ahead pass easier.

Jasmine ran her hand over the phone number Rhett printed at the bottom of the page. She looked down at Rebel with a smile.

"Let's send a picture to your dad."

Chapter Three

JACOB PULLED into the drop-off lane at the airport in Jackson. Rhett's FBI counterpart, Dan Nguyen, waved from where he was waiting for them with his suitcase at his side. They would both be testifying before Congress on extremist groups within the United States. Rhett would also spend the next few weeks training new agents who would work undercover within some other groups.

Jacob got out and went to shake Dan's hand while Rhett grabbed his pack from the back. His worn backpack looked even more tattered next to Dan's pristine black rolling bag. They couldn't be more different. Dan was precise, down to his perfectly pressed shirt and close-cropped hair. Rhett wasn't sure of the last time he'd washed the jeans he wore. Despite their differences, they worked well together, and Rhett respected his fellow agent. More importantly, Dan was part of a very small group of people he trusted.

Rhett snapped the hair tie on his wrist. "You ready?" he asked Dan, jerking his head toward the sliding doors. The sooner he got away, the less he'd be tempted to turn around, pick up Rebel, and disappear.

"You let me know if you need anything, okay?" Jacob clapped his hand on Rhett's shoulder.

"You're not my handler anymore."

"No, but I am your friend."

Rhett felt like a heel. Jacob was trying to be a good friend. Just because he wasn't in the mood to have people or friends around him didn't mean he couldn't acknowledge Jacob's gesture.

"Thanks. I don't want you to think I don't appreciate everything you've done for me. Setting it up for Rebel to stay with Dr. Owens takes an enormous weight off my shoulders. The next two weeks are going to be hard enough as it is. Knowing Rebel will be in good hands will make it easier."

"You can trust Jasmine."

Rhett nodded. Trust wasn't something that came easily to him, especially after the last few years, when vile people fueled by hate surrounded him. Sometimes it was hard to remember there were good people in the world. But he knew with absolute certainty that Jacob was right. Even though he'd just met her, Rhett knew in his heart he could trust Jasmine.

He shook Jacob's hand and headed into the airport. The security lines were thankfully short, and he and Dan were buckled into their seats in less than half an hour. Rhett closed his eyes and pretended to sleep to avoid having to talk. There would be enough talking in the days to come.

Eyes closed, he replayed his encounter with Jasmine Owens. He liked the way her dusky-pink lips curved into a smile, revealing dimples on her cheeks. Rebel was an excellent judge of character. His unease about leaving the only family he had left with a complete stranger evaporated when he saw the way Rebel responded to her. Coupled with his own response, he knew Rebel would be okay. Rhett wondered if she'd read the letter he wrote yet. Now that he'd met the woman taking care of Rebel, he hoped she would honor his request and send him pictures. *Hope*. It was something he hadn't felt a lot of for a long time.

"Nervous flyer?" Dan asked, looking down at where Rhett fingered the elastic around his wrist.

Rhett looked down. He hadn't realized what he was doing.

"Not really, I was just… thinking."

"Anything in particular?"

"It's hard not to replay everything, getting ready for this testimony," he said.

"I never imagined the Fourth of July would be a holiday that gave me nightmares," Dan admitted.

Rhett frowned. "You've been having nightmares?"

Who hadn't been affected by the events that took place that night? If he'd done more, could he have avoided all this?

"Just a couple, right after that night." Dan exhaled. "If it hadn't been for you getting the coordinates to us, it could have been so much worse."

Rhett didn't have a response. He'd had too many nightmares himself about what could have happened if backup hadn't arrived in time.

"Sir, what would you like to drink?" The beverage service interrupted their conversation and allowed Rhett to switch to safer topics for the rest of the flight.

The plane began its descent into the nation's capital, and Rhett felt the familiar weight of responsibility settle into his bones. He turned his phone on while they were taxiing toward the gate and frowned when he saw the text notification from Jasmine. Worry washed over him as he opened the message, only to chuckle a second later.

It was a picture of Rebel with Jasmine. His tongue was hanging out in a canine version of a big loopy grin. Jasmine was crouched down next to him with her arm around him and her tongue stuck out, mimicking Rebel's.

"What's so funny?" Dan asked.

Rhett turned his phone around to show him the picture.

"Aww, that's adorable. I'm glad it worked out for Dr. Owens to have her practice open just in time for her to take Rebel for you."

Dan's phone dinged, and he looked at his message, his face breaking into a big smile.

"Anything you want to share?" Rhett asked with a raised eyebrow.

"Just a message from Reid."

Reid Ellis was another former resident of Colton who'd found his way home, just like his brother Dax. He'd given up his job as a high-profile prosecutor in Chicago and was working in the county prosecutor's office, but his genuine passion was working with Primus Wallace, the owner of the Buckthorn, learning to make whiskey alongside the proprietor of the legendary juke joint. Reid had been the reason Dan continued to spend time in Colton after their case ended. They both checked in on Rhett, offering their support while he rebuilt his life.

Rebuilding friendships or forging new ones was something Rhett was struggling with. It was disappointing to discover how many of his old friends didn't question his association with people who espoused hateful beliefs, and some exposed their own affiliations with other hate groups. The discovery left Rhett questioning his own judgment. He'd been very careful about who he let into his life since then. Dan and Reid were two of a small circle of people he considered friends now. Rhett appreciated their kindness, but he wouldn't burden them with his issues.

"You two really clicked," he observed.

Dan dropped his head back against the headrest with a tender look on his face. "I wasn't looking for a relationship, especially with my career and the life I have right now, but...." He shook his head with a slight smile. "When you find someone that you… love, well"—he spread his hands wide—"I'm not going to risk losing a lifetime of happiness."

Rhett's eyebrows shot up. "Wow, I didn't know things were that serious between the two of you."

"I'm thinking of moving to Colton and making the commute to Jackson."

"That's great. I'm happy for you both."

Dan opened his mouth to speak and stopped before he finally said, "You know, you can find some happiness too."

"I'm not interested in having a relationship right now."

Rhett jumped out of his seat joining the crush of their fellow passengers preparing to deplane, to avoid continuing the conversation. By the time they retrieved Dan's bag from baggage claim and got a ride into their hotel in the city, Rhett was ready to crawl out of his skin. There was too much concrete and too many people around for his liking.

Rhett threw his pack in the chair in the corner of his hotel room and sank down on the edge of the bed, eyeing it for a minute before he got back up again. He didn't own a suit, but he should unpack the last decent pair of slacks, blazer, and dress shirt he owned. He made quick work of hanging up the clothes he'd be wearing for his testimony and shoved everything else in a drawer.

A stiff wind blew off the Potomac, and the sun sat low in the pale blue-gray sky. This far north, spring's grip was tenuous, and Rhett wasn't interested in fighting the wintery chill just to wander aimlessly around the city. He checked the time. Dan had invited him to come out for dinner with a few other agents. He wasn't one for socializing on a good day, and he'd have to spend enough time with people in the coming weeks. Rhett had declined Dan's offer, clinging to his solitude for as long as he could.

Rhett paced the hotel room, glancing at the phone he'd tossed on the bed. After a few minutes, he kicked off his boots, pulled his hair into a haphazard knot on his head, and positioned himself so that he was sitting up against the headboard. Opening his phone to the picture that Jasmine had sent brought another smile to his face. Fingers moving quickly over the keyboard, he sent a text thanking her. His phone vibrated with a request for a video chat a second later.

Looking down at the name with surprise, Rhett quickly sat up and huffed out a laugh when Rebel's face filled the screen.

"Hey, buddy. You look like you're doin' just fine," Rhett said.

Rebel barked and put his paw up as if he were waving hello. The camera became shaky for a moment. Rhett drew in a sharp breath when Jasmine's face filled the screen.

Her eyes were shining with happiness. Tendrils of hair worked their way loose from her topknot, framing her face. He hadn't noticed the smattering of tiny freckles that dusted over her nose before, and now he couldn't stop looking at them, wanting to reach out and trace their path with his fingers.

"Hi. Rebel wanted to make sure you arrived safely," she said.

Rhett returned her smile. It was a strange feeling. Those particular muscles in his face had gone unused for far too long. "Yep, all settled in."

An awkward silence followed while they just smiled at each other. Rebel came back into the picture, nudging Jasmine's shoulder with his nose.

Jasmine started stroking Rebel's back as she spoke. "Thank you for the letter that you left. I wanted to reassure you Rebel will be okay. I will treat him as if he were my own."

Rhett nodded, swallowing past the lump that formed in his throat. "Appreciate that. I didn't think to ask, do you have any pets? Like I said in my letter, Rebel is good with animals. He's never chased a cat or barked at another dog… he's really well-behaved."

"Rebel is just fine. You don't have to worry. I can already tell that he's going to be a great helper around here." Jasmine's smile faded. "I don't have any pets right now. I lost my Daisy before I left Ohio."

"Was Daisy a dog or a cat?"

Jasmine's smile returned. "A corn snake."

She chuckled when Rhett shuddered. "I guess that means you don't like snakes."

"No, ma'am," he replied, making a face.

"I got Daisy for my tenth birthday. She was my first real pet. Learning how to take care of her is what got me interested in veterinary medicine."

"Are you going to get another one?"

Jasmine cocked her head. "I don't think so. Daisy was a wonderful pet, but I think I'd like a dog when the time is right."

Rebel pushed his nose into the camera again. Rhett exhaled, releasing some of the tension from the trip. "Thanks for calling. I… would it be okay if we did this again?"

"Of course. You've got my number. Call anytime you want to see Rebel."

Or you. He'd never been much of a talker, but he wanted to keep talking to Jasmine.

He was trying to think of a way to keep the conversation going when there was a noise in the background. Jasmine looked over her shoulder. "It looks like I've got a client. Check in again soon, okay?"

"Yeah, sure."

The screen went dark, and Rhett's mood darkened along with it. Finding Jasmine attractive was unexpected. Rhett knew when he took the undercover assignment there would be sacrifices. He thought he could handle it, but since his assignment ended, he was struggling to make peace with the things he'd been compelled to do and the people he'd hurt along the way. There was no way he could burden Jasmine with his scars.

Another message came through on Rhett's phone. Rebel was up on his hind legs, his paws on the exam table, nose to nose with a tiny kitten. The message said *I told you he'd be a great helper*.

Rhett's phone vibrated with an incoming call. He frowned and stared at the number he'd been avoiding calls from for months now.

Just like he couldn't bring himself to go in his grandpa's cabin, Rhett hadn't been able to respond to his parents when they reached out to him. They'd apologized over and over for the way they'd treated him when they thought he was something that he wasn't—a racist. His parents were liberals who took pride in their memberships in organizations that fought for racial justice, like the Southern Poverty Law Center. Thinking their son believed in everything they abhorred had devastated them. When they learned the truth, they were just as crushed. That made it worse. He couldn't stand the pity and sadness in their eyes every time he saw them, so he'd started making up excuses for not spending time with them or seeing them at Thanksgiving and Christmas.

Even before his assignment, spending the holidays with his parents was awkward. His parents were working to make up for being absent in his life when he was growing up. They got married young and had a child before they were ready to settle down. They weren't ready to give up their carefree lifestyle and hanging out with friends for the responsibilities of parenting, leaving his grandpa to raise him. By the time they settled down and realized they wanted a relationship with Rhett, he'd moved on. His grandpa was the only family he wanted, and in Rhett's mind, his grandpa would live forever. He'd counted on his grandpa to be there for him when his assignment was over. Grandpa was the only person he knew he could burden with his troubles.

Rhett rubbed his chest, trying to ease the tightness that wouldn't go away. He'd been arrogant, thinking he could pick up his old life and things would be like they were before. Some veterans in the agency had tried to warn him, but he was young and cocky and thought he was tougher or better than they were. Instead, he was drifting. No matter how hard he tried, he couldn't seem to find his footing. Yes, there were people in his life who cared about him, people who wanted to help him, but he didn't feel like he was worthy after the lies he'd told, no matter how noble his intentions were.

His life was too messy right now, and as much as he wanted to figure it out before he let anyone in, he wouldn't burden anyone with his problems. They were his, and it was his job to figure out what he wanted to do next. But he couldn't stop thinking about calling Jasmine again, wanting to see her smile, hear her laughter that was filled with so much hope and happiness.

He put his phone aside. He would allow himself one call a day. It was all the temptation he could afford.

CHAPTER FOUR

THE COLTON Farmer's Market was in full swing on Saturday morning. Spring had arrived with a bright blue cloudless sky and warm air scented with hyacinth. People were happy to be out and about, mingling in the park. Some were there to shop, and others were out looking for an opportunity to catch up with friends and gossip. Jasmine watched the scene play out from the table she'd set up with flyers for a free spay and neuter clinic she planned for next month. Several students from the veterinary assistant program at the trade school in Greenwood had volunteered to help with the event. Jasmine hoped it would bring in new clients and get the word out in the community about the clinic.

The park buzzed with activity as people wandered through tables filled with fresh produce, flowers, and crafts. There was a line at the booth where Opal, Pearl, and Ruby, the three sisters known as the Jewels, sold cordials and syrups.

Ruby waved at her and called out, "Don't you worry, honey. I put aside a bottle of elderberry syrup for you."

"Thank you, Ms. Ruby," Jasmine shouted back.

Jacob was pushing his son, Dante, in his stroller with his wife, Mae, at his side, headed in her direction. Their progress was slow, as everyone wanted to shake Mae's hand or ask a question. The community appreciated and respected their mayor, and there was no doubt in Jasmine's mind that Mae would serve another term.

When they finally reached her table, Mae pulled Jasmine into a hug.

"I just got the most amazing yarn the other day. I've been waiting forever for it to get here," Mae exclaimed. "And the colors." Mae swooned, putting her hand over her heart. "I need you to help me decide what I'm going to make with it at knitting club on Tuesday."

"It didn't take forever," Jacob said, chuckling. "It was just two weeks."

Mae came over and stepped between Jacob and the stroller. She put her hand on his cheek and said in a low, sexy voice, "Two weeks can seem like forever when you're waiting for something you really want."

Jacob growled low in his throat and captured Mae's lips in a searing kiss.

"Watch out, you two. That's how babies get made," someone in the crowd called out with a laugh.

Jacob let his wife go. The two exchanged a look that touched Jasmine's heart. No one she'd ever been with looked at her that way. She thought about the video chat with Rhett the night before. There were moments when she thought she caught a look of… interest or heat in his eyes. It was hard to tell. Or maybe she didn't want to be wrong and end up disappointed.

"Who is making you smile and blush like that?" Jacob asked.

Jasmine suddenly became very interested in straightening the flyers on her table.

"Nothing," she said.

Mae elbowed her husband in the ribs. "Stop it. You're embarrassing her."

"Well, I'm not the one who started it," Jacob shot back with a heated look in his eyes.

Jasmine felt a slight pinch of jealousy that surprised her. Romance wasn't on her list of reasons why she had wanted to move to Colton, but dating again was part of her recovery from past disappointments.

Mae opened her mouth to argue and stopped when Dante started to cry.

"Hey, little man. What's wrong?" Mae crooned, taking him out of the stroller.

"Is it his diaper? Is he hungry? What's wrong?" Jacob instantly went on high alert.

Mae's father, Joseph Colton, came toward them with his arms outstretched. "Nothing's wrong that his grandpa can't fix."

He took Dante from Mae's arms and the baby quieted, snuggling into his grandpa's chest.

Jacob looked at Joseph in awe. "I don't know how he does it. Every damn time."

Joseph laughed. "I'm not giving away any of my grandpa secrets."

"Dad, have you met Jasmine Owens yet?" Mae asked.

Joseph held out his free hand and shook Jasmine's. "Welcome to Colton. I've been meaning to come by and say hello. It's been at least twenty years since we've had a vet in this community. We're happy to have you here."

"Thank you," Jasmine said.

"You two enjoy the market. I'll take care of Dante for a while," Joseph said to Jacob and Mae.

"Thanks, Dad," Mae said, giving her father a peck on the cheek.

Joseph waved, heading through the park, holding his grandson with one arm and pushing the stroller with the other.

"Your dad could be the poster child for proud grandpas." Jasmine laughed.

"You should see her mother," Jacob said. "How are things going with Rebel?"

Jacob knelt down and patted his leg. Rebel lifted his head and yawned, slowly getting up from where he'd been napping under the table.

"Have you heard from Rhett?" Jacob asked.

"He's been calling to check in on Rebel." Jasmine offered no more details. Jacob was just as overprotective as her big brother, and the last thing she wanted was an interrogation into her personal life.

"Let us know if there's anything we can do to help," Mae said.

"Thanks, I will."

Mae threaded her hand through Jacob's arm and led him over to the next booth. Jasmine blew out a sigh of relief and a silent thanks to Mae for leading Jacob away. Rebel trotted back to her side and sat down, resting his head on her thigh. Jasmine ran her hands through his soft fur. Yes, she found Rhett attractive. They'd continued to talk after the first video chat, quickly slipping into a routine where Rhett called every night. Even though he said it was to check in on Rebel, they continued to talk long after he said hello to his faithful friend. Nightly phone calls from Rhett quickly became her favorite part of her day. It didn't matter what subject they talked about; it was just about spending time together, even if it was through a screen.

A vendor who sold flowers came over to her table, carrying a gigantic bouquet of tulips in shades of pink and white. "Excuse me, Dr. Owens?"

"Yes."

The vendor held the bouquet out to her. "These are for you."

Jasmine looked down at the flowers and then around the park.

"I… thank you. These are lovely."

The vendor smiled with a wave and walked back to her stand.

A few minutes later, her phone buzzed with a text message.

I hope you are having a good day at the farmer's market. I wish I could be there to give you these in person. Thank you for taking care of Rebel for me.

Jasmine didn't know how long she'd been sitting there, clutching her bouquet and grinning at her phone, before someone cleared their throat, bringing her back to reality.

She looked up to find her brother standing at her table, his hands resting on the duty rig around his waist. The sunlight glinted off the gold braid around his hat and his badge. He was looking at her with a raised eyebrow.

He pointed at the flowers. "You want to tell me where those are from and what has put that goofy smile on your face?"

"Absolutely not. It's none of your business."

They stared each other down for a minute before her brother sighed. "All right. But you know I'll find out eventually."

"We agreed to respect each other's privacy when I moved here, remember? Just because you're the sheriff, Isiah, doesn't mean you need to know everything that's going on."

"Maybe not, but with my little sister, you can't blame me if I'm a little overprotective."

Rebel chose that moment to lift his head and look at Isiah, giving him a little snort.

Isiah laughed. "Maybe you don't need my help. Looks like you have a guardian to keep you safe."

In the time she'd spent with Rebel, Jasmine had seen no trace of aggression, but her instincts told her that if she was in any danger, those protective instincts would come out in full force.

She stroked Rebel's head. "He's a good companion. Rhett has him trained so well. I'm really impressed."

"Does this mean you might consider an upgrade?"

"Daisy was a sweetheart."

Isiah made a face and shuddered. "Yuck. That snake was so creepy."

"Quit being so dramatic. She got out of her enclosure one time, and you've never forgiven her for it."

"That's because I found her in *my bed*!" Isiah exclaimed.

Jasmine covered her mouth, trying unsuccessfully to suppress the laughter that always came with the memory of Isiah running through the house screaming like a little girl. She did her best to school her expression while her brother glared at her.

The lapel mic on Isiah's shoulder crackled to life. He wagged his finger at her. "One of these days, I'm going to get you back."

Isiah jogged toward his cruiser parked in front of Town Hall. They might tease each other and have an occasional argument, but they were close, and Jasmine was happy to have family close by. It was different from living back home, with her parents constantly checking in and hovering. They did it because they cared, and Jasmine was grateful for all the support they gave her while she got back on her feet again after a tough start to her career in veterinary medicine. Her brother worried about her too, but he respected her boundaries—at least most of the time.

She pulled out her phone again and posed for a selfie with the flowers and sent it to Rhett with a message thanking him.

A family approached her table, asking for advice on what breed of dogs would be best for their five-year-old with allergies, who had been desperately begging his parents for a puppy. Jasmine was happy to help and spent the next hour talking about the differences between a poodle and a Portuguese water dog and other breeds that were hypoallergenic. Other people came by, asking about her practice and picking up flyers for the spay and neuter clinic. A couple of farmers who were vendors at the market came by and were happy to discover that her clinic was a mixed practice that worked with both small animals and some large breeds. Of course, as a vet in a rural area, she would always help whatever animal was in need.

The park began to clear out, and vendors were closing down their stalls when Ms. Ruby, the youngest Jewel sister, approached her table with a small bottle filled with dark purple liquid.

"Here you go, honey," Ms. Ruby said.

Jasmine reached for her tote bag. "How much do I owe you?"

Ms. Ruby waved her off. "Not a thing."

"You have to let me give you something, Ms. Ruby."

Ms. Ruby tapped her lips. "How about you let me dig through your yarn stash? I'm looking for some small bits for a scrap scarf."

Jasmine held her hand up. "Deal."

"Any chance I can get you to make one of those scarves for me?" a low, gravelly voice asked.

Ms. Ruby's head whipped around, and her eyes widened. Robert Ellis touched the brim of his Biloxi Shuckers hat.

Jasmine had met the older man on her first visit to Colton. She instantly liked Uncle Robert, as her brother and his friends called him. He'd introduced himself as Uncle Robert when they met and explained that was what the "young" folks called him. He was a kind man who had returned to his hometown after leaving whatever government agency he'd been working for. Some folks said he was in the FBI; some thought he'd been in the foreign service. Her brother said it was the CIA. Isiah called him a man with "resources and secrets." And it was obvious Isiah held him in high regard.

"Ruby." He turned to Jasmine. "Dr. Owens. Looked like traffic at your booth was good today."

"It was. How was your day at the market?"

Uncle Robert glanced toward the bed of his vintage pickup truck, which was filled with empty crates. "Yup, I sold out of just about everything." He set a basket of vegetables on her table.

"I divided up what was left between you and Doc Colton. We've gotta take care of the folks that take care of us and our animals." The basket he'd brought overflowed with greens, spring lettuce, sweet potatoes, and a few other vegetables. "It's early yet, but there'll be cucumbers in a few more weeks."

The minute Jasmine stood up, Rebel did the same, staying at her side as she went to give Uncle Robert a hug.

"Thank you," she said.

The kindness and support she'd received from the community since she moved to Colton touched her deeply and reaffirmed she'd made the right decision to make Colton her home.

Uncle Robert looked at Ms. Ruby. "About that scarf? How much do you charge?"

Ms. Ruby stared at him for a minute before she answered in a soft, shaking voice, "I think it's too late for me to make anything for you." She cleared her throat. "Besides, spring is here. You don't need a scarf."

"That might be true, but maybe I want one anyway," Uncle Robert said.

The way he said it made Ms. Ruby's eyes grow wide.

"Ruby, we're fixin' to close up," Ms. Ruby's sister, Opal, called from their booth.

"Bye, honey," Ms. Ruby said to Jasmine.

With one more glance at Uncle Robert, she walked away. Uncle Robert dropped his chin to his chest with a sigh. "I'm an old fool," he muttered to himself.

"For what it's worth, I thought it was a good line," Jasmine said.

Uncle Robert gave her a wry smile. "I might be a little rusty in the flirting department."

"You and me both."

He pointed to the bouquet on her table. "Looks like whatever it is you're doing is working."

She could feel the heat in her cheeks.

Uncle Robert patted her shoulder. "I didn't mean to tease."

"No, it's fine. It's new, and I don't really know if… it's new," she repeated.

"I understand. Here, let me help you take that table back to the clinic."

Jasmine put the leftover flyers in her tote bag and picked up the crate of produce so Uncle Robert could fold the table legs.

"It's none of my business, but for what it's worth, Rhett Colton is a good man. He might be a broken man right now, but that won't last. He's gonna be okay," Uncle Robert said as they walked toward the clinic.

Jasmine smiled as she unlocked the door. She shouldn't be surprised that Uncle Robert knew it was Rhett. The man had an uncanny way of knowing just about everything that was going on.

"I can take that now," Jasmine said, setting the crate on the counter and taking the table from his hands. "Thanks, and I agree. Rhett is a good man. It's kind of hard to get to know him when we're talking through a screen. I wouldn't mind getting to know him better when he comes back."

Heat rose in Jasmine's cheeks when Uncle Robert declared, "If that boy has any sense, he'll sweep you off your feet the minute he gets home. It's what I wish I'd done when I came home." The tinge of sadness in his voice and the flash of pain in his eyes told their own story.

"Maybe it's not too late?" she said.

Uncle Robert's lips tipped up in a half smile. "Maybe." He knelt and scratched Rebel's head, chuckling when the appreciative canine pressed his head against his hand, begging for more. "You know, I've been thinkin' about getting a dog. Someone to keep me company."

Jasmine suspected he'd rather spend evenings on the porch with Ms. Ruby instead of a dog, but she kept that opinion to herself.

"Let me know if you want to go to the shelter in Greenwood. I'd be happy to come along and help you look."

"I just might do that."

Tipping his hat, Uncle Robert said goodbye. Jasmine watched him walk across the park, his hands in his pockets and his shoulders low. Rebel let out a whine and pressed himself against her leg.

"Yeah, I know," Jasmine said. "Come on, boy. Let's go for a walk and have some dinner before your dad calls."

Rebel followed her upstairs, waiting patiently while she put the tulips Rhett had sent to her in a vase. She reached out and ran her finger over one soft petal. Some of the blooms were the fancy ones that almost looked like roses. The mix of light pink and dark pink blooms, some with delicate stripes mixed with translucent white ones, created an enchanting bouquet. Tulips just became her favorite flower.

When they returned from their walk, Jasmine fed Rebel and made a salad with the spring lettuce from Uncle Robert. She curled up on the couch and positioned the flowers where Rhett could see them when he called. Rebel jumped up on the couch next to her at her invitation. Jasmine glanced down at the T-shirt she was wearing and wished she had something that was a little more flattering in her wardrobe, but that would mean owning something more form-fitting, and she wasn't sure if she was ready for that.

Her phone rang, and Rhett's name flashed on the screen.

"Thank you for the flowers," she said when his face appeared.

Rhett smiled. "They look beautiful," he said.

There were dark circles under his eyes, and his face was pinched and drawn.

"Tough day?" she asked.

He sighed. "I had to go over what happened the night they kidnapped Mae again. I hate reliving that night."

Jasmine wanted to crawl through the screen, wrap Rhett in her arms, and smooth away the lines on his forehead. She reminded herself what happened the last time she'd tried to take away someone else's pain and remembered that while she could heal an animal, she couldn't always save another human being.

His eyes met hers through the screen. "When I come home, I'm going to buy you another bouquet so I can give them to you in person."

"You're trying to change the subject."

"How did I know it wouldn't work with you?"

His drawl was low, with the same quality she'd heard in Uncle Robert's voice. A hint of sadness mixed with… longing. But the look in his eyes made her stomach tumble and fall.

"When you get back, we'll have a lot of time to talk face-to-face."

"What if…." Rhett paused and leaned closer to the screen. "What if when I get home, I want to do more than talk?"

Jasmine wondered if Rhett somehow knew she'd imagined kissing him. Lately, she'd wondered what it would be like to run her hands over his bare shoulders, what it would feel like to have his arms around her.

Jasmine grinned mischievously. "I… I would be open to talking about that."

Chapter Five

WHAT HAD possessed him to say he wanted to do more than talk? Despite knowing that he shouldn't, he couldn't help himself. His conversation with Jasmine the night before had Rhett even more eager to return to Colton. Now there was someone he looked forward to seeing when he came home. All he had to do was get though one more hearing.

Rhett tried not to crawl out of his skin while another senator questioned whether the number of hate groups in the country they'd claimed was really correct. He clamped his jaw shut and tried to school his expression while the expert sitting at the long table in the hearing room repeated the facts and data again. The only thing keeping him sane was replaying the conversation he'd had with Jasmine a few nights ago. Flirting didn't come naturally to Rhett; he'd always hated that part of dating. He'd done it when it was necessary while he was undercover and felt grimy after he'd done it.

Jasmine was different. She found a way to get Rhett out of his own head and made him feel like the man he used to be, whole and unblemished by the past. He needed to finish this trip and get back home so he could see her, talk to her, in person.

His conversation with Jasmine kept him sane the next day during another round of testimony. The hours and questions dragged on. Just when Rhett thought he couldn't stand it anymore, it was over. He walked outside and took a deep breath, squinting up at the bright blue sky.

"You okay?" Dan asked.

Rhett nodded at his counterpart. "Yeah. You?"

"I'm good." Dan ran his hand over his face. "What a shit show."

"I don't know how some of these guys can look an expert in the face and tell them they're wrong."

"I swear to God, when that senator brought up how some of your family members were arrested and questioned your loyalty, I almost lost it."

"Hypocrisy at its best," Rhett said.

"I wish we could go public with that asshole's file and show the world who he's been hanging out with."

Rhett sighed. "You and me both."

Dan's phone rang, and his frown transformed. "Hey, babe. Yeah, we're done." He nodded and looked at Rhett. "Reid says hi."

"Tell him I said hi. I'll let you talk," he said, gesturing toward the path along the Mall. A walk under the cherry blossoms would help take away the day's stress.

"Excuse me, sir," a young Black man called out, jogging toward him. Rhett stopped. "I tried to find you after the hearing. Will you please come back to the Capitol with me?"

"What's this about?" Rhett asked.

"There's a senator who wasn't in the hearing today who would like to meet with you. It wouldn't be long. He'd like just a few minutes of your time."

Rhett pinched the bridge of his nose and inhaled. "Yeah, okay, fine."

He followed the young man back into the Russell Building, through security again and past the hearing rooms. "I hope you don't mind taking the stairs. It's faster this time of day."

"No problem," Rhett said.

He didn't care who it was that wanted to meet with him. Rhett just wanted to get it over with. He'd had his fill of bureaucratic bullshit for the day.

When Rhett saw the nameplate on the wall next to the doorway where the young man stopped, he almost tripped.

The young man held his hand out. "I didn't introduce myself before. I'm Amari Paige, one of Senator Jacobs's staff assistants."

Rhett shook his hand. "I can't go in there," he said in a quiet voice.

Amari gave him a sympathetic look. "I know it's been a long day."

"It's not that. I'm not… I don't know how to say it… worthy."

"That's not how the senator feels. Please, he doesn't have much time, but he wanted to see you."

Amari opened the door and gestured for him to go in. They walked through an outer office buzzing with activity and stopped at another door. Amari knocked, and a deep voice said, "Come in."

When he opened the door, Rhett froze. Amari gave him a gentle push and then closed the door behind him, leaving him alone with the senator.

Senator Lawrence Jacobs was a civil rights icon, the son of sharecroppers. He had been on the front line of the civil rights movement, putting his own life in jeopardy to ensure the right to vote for Black Americans. He slowly unfolded himself from his desk, moving slowly now that he'd reached his eighties. His dark brown face bore the stress from a lifetime of fighting for rights others took for granted. He was a small man physically, slightly stooped with age, his head completely bald.

"Thank you for taking the time to meet with me," Senator Jacobs said.

"I…." Rhett was at a loss. This man, this legendary figure, was thanking him for taking the time to come see him. "Thank you, sir. I don't know what to say."

The senator shook Rhett's hand and gestured toward the chair in front of his desk.

Rhett looked around the room as he sat down. Pictures and mementos chronicling a lifetime of service lined the walls.

"Have a seat. I wanted to be at your hearing today, but my schedule didn't allow it. I don't serve on that committee, but I was watching," he said, lowering himself back into his seat. The senator folded his hands on his desk and looked at Rhett with his dark soulful eyes. "You did a good job keeping your cool in there today. I bet there were a few times when you wanted to rip some of my colleagues to shreds."

Rhett cleared his throat. "Yes, sir."

The senator nodded with a slight smile. "This isn't simple work. There were many days when I wondered if I could get up again. But people like you, who volunteer to live with hate, I don't know how you managed it."

"It's nothing compared to the lifetime you've spent in service, sir."

"It all adds up. Every moment of service and sacrifice counts. That's what I wanted to tell you. I saw something in your eyes today when I was watching the hearing. Never think what you did wasn't enough, Agent Colton."

The senator tapped the folder on his desk. "I've read your reports." He pulled out another file. The edges were worn with age, with stains on the cover. "And your grandfather's."

Rhett had seen copies, but seeing the original file sent a chill down his spine.

The senator folded his hands again and leaned forward. "We do what we can, Agent Colton. No one is perfect, no one has all the answers. What I saw in that hearing room today was a young man who was carrying the weight of the world on his shoulders."

"I didn't get all of them," Rhett whispered before other words rushed from his mouth. "My cousin Larry is already recruiting, trying to rebuild. I can't…. What if something happens to someone I care about because I didn't do enough? I try to see the bigger picture, and it's overwhelming. There are days when I think if I can just get rid of one more, it will make a difference, and then I realize… it's like tossing pebbles in a well."

"I think I can safely say we all feel that way from time to time," the senator said in a solemn tone. "It's not up to you to take on this work by yourself. When I marched in Alabama and Mississippi, I wasn't alone. I marched arm in arm with others committed to the cause the same way I was." The senator sat back with a weary sigh. "Do you know what you want to do next?"

Rhett shook his head. "I'd like to stay with the agency, but I'm not sure how much good I can do now that I'm not able to work undercover."

"You take your time and think about it. There are always ways to give in service, both large and small. Like I said, it all counts. Go home, spend time with your friends and family. You got anyone special waiting for you in Colton?"

Rhett thought about Jasmine.

"That smile tells me the answer is yes," the senator said with a twinkle in his eye.

"There's someone. We just met, but she's… special. Talking to her, I'm able to see a future where I can be happy."

"That sounds like a very special person, and I'm glad you have someone in your life to support you and share the burden with. I couldn't have done the work I have if I didn't have my Lillian at my side." The senator stood. "I wish we had more time, but I have another meeting I need to get to."

Rhett jumped up and, without thinking, offered his elbow to the senator as he moved stiffly toward the door. Senator Jacobs gave him a sharp look and then put his hand on his arm. "You're right, I am getting old. I can see the arc of history in parallel to my life. But you, your path is just beginning. People like you give me hope that when I'm gone, the world will be a better place."

Rhett opened the door, and the senator waved away the staff members hovering nearby.

"This young man can escort me to the meeting. Amari, will you please bring my briefcase?"

"Yes, sir," Amari said.

The three walked slowly down the hallway toward the elevators. The senator's grip was tight on Rhett's arm.

"You know, I've been to Colton," the senator said. "We stopped on our way to a march in Jackson. Richard Colton made sure we had places to stay and food in our bellies." He chuckled. "I had hair back then, and Mr. Colton arranged for all of us to get haircuts at the barbershop in town."

"The barbershop is still there, and Richard Colton's granddaughter is our town librarian."

"And you have a new mayor who is doing a great job revitalizing the town," Senator Jacobs said.

"We're all proud of Mae Colton. She's doing everything she can to make Colton a better place to live."

"And so are you."

They reached the doorway of the meeting room. The senator let go of Rhett's arm and shook his hand. "I don't get many opportunities to meet the folks who are out in the field. Thank you, Agent Colton."

Rhett struggled to get past the lump in his throat. "Thank you, sir."

Senator Jacobs reached into his pocket and pulled out a business card. "You stay in touch with me. And if things work out with the young lady you're talking to, I expect an invitation to the wedding." Senator Jacobs turned to his assistant. "Are you ready, Amari?"

"Yes, sir." Amari shook Rhett's hand, and the two men went into the meeting room.

Rhett stood outside the meeting room for a few minutes, trying to compose himself. He walked numbly back outside, blinking up at the sun once again.

He was still trying to process the conversation with Senator Jacobs when he called Jasmine that night.

"You were great today," Jasmine exclaimed, answering his call on the first ring.

"You watched?"

"I did."

"Most people can't find C-SPAN." Rhett snorted with a laugh.

"More people should. I wish the networks covered it. What you and the others testified about is important. I don't know how you stayed so calm through all that questioning."

Rhett leaned back, resting his head against the headboard, finally able to relax for the first time that day, seeing Jasmine's face on his screen.

"A couple of those senators didn't make it easy. They always want to put on a show for the cameras. The closed-door hearings were easier," he said.

"Well, you wouldn't know it from what I saw on TV. Rebel and I were really proud of you, weren't we?"

Rebel popped up on the screen next to Jasmine, giving her a wet kiss.

"Senator Lawrence Jacobs asked to meet with me after the hearing," Rhett said.

Jasmine's eyes widened. "Oh my God," she said in an awed voice.

"It was surreal. Amazing. I can't put it into words."

"I can't imagine what that must have been like. Why did he ask to see you?"

"I… I think he wanted to thank me. He talked about how hard it is doing civil rights work. He told me he came to Colton once on his way to a march in Jackson. It was… incredible."

Jasmine smiled. "You sound… hopeful."

"I do?"

Jasmine nodded. He thought about it for a moment and realized that was exactly what he was feeling.

Chapter Six

"HOW WAS your day today?" Rhett asked.

Jasmine tucked herself into the corner of her sofa and hugged her knees to her chest. "It was okay."

She'd been looking forward to her nightly phone call all day. It was amazing how quickly you could make a routine. Rebel was curled up on the sofa with her, his head resting on the back cushion, looking out the window at the park below.

Rhett frowned. "Just okay?"

"I have to remind myself that it takes time to build up a practice. Today was pretty slow, but I know it won't always be that way. I have a call out to the Anderson farm to look at one of their goats tomorrow. I'm hoping they will see that I know what I'm doing and I'll get more calls from them in the future."

"The Andersons are good people. You won't have any problems there. I'm sure once word gets around, you'll have a full schedule. Colton has been missing services like your clinic and the medical clinic for too long now. It's good for the community."

He sat up straighter against the headboard. "I have to tell you, I worry about you. Are you going to be making any more calls out to any farms? Some of those farmer folks are… old-fashioned. They might not be too friendly to a female vet."

"Or a Black female vet?" she asked.

Rhett nodded.

"I appreciate it, but I know what I'm doing. This isn't my first time working out in the field. I've dealt with clients who questioned my abilities before. There have been a few times where someone didn't want me anywhere near their animal without giving me the third degree first, and even then…." She shrugged.

"Will you promise me you'll let me know if you ever need any help?"

"You're forgetting my brother is the sheriff, and Jacob and Dax have appointed themselves honorary big brothers. I have more than enough people watching over me," Jasmine said with a wry smile.

"I didn't know you knew Dax and Jacob that well."

"Isiah brought Jacob and Dax home from boot camp with him. Of course, the minute my parents found out that Jacob's parents passed away and Dax wasn't close with his own family, they unofficially adopted them. I immediately gained two more overprotective big brothers." She laughed, shaking her head. "God forbid a date showed up at the house when they were home on leave."

Rhett chuckled. "I would have liked to see that."

"They might annoy me sometimes, but I know they'll always be there for me if I need them. It was one of the big reasons I moved to Colton, to have family and friends close by. We have family dinner every couple of weeks at Dax and Callie's. Maybe you'll come with me when you get back."

Rhett's smile slipped. "I, uh… maybe."

Jasmine kicked herself. It was too soon; she was just getting to know Rhett.

"I'm sorry. I shouldn't have—"

Rhett interrupted her, blurting out, "I've been wondering, what kind of food do you like?"

"Oh, um, I like just about everything, but I'm not great with spicy food. My brother snuck some wasabi into my sushi one time, and I thought I was going to die. I drank a gallon of milk, and I still had heartburn a day later."

Rhett laughed.

"It's not funny." Jasmine pouted.

"Make sure you never order Tillie's pepper greens at the Catfish Café. They might just put you in the hospital."

Jasmine nodded. "Duly noted."

"I suppose growing up in Chicago, you got used to eating out at fancy restaurants. I'm afraid there's not much sushi around Colton," Rhett said. "But I'd like to take you out to dinner when I get back. We could go to Memphis or Jackson. I don't own a nice suit, but I'd get one, and you'll have to explain what all those forks are for, but I can take you somewhere nice."

"I never enjoyed having to get all dressed up to go out to dinner. It doesn't matter what the place is, Rhett. It's the company."

A slow smile spread over Rhett's face. He took the hair tie off his wrist and pulled his hair back. "I just wish this trip was over."

"You only have a few more days."

"If everything goes well, I'll be home by the end of the week."

EVERYTHING DID not go well. Rhett was called back to testify two more times in House and Senate meetings. There were a few stubborn senators who thought if they asked enough stupid questions, they could get him to change his story or, worse, get him to have a breakdown so that they could discredit his testimony, claiming he was emotionally unstable.

There were more meetings with lawyers from the Department of Justice to review his testimony for upcoming trials. They'd arrested over thirty people on various charges after the night of the failed kidnapping attempt. And while Rhett should have been proud of that, he couldn't stop thinking about the others who'd slithered away, like copperhead snakes seeking shelter in the cool shade of the kudzu vines.

There were extra training sessions for the new batch of agents who would go undercover, embedding into domestic terrorist groups around the country. Rhett requested those training sessions, wanting to make it absolutely clear what the risks were and the sacrifices they would be making. He'd been so confident when he went in. His confidence quickly disappeared when he was faced with the reality of the work he'd committed to do.

Each meeting ended with someone asking the same question: "What are you going to do next?" Rhett hadn't allowed himself to think about the future while he was undercover. When his mission ended so abruptly, he wasn't prepared to be thrust back into a normal life. Now he was paralyzed by the possibilities. Did he want to stay with the bureau? Would he be able to stay in Colton and build a life there? The options swirled in his head, keeping him up at night. When he got home, he'd have six months of leave ahead of him to figure it out.

The only thing that kept him grounded and gave him hope was Jasmine and their nightly calls. Seeing Rebel was reassuring, but it was Jasmine's smile that kept him going. For the first time, he looked forward to going home. He knew it wasn't true, but he felt like he had someone to come home to. He pictured Jasmine as she described the animals she'd treated that day. He laughed so hard his stomach hurt while Jasmine imitated a pair of guinea pigs that were brought in for a checkup talking to each other.

When she finished, she asked, "How are you doing? Did you have a good day?"

Rhett would be in DC for a few days longer than he'd planned, and his anxiety about getting back to Colton increased with each minute that passed.

"Honestly"—he snapped the elastic band around his wrist—"I'm wondering what good any of this is doing. There are so many hate groups out there, it feels like my part in all this was just a drop in the ocean."

"You're doing a lot of good, and you've already done so much." She paused before saying in a more serious tone, "There's something I've been wanting to ask you."

"You can ask me anything. I like talking to you," Rhett said.

"Why did you do it?" she asked. "What made you go undercover?"

"Oh, that question." Rhett couldn't decide if he was disappointed or relieved that she asked.

Jasmine wrinkled her forehead. "You don't have to tell me if you don't want to."

Rhett thought about it and realized he wanted to share the story with Jasmine. He gave her a small smile. "I went undercover for my grandad. He did some things in his past that he regretted. He did his best to make amends, but he never felt like it was enough. I wanted him to be at peace."

Jasmine's gaze was sympathetic. Normally when people gave him that look, it made Rhett uncomfortable. With Jasmine, her compassion made him feel human again.

"That's a big burden to carry, Rhett," she said softly.

"My grandad was the most important person in my life. I just wish… I just wish he'd lived to the end of my mission so I could have seen him again."

Jasmine's eyes grew wide. "Oh, Rhett, I'm sorry."

"I miss him every day."

"Of course you do. If I were with you right now, I'd give you a hug."

Rhett smiled faintly. “I’d take that hug.”

Jasmine’s eyes sparkled. “I’ll be able to give it to you when you get home.”

“Just a couple more days.”

Chapter Seven

JASMINE MIRRORED Rhett's pose, leaning against her headboard, her laptop balanced on her lap. Rhett had just asked her if she missed her friends back home.

She thought about it for a moment, trying to come up with an answer that didn't make her sound pathetic, but in the end, she chose to tell him the truth.

"I didn't make any friends at school. I was working a lot of hours between classes, studying, and my mentorship program. There wasn't much free time left at the end of the day. I'm not… I've never really felt like I knew what my place was. I didn't have a large group of friends to hang out with. A lot of that was my fault, as I spent a lot of time with my boyfriend." She stroked Rebel's soft fur. "Even though I work with people every day, I don't always know that I'm good with people outside of work."

"You're good with me."

Her stomach dipped in sync with the way the words fell from his lips.

Rebel pushed his snout into the screen, making Rhett laugh.

"Rebel is wondering when you're coming home," she said.

"I'll be back in Colton at the end of the week."

Jasmine wanted to jump up and do a little happy dance.

"Rebel will be happy to welcome you home."

Rhett's Adam's apple bobbed. "Will you be happy to welcome me home?"

"I will. Is it weird that I'll also miss our phone calls?"

"We don't have to stop if you don't want to."

Jasmine could feel the heat rise in her cheeks. The steps to this dance she and Rhett had started were unfamiliar to her. She'd never been a great dancer to begin with. Did she want something more with Rhett? What would her family think if she brought home a White boy who had been undercover with White supremacists? Her parents were pretty easygoing people, but that might ask too much of them. Even with all the potential obstacles running through her head, she couldn't deny her attraction to Rhett. It took her by surprise and grew with each of their nightly phone calls.

"We… we don't have to decide anything. We can just see how it goes when you come home." Jasmine cringed. She didn't want to sound too eager. One step forward, one step back. Was this a waltz? She had no idea. "Are you going to be staying at your grandpa's cabin?"

Rhett had talked a lot about the little fishing cabin he'd inherited from his grandfather.

"Yeah, I need to get going on the repairs the place needs." He sounded more resigned than excited by the idea.

"Is there anything I can do to help?"

"Nah, I'll be fine."

"Let me know if you change your mind. I'd be happy to help."

"You've already done so much for me. I'll never be able to repay you for taking care of Rebel for me."

"I'm glad Jacob asked me to help. I'm going to miss this guy when you come back," she said, scratching Rebel behind the ears.

"We'll just have to make sure we come to visit."

A low rumble of thunder interrupted them. The lights flickered, and Rebel lifted his head, sniffing the air.

"You okay?" Rhett asked.

Jasmine wrapped her arms around herself. "I hate thunderstorms."

"Rebel will keep you safe."

I wish it was you.

Jasmine jumped when another boom of thunder crashed closer. There was a knock on her door. "That will be my brother."

Rhett nodded. "Okay, I'll see you tomorrow."

Jasmine ended the call and dashed to open her door.

"You know I'm a grown woman and I can deal with a thunderstorm by myself, right?"

Her brother stepped over the threshold and pulled her into a hug.

"I do, but that doesn't mean I still can't come and check on you."

Jasmine wouldn't admit her brother was right. She was happy that he came.

"Come on, I'll make emergency hot chocolate," Isiah said.

When they were little, her brother started the tradition of making hot chocolate whenever there was a big storm. Peppermint vodka became part of the tradition on trips home when Jasmine was in college. It was the familiarity of the routine as much as the sweet treat that helped her stay calm during a storm.

Rebel trotted over, and Isiah crouched down to pet him. "Hey, buddy. Are you doin' a good job taking care of my little sister?"

Isiah chuckled when Rebel replied with a short bark.

"It looks great in here, sis," he said, wandering into the living room. He stopped and picked up the book she left laying open on the couch. "You and your Jane Austen. Don't you ever get tired of reading *Pride and Prejudice?*"

Jasmine snatched the book out of his hands and clutched it to her chest. "Absolutely not. Some people read Aristotle or Voltaire, looking for wisdom, but Jane Austen is the one who had all the answers to life's mysteries."

"Oh Lord, here we go again."

"I'm not the one who started this. You could have left me and Jane alone. We're perfectly happy together." She put the book back on her bookshelf next to all the other books Jane Austen wrote. "You're still salty because you finally read *Emma.*"

"It's not funny," he said, moving her out of the way, taking over stirring the chocolate chips into the pan of warm milk.

Jasmine laughed. "I still can't believe I got away with calling you Mr. Knightly for months before you figured out why."

"I am not Mr. Knightly."

"Hate to break it to you, but that's exactly who you are. Always correcting and holding people to high expectations."

Before it could escalate into a full-blown sibling argument, another flash of lightning made Jasmine jump, illuminating the apartment in an eerie white glow.

"Do you have any candles?" Isiah asked.

Jasmine opened a drawer in the kitchen. "Of course I do."

She started rummaging through the drawer, pulling out a couple of candles and a flashlight.

"Good to see you have supplies handy," he said while she went around the room and lit the candles set out on the coffee table and the bookshelf in the living room.

"As if you would let me get away without being prepared."

Isiah had always been a stickler for following the rules and being safe. It made perfect sense he would end up working in law enforcement. But it shocked Jasmine when he announced he was giving up his job as a fire marshal in Chicago to move to a town in the Mississippi Delta. She was also just a bit jealous. It was always her dream to live in a small town, something her siblings teased her about growing up. She'd followed her dream to become a veterinarian when she went to Ohio State university, one of the top veterinary schools in the country. After six years of hard work, she moved back to Chicago less than a year ago with her illusions shattered. Her brother's newfound fondness for small-town life felt like salt in a wound.

He set two mugs of hot chocolate on the kitchen island and went over to the small bar cart she'd set up in the living room, returning with a bottle of peppermint vodka and adding a generous splash to her mug and a small one to his. Isiah returned to his seat and took a drink with an appreciative nod.

They sipped at their hot chocolate while the time between thunder and lightning shortened until there was no separation between the two. The lights flickered again and then went out.

She reached for his hand. "Thanks for being here. I'm glad you found Colton for both of us."

Isiah shook his head with a wry smile. "In a million years, I never expected to be here, and now I can't imagine living anywhere else. And I'm happy you're here now too, sis. I know it may have seemed like I kind of took over your small-town dreams. I never planned that when I came here. I'd fallen under Colton's spell. This place is special, and it feels good to know I'm part of a community effort to help this town thrive."

"I'll admit I was jealous as hell when you came home and told us you were moving here."

Isiah put his arm around her shoulder and gave it a squeeze. "What would Mom say?"

"Sometimes the best things come from something unexpected," they both said in unison.

There was a low buzz, and Isiah pulled out his phone, the light from the screen illuminating his turned-down mouth.

"Aren't you off tonight?" Jasmine asked.

"A small-town sheriff is always on duty."

"I'm glad you have a deputy to help now."

"So am I. Going from a one-man operation to having a deputy made a difference, especially…" Isiah pressed his lips together, shaking his head.

"What's wrong?"

"Compared to a lot of small towns, Colton's been pretty lucky with drug problems. But the last few months, we've had a few incidents with people who are using fentanyl, meth, anything they can cook up or steal."

Jasmine sucked in her breath. "People who use illicit drugs could be dangerous and unpredictable." She worried about her brother's safety under normal circumstances, and knowing he was having to deal with a new drug problem added to her concerns.

"I want to talk to you, Doc Colton, and Emma about making sure your drug supplies are secure."

Everyone in town was thrilled that Colton's medical clinic recently reopened and a doctor was on hand again. Jasmine had only met Dylan Colton, the town doctor, briefly. Dylan came across as quiet and serious, the complete opposite of his outgoing brother, Taylor.

"I was going to stop by the pharmacy tomorrow. I'll mention something to Emma while I'm there," she offered.

Isiah's phone buzzed again with another message. At the same time, they could hear the siren start from the firehouse down the street.

"I better go," Isiah said, reading the message. "There's a tree down on Magnolia Street, took out some power lines. Nate might need help."

Jasmine gave her brother a quick hug. "Be careful out there."

"I'll check back with you later. Make sure you lock your door behind me."

Jasmine leaned against the door after she turned the lock. No one could ask for a better brother, but sometimes he forgot she was a grown woman who could take care of herself. She felt a tiny pang of guilt that she was happy he got called away before he could give her the third degree on her romantic life. It was inevitable whenever they were together. It wasn't as if she had anything to report, anyway. Her social life was pretty much nonexistent since she left Ohio. She was making friends in Colton, but she hadn't gone on any dates yet. Maybe that would change when Rhett came home.

Chapter Eight

RHETT'S FINGERS tapped against his bouncing knee, his fingers twisting the hair tie on his wrist. Eventually, he took it off and pulled his hair up off his face. Five minutes later, he took it out again. Twenty minutes was all that separated him from Jasmine and Rebel.

"Where do you want me to drop you off?" Dan asked.

Rhett watched the empty furrows in the fields fan out as they made their way back home.

Only it wasn't home. *Home* was a concept that he'd struggled with before he left for DC. Now, after just a few weeks, he was even more uncertain about what that looked like for him.

"If you can drop me off at the vet's office, that would be great."

"Of course, I forgot. You must be excited to see Rebel again."

And Jasmine.

It took all his self-control not to jump out of the car and run the rest of the way to Colton so that he could see her in person. He needed to know for sure she was real and not just an image on the screen. Just for one moment, he needed to have that moment. *It would be enough*, he told himself, even though his heart whispered, *Liar.*

"Thank you for the ride. I figured you would stay in Jackson."

Dan smiled, his hands flexing on the steering wheel. "I want to see Reid. It's been over two weeks and—"

"You can't wait to see him again." Rhett voiced his own feelings.

"Yeah. I wasn't sure I'd ever find… my person. Now that I have, I can't stand a minute without him."

"Do you worry about his safety?"

Dan's brow furrowed. "In what way?"

"With your job, there are people who want… revenge. Aren't you concerned about the people around you getting hurt?"

"No, not really. I'll always worry about my family and Reid, but not because of my job. Isn't it part of loving someone that you worry about them?"

Rhett reflected on Dan's statement for a moment. "I guess so, but I don't want to be a burden. I don't want to be the person someone has to worry about."

Rhett ignored the sharp look he got in return. Dan didn't understand.

Soon enough, green fields gave way to low brick buildings and clapboard cottages. They turned the corner into the town square, and Rhett's gaze was drawn to the vet clinic at the end of the block. Dan barely came to a stop before he grabbed the door handle and opened it. He pulled his pack from the back seat and waved goodbye as Dan took off again.

He'd been thinking about this moment every day since he left, and now that it was here, he was frozen, afraid to take the next step.

EVERY TIME someone came into the clinic, Jasmine rushed out to the lobby to see if it was Rhett. Each time, she admonished herself for being overeager. It wasn't as if she was going to throw her arms around his neck when he walked in, even if she'd thought about it more than once.

"Anything I can help with?" Imani asked when Jasmine lingered at the front desk, eyeing the front door.

It thrilled Jasmine when Imani Burke applied for the veterinary assistant's job. Imani recently graduated from a veterinary assistant program at a community college nearby, and Jasmine was pleased to guide another Black woman coming into her profession. Jasmine would do everything she could to make sure Imani had the support and mentorship she'd never received in her first job out of veterinary school.

"No, I just thought I heard someone come in," Jasmine said, reaching down to pet Rebel on the head. The dog made each trip out to the lobby glued to her side, as if he knew his owner was coming today.

"You don't have an appointment for another hour, if you want to take a break."

"How about I head over to the Catfish Café and grab us some lunch?"

Imani stood from the reception desk. "I'll go. It's the least I can do for y'all giving me this job."

"I didn't give you this job. You earned it, Imani. And you don't have to keep thanking me. You're doing a great job, and I appreciate having you here."

Pink tinged Imani's cheeks, and her smile widened to a grin.

Jasmine pulled a twenty-dollar bill out of her pocket. "I'll have the meat loaf sandwich, if you don't mind."

Imani took the money from her hand and headed toward the door. She pulled up short when she got there and gasped, turning back to Jasmine, wide-eyed. "Rhett Colton is headed this way. I'd better stay and make sure everything's okay."

"Imani, you know Rhett was working undercover. He's not really a racist."

Her assistant frowned. "I know, I just… the way he acted, it seemed so real."

Imani seemed shocked when Jasmine introduced her to Rebel and explained why she was taking care of Rhett's dog. The young woman was well-aware of Rhett and the group he'd been hanging out with, having encountered them in her town about thirty miles south of Colton. Unlike Colton, the leadership in Imani's hometown turned a blind eye to the White supremacist activities happening right underfoot. Thirty miles could make a difference between progress and the past.

Before Jasmine could reassure Imani again, Rebel let out a high-pitched whine and ran toward the front window, his whole body wiggling with excitement.

Jasmine tracked Rhett as he made his way toward the clinic. Her heart was beating in her chest so hard, she thought for sure Imani could hear it. It was easy talking to Rhett with a screen between them and Rebel as the reason to reach out and touch base. What was going to happen now?

Imani shifted next to her when Rhett crossed the street.

"If you want to go out through the back, you can," Jasmine offered.

Imani nodded and scurried out to the back. Jasmine felt a brief pang of guilt for being happy Imani took her up on her offer. She wanted it to be just the two of them when she saw Rhett again.

Rebel did a little dance as Rhett approached the door. As soon as he came in, Rebel rushed to him with happy whines and yips. Rhett dropped his pack and knelt down, accepting the wet kisses while running his hands through his fur and whispering to his companion. Eventually, Rebel settled in his arms, panting, his tongue hanging out in a contented canine grin.

Rhett looked up, still crouched on the ground. "Hi."

"Hi."

All the things she'd thought about saying, had wanted to say in that moment, disappeared when Rhett looked at her. Her breath caught. His gaze was stormy blue mixed with gray. To Jasmine, it looked as if he were fighting not to be swept out to sea.

He stood up and shoved his hands in his pockets. A lock of hair pulled free from his ponytail and brushed against his cheek. Jasmine's fingers itched to reach out and tuck it behind his ear.

"How was—" Jasmine started.

"Thank you—" Rhett said at the same time.

They both laughed.

"How was your trip?"

Rhett's expression grew serious. "I did what I needed to do."

Jasmine wasn't sure how to respond to that.

"Thank you for taking good care of Rebel and for… talking to me. It helped make the days a little easier to get through."

Her heart did a dance similar to Rebel's when he saw Rhett. She hadn't expected or wanted to jump into a romantic relationship when she moved. Now the idea held a lot more appeal than it had in a long time.

Rhett looked around the waiting room. "How are things going here?"

"Good. Slow, but good. I've hired a vet tech. Imani's helping at the front desk, but I interviewed someone today as a receptionist who can also help out with the night shift. I'm going to offer him the job. Money might be tight for a bit, but I'm going to take the risk. Business will get better once people get to know me.

"You've made a lot of progress in a short amount of time."

"Some days, it feels like a lot has happened in a short amount of time. Other days, I look around and wonder why I haven't accomplished more. I have to remind myself that it's only been a few months since I moved to Colton."

"When I left for DC, two weeks felt like a lifetime"—Rhett's voice softened—"and it would have been if it weren't for you. I… I don't know how to tell you how much our nightly phone calls meant to me."

"I'm glad I could help, I… now that you're back, well… we don't have to stop talking just because you're back."

Rhett's gaze brightened. "I'd like that."

Rebel came back to Jasmine's side. She knelt down to give him a hug and said, "I'm going to miss you."

"We'll make sure we come back to visit."

Jasmine looked up at Rhett, and their eyes locked. They shared a smile, and just when Rhett started to say something, the bell over the door interrupted him.

A woman came in with a pet carrier and an anxious look on her face. "Are you Dr. Owens?" she asked. "I don't have an appointment, but Cletus got into a fight."

A pitiful *meow* came from the carrier.

Jasmine jumped up. "I am. Come on, let's get Cletus back to an exam room and take a look."

Rhett leaned down and brushed his lips against her cheek as she walked past. "Thank you. You were exactly what I needed"—he glanced down at Rebel—"what we both needed."

Her stomach did a little flip-flop. She smiled and whispered, "Call me tonight," before turning to the woman and ushering her into an exam room.

WHEN SHE finished with Cletus, Imani brought her lunch into the office and asked with a worried look, "Did everything go okay with Rhett? He didn't try to do anything to hurt you, did he?"

"No, of course not. Rhett would never do anything to hurt me." Jasmine frowned. "He's not a dangerous man. He said and did the things he did to help this community."

Imani's shoulders slumped. "You're right. I shouldn't have said that."

Jasmine took a deep breath and released the anger Imani's questioning caused. "He just came back from testifying before Congress and training other agents who are going to be making the same sacrifice he did, going undercover with other White supremacist groups. I don't mean to dismiss your feelings. I just… can you imagine how hard it was for him to spend that much time undercover with everyone thinking he was someone he wasn't?"

Imani shook her head. "No, I can't, but I know what it's like to not feel safe in my community because of those folks."

"There's enough hurt and pain for everyone, isn't there?"

"Agreeing on that is a good start," Imani said.

"I won't push. All I'm asking is if you can try to see Rhett for the man he is, not the role he played."

Imani nodded. "I can do that."

She gave her a grateful smile. "Thank you."

Rhett was on Jasmine's mind for the rest of the day. She wondered if he was getting settled in back at his grandpa's and how long it would be before she saw him again. He spoke so lovingly about the place he grew up. She couldn't wait to see it. The afternoon dragged on until, finally, it was time to close for the day and head home.

As soon as she said goodbye to Imani and locked up, she ran up the stairs to her apartment and changed into her running gear before heading back out, hoping to burn off her restlessness with a long run. She circled the park before heading out of the town square, across Mockingbird Bridge, and out to the country road leading away from Colton. Her breaths came out in little puffs in the chilly night air. Her footsteps slowed when she reached a fork in the road. Looking up at the sky, there were so many stars, they created a veil of white overhead. She was wondering if Rhett was admiring the night sky, too—and which road would take her to Rhett's cabin—when a large SUV with the sheriff's logo came down the road and pulled to a stop.

The window rolled down, revealing her brother. "Hey, sis."

"All quiet on the streets of Colton tonight?"

Her brother nodded. "So far." He looked around and turned back to her. "It's dark on these back roads after sundown. You need to be careful running out here. You should wear something reflective."

Jasmine looked down at her black shorts and gray running tights. She hadn't even thought about what she threw on when she left; she just wanted to run.

"Want a ride back into town?" Isiah offered.

Jasmine looked down at her watch. It was just past seven. If she rode back with Isiah, she'd have time to shower and change before Rhett called. If he called.

"Sure," she said.

She jogged around to the passenger side and climbed in. The bright lights from the large display screen attached to the dash cast an eerie glow in the darkened cab.

Isiah glanced at her as he drove back into town. "I heard Rhett Colton came back today."

"He did. He came by to pick up Rebel this morning."

"That's good."

Jasmine gave him a sharp look, and he cleared his throat.

"I just meant that now you won't have to take care of him… I mean, Rebel."

"Isiah, don't start with the protective older brother shit. We agreed when I moved here that we would respect each other's privacy."

"Yeah, okay, you're right. I just want you to be careful. Rhett's been through a lot, and he's—"

"He's broken," Jasmine finished.

"And it's not your responsibility to fix him."

"That's not—" Jasmine protested.

Isiah's snorted laugh interrupted her.

"What are you laughing at?"

Isiah pulled up in front of her clinic and shut off the engine. He leaned against the steering wheel. "Jas, you've been trying to fix everything and everyone since you were born, and it's a great quality to have, but you give too much of yourself sometimes. Don't try to rescue Rhett the way you try to rescue every other stray you come across."

"What about you, Mr. Knightly?"

"Stop calling me that," her brother said between clenched teeth.

She'd started referring to him as the hero of Jane Austen's classic *Emma* when he kept telling her stories of his encounters with Presley Beaumont.

"It's different," he huffed.

"Is it?" she challenged.

Isiah bowed his head for a minute before muttering, "Maybe not."

Jasmine reached out and put her hand on his shoulder, giving him a gentle shake. "Like I said, it runs in the family."

"Be careful, okay? Rhett went through hell for two years, surrounded by hate every day. You may not be the help he needs."

Chapter Nine

Lively chatter drowned out the clack of knitting needles in the Spring Street Bookstore and Coffee Shop. It had thrilled Jasmine to discover the town mayor was also a knitter. Callie Ellis, the town librarian and shop owner, offered to keep the little shop open later on Tuesdays so they could meet up for wine and knitting. They'd only met twice when Ms. June joined them. Known as Colton's free spirit, Ms. June had been a bit of a recluse until the last year. When Mae Colton was appointed as mayor of the town, Ms. June started showing up at the mayor's office with a list of improvements for the town. While she meant well, her suggestions were often unrealistic, like the time she wanted to have all the businesses in the town square paint their storefronts colors based on the proprietors' astrological signs. No one minded, though, because it was nice to welcome the retired professor back as an active member of the community.

Ms. Ruby and Emma Walker, owner of the drugstore, soon followed. Then, to everyone's surprise, Ashton Beaumont showed up, asking if a crocheter was allowed within their midst.

Ashton was watching his sister, shaking his head at the tangled mess Presley made of the scarf she was trying to craft. Presley had started joining her brother on Tuesday nights. Jasmine wasn't sure exactly sure why, since she did not have a knack for needlework.

Jasmine focused on the hat she was knitting, unwilling to admit she chose the deep blue and green variegated wool because it would look good on Rhett.

"Oh, I give up," Presley wailed, dropping the tangled mass of yarn into her lap.

"Here, honey, let's see if we can set you straight again," Ms. June said.

"Thank you, Ms. June, but I don't want you to waste your time. I'm afraid knitting just isn't for me."

"Maybe you'd be better at crochet," Ashton offered.

Presley shook her head. "No, that's your thing. To be honest, I'm just here for the company, anyway."

"Well, we're happy to have you." Ms. Ruby patted her shoulder.

"Really?" Presley looked at her, wide-eyed.

Ms. Ruby chuckled. "Yes, really."

Presley started blinking rapidly. "Thank you, ma'am."

Even though she'd just met Presley when she moved to town, Jasmine felt like she'd known her for a long time. When Isiah told her how Presley tried to rearrange the library books by color, Jasmine thought it was kind of funny. When she heard that Presley had suggested having actors pick cotton outside of Halcyon, the plantation house on the outskirts of town, Presley's lapse in judgment horrified Jasmine at first. Then, over time, the anecdotes her brother shared changed, and by the time Jasmine moved to town, she encountered a woman who was genuinely trying to better herself.

"I hear you made a call out at Mockingbird Farm the other day. What'd you think of those Anderson brothers?" Mae asked, waggling her eyebrows and fanning her face.

"Hush, Mae. You're an old married woman now," Callie said.

"Old woman my"—Mae glanced at Ms. Ruby and Ms. June—"well, anyway, I'm still in the honeymoon phase, and just because I'm married doesn't mean I can't appreciate a fine-looking man when I see one."

Ms. June and Ms. Ruby leaned their heads together and tittered.

"Seriously, how are y'all getting along with folks?" Mae asked. "Some farmers around here are pretty old-school in their thinking."

"Most have been happy to have a vet servicing the area again," Jasmine replied. "There are always a few who want to quiz me and put me through my paces, so to speak. The same thing happened back in Ohio. It's part of the job." She shrugged.

Presley frowned. "But it doesn't mean it's fair."

"Just be careful," Emma said, keeping her eyes on her needles. "I know they rounded up a lot of folks when my dad… when Mae was kidnapped, but that doesn't mean there aren't more. I worry about you going out on calls by yourself."

Everyone in the room looked at Emma with sympathy. Ms. June reached over and patted her arm. Emma's dad ended up being the ringleader in Mae's kidnapping. He was killed that night, and no one in Colton, not even his daughter, mourned his passing.

"Don't worry, Emma. I'm usually carrying when I go out on calls. And if I had to, I suppose I could use my tranquilizer gun, but it wouldn't be very effective."

"Oh, dear. Have you ever had to use it?" Ms. June asked.

"No, I haven't, but I have seen my mentor tranquilize an unruly bull who wasn't too keen on being examined when I was in school."

Ms. June gasped, her hand going to her chest. "How frightening."

Jasmine shook her head with a slight smile. She decided Ms. June wouldn't handle hearing any more about the encounter or how thrilling it was at first. That was at the beginning of her time at the practice in Ohio, before she knew the truth. Her smile fell, remembering how disillusioned she'd been when she discovered the only reason they included her on the visit was to get photos they could use as publicity for the practice. They wanted to give the illusion that they were inclusive and progressive, but the reality was far different.

"You okay?" Presley asked.

"Yeah, I just got lost in my thoughts for a minute."

"Do you miss your old practice?" Callie asked.

"No," Jasmine said, a little too emphatically. She focused on the intricate cable stitch, ignoring the curious stares.

"Well, if you don't want to talk about the past, do you want to tell us who you're knitting that hat for?" Mae asked.

"Mae," Callie and Emma exclaimed in unison.

"That is none of your business," Callie finished.

Mae put her knitting down and looked around the room. "Don't tell me you all don't want to know what's going on between Jasmine and Rhett. I've been tryin' to fish it out of her all night, and none of y'all are any help."

Ms. June started sputtering and choking on the swig of kombucha she'd just taken while Ashton thumped her on the back.

"Lord, Mae, you could give direct directions," he said, chuckling.

Jasmine felt the heat rise and bloom across her cheeks. She gripped her circular needles so tightly, she expected the thin bamboo tips to splinter in her hands.

"We're just friends," she managed to say in a way that she thought made her sound noncommittal.

"Good for you, honey. I suspect that boy needs a friend," Ms. Ruby said.

Mae wrapped her arms around herself. "This whole town owes him for what he did. I'll never be able to thank him for getting the coordinates for where I was being taken to Jacob and Dan. He did everything he could to keep me from…." She shook her head, biting her lip.

Callie wrapped her arm around her best friend. Ashton noticed a tear slipping down Ms. June's cheek and handed her a handkerchief. The entire community felt the impact of that horrible night.

"Is there anything we can do for him?" Presley asked.

"I really don't know. Just treat him with kindness. I've noticed some folks still keep away from him when they see him on the street. Everyone must know that he was undercover by now, but—"

"Jacob and I have noticed it too," Mae said.

"That ain't right," Presley said with a frown. "If folks will put up with me after all the foolishness I've done, they should treat Rhett like a hero."

"I don't think that's what he wants, but if we can all try to be just… normal around him, maybe that would help."

Everyone nodded in agreement.

Callie and Mae, with babies and husbands waiting for them at home, were always the first to leave. Not long after Callie's and Mae's departure, Ms. June and Ms. Ruby took their leave, walking home together since they lived within a few houses of each other.

Ashton looked around the room as they were packing up. "You know, it would be nice if we could have a yarn shop in this town. It could be smaller than this and still big enough to host us all on Tuesday nights."

Mae nodded enthusiastically. "Any new business in town would be wonderful. Wouldn't it be great to walk around the town square and not see a single storefront papered over?"

"I know I'm new," Jasmine said, "so maybe you have already tried something like this, but have you done any advertising?"

Presley wrinkled her nose. "Like place an ad for a new business?"

"Sure, why not?" Jasmine said.

Ashton rubbed his hands together. "I like this idea. I'll talk to the rest of the board of the Colton Foundation. We have money set aside to give grants to small businesses. We can use that as an incentive."

"Let me know if there's anything I can do to help," Jasmine offered.

Callie had left a key with Presley to lock up the shop when they finished. They stood on the sidewalk for a few minutes, chatting about whether Colton could support a small yarn shop. They all agreed that if the shop also offered fabric and quilting supplies, it would be a hit with the crafters in the community. Presley and Ashton both gave her a hug before saying goodbye, and Jasmine turned toward her apartment, glowing with happiness. It felt good to have friends, and it lifted her heart knowing she'd settled into a community that really cared.

Just as she put her foot on the bottom stair, a movement in the park caught the corner of her eye. She changed course and headed toward the two figures sitting by the water. Rebel jumped up and trotted to her as she walked toward them.

"Hey, what are you two doing sitting here in the dark?"

Rebel licked her hand. Rhett stood up and came over.

"I… we… I was going to wait for you and offer to walk you home after your meeting. I was thinking, and I didn't notice you'd finished. I guess I'm not a very good escort."

Jasmine linked her arm through Rhett's. "I disagree. You're thoughtful, and I'm glad you're here. But you should have come in instead of waiting out here."

"I didn't want to make anyone uncomfortable."

Jasmine pulled back. "Why would anyone be uncomfortable?" She reached up and forced his eyes to meet hers when he answered with a shrug. "I know there are still folks in town who are having a hard time believing they can trust you, but Rhett, everyone in the knitting club is a friend. They only want to show their appreciation."

"It makes me uncomfortable," he admitted.

Jasmine let her hand fall from his face and wrapped her arms around him. "I'm sorry. I didn't mean to push."

Rhett sighed and held her for a minute before he let go. "Thanks for letting me walk you home."

Jasmine wrinkled her nose. "That wasn't much of a walk. Do you want to come upstairs and have some late supper with me?"

They'd reached the bottom of the staircase leading up to her apartment, and he blurted out, "I should go." But as Rhett stepped back, Rebel bounded up the stairs and sat down in front of her door.

"It looks like the decision's been made for you." Jasmine laughed, tugging on Rhett's hand as he followed her up the staircase with heavy footsteps.

She barely got the door open before Rebel ran inside and jumped up on the sofa, resting his head on his paws.

"Well, someone has made himself at home."

"Rebel, get down," Rhett ordered.

"It's okay, Rebel. You can stay."

Rhett stood awkwardly in the entryway, his eyes darting around the room.

"Come in," Jasmine said, giving him a gentle nudge. She steered him toward one of the barstools at the kitchen island.

He ran his hand over the honed marble countertop. "This is really nice."

"Thanks. Between Taylor Colton and his crew and Jacob, I feel very spoiled." Jasmine went to work, pulling out a container of potato soup she'd stashed in the freezer. "Taylor's your cousin, right?" She drummed her fingers on the countertop, waiting for the microwave to work its magic.

"Yeah, Taylor and Dax Ellis. We're all third or fourth cousins," Rhett replied. "Coltons are a tangled mess of kudzu vines. It's almost impossible to find the root, but we're all connected."

"My family is all over the place, mainly Illinois and Michigan, with a few relatives in California. We don't see each other often unless there's a wedding or a funeral, though."

"Is it just you and Isiah?"

"Yep, it's just us. Isiah has perfected the role of overprotective and annoying big brother."

Rhett chuckled. "I'd like to see him try to boss you around."

"It usually doesn't end well."

Jasmine set a bowl of soup in front of him. "How about a cold beer to go with this?"

"If you don't mind, could I have a cup of tea?"

"Of course. I have regular, chamomile, and some Earl Grey. Do any of those sound good?"

"Earl Grey, please."

By the time Jasmine put the kettle on and pulled out a couple of mugs, Rhett had emptied his bowl. Without asking, she refilled it and slid it in front of him. As long as she had the chance, she was going to get as much food into him as possible, so she grabbed a chocolate bar she'd been saving for the next time she was having PMS and needed a chocolate fix. She set it down on the table along with his cup of tea.

"Do you have a big family?" he asked when she settled on a stool next to him with her cup of tea.

"Average, I guess. My brother and I have a few first cousins, but we don't hang out that much. Are you close to your cousins?"

Rhett's mouth turned down. "I used to play with Taylor and Dax when we were kids, but we lived in Jackson, so I didn't see them very often. Most of the other family around here don't want to have anything to do with me since I'm responsible for having a lot of them arrested."

Jasmine put a comforting hand on Rhett's arm.

Rhett brushed his empty bowl away and leaned his elbows on the table. "I don't care that they were family. The members of my family that were arrested are dangerous, hateful people. My only regret is my cousin Larry weaseled out of any trouble."

"You did a good job, Rhett. Eventually, your cousin will get caught."

He put his hand over hers and smiled. "How do you do it?"

"Do what?"

He shook his head, still smiling. "You're one of the most positive people I've ever met."

"My brother used to give me a hard time about how sunny I always am. My family used to treat me like I was going to fall prey to every con man in town." Jasmine sat up straighter and looked Rhett in the eye. "They know I can take care of myself now."

Rhett's forehead creased. "What happened?"

Jasmine thought for a minute and decided she wasn't ready to share that part of her story yet. "Nothing I want to talk about, at least not yet." Jasmine reached out and put her hand over Rhett's. "The important thing is, I've learned that no one is perfect or happy all the time. And that's okay, as long as you take care of yourself and be brave enough to ask for help when you need it."

Rhett turned his hand over so his hand pressed against hers. His palm was both smooth and rough at the same time.

Looking down at where their hands joined, her skin tingled where they made contact. She'd never been bold in a relationship, but Jasmine knew it was up to her to make the first move after she'd just talked about being brave. Before she lost her nerve, Jasmine took her own words to heart.

Sliding off her stool, she moved to stand between Rhett's knees. He let go of her hand and pressed his to her back, gently drawing her closer. She was a puzzle piece that just locked into its mate. Alone, one piece made little sense, but once it connected with another, a picture formed.

Sweet orange with a hint of vanilla mingled in the air between them. Rhett's breath was warm, and his lips were soft as they ghosted over her cheek before they connected with hers.

She reached up and briefly brushed her lips. When she saw the heat flare in his eyes, she dropped her hand and took a step back.

"I shouldn't have done that," he said.

"It's okay, I… I'm… I haven't—it's been a long time since anyone kissed me."

Rhett's lips curled into a half smile. "Sweetheart, that wasn't a kiss."

*He's flirting with me. T*he realization filled her with a mixture of nervousness and joy. She'd never been very good at flirting, but right now, Jasmine wished she'd taken a masterclass because she wanted to flirt with Rhett, and she wanted to be good at it. And she wanted Rhett to kiss her.

Now was the time to say something, something seductive to let him know what she wanted, but when she opened her mouth, the only thing that came out was "Oh."

His expression grew pensive, and he announced, "I have to go."

"You can stay," she said in a breathy voice.

She reached up and cupped the side of his face, wishing he would let her help him heal. She could see in his eyes that he was still holding onto his pain, keeping it close to his heart, and that he'd already made the decision to leave.

Chapter Ten

Rhett approached the clinic from across the park, still feeling like an ass for running away from Jasmine the night before. He looked down at the bouquet he was strangling in his hand and, loosening his grip, he took a deep breath. Signaling Rebel to wait for him, he opened the door to the clinic.

A young man was behind the counter at the reception desk, checking in a man and his son with a cute little gray rabbit in a carrier. Once they checked in, he moved forward. The young man grinned at Rhett, his eyes flickering to the flowers.

"Let me guess, you must be Rhett." He held his hand out. "I'm Zach, Dr. Owens's new receptionist."

Rhett shook Zach's hand. "Nice to meet you." Rhett glanced at the little boy holding the carrier in his lap. "I'm sure Dr. Owens is busy. I just wanted to drop these off."

Zach shook his head with a smile, leaned over the counter, and whispered, "She's in her office. I can give you five minutes."

He pointed Rhett in the right direction, and he went back and knocked on the door.

"Come in."

Rhett opened the door and held out the flowers before poking his head in.

"Zach says I only have five minutes, and that's not long enough to apologize for running out on you yesterday," Rhett said, "so I'm hoping you like daffodils and you'll come on a date with me this weekend so I can apologize properly."

Jasmine got up from her desk and took the flowers out of Rhett's hands.

"Daffodils are my favorite, and I'd like to go out with you this weekend."

He let out the breath he didn't realize he'd been holding and gave her a kiss on the cheek. "I'll call you tonight."

She nodded. "Thank you for the flowers."

Rhett nodded too, then backed out of the door.

"Hope the flowers worked," Zach said with a wink when Rhett passed through the waiting room.

Rhett gave him a quick wave on his way back outside, where Rebel was patiently waiting on the sidewalk.

"Don't let me screw this up, okay?" he said to Rebel before rubbing his head.

SUNLIGHT GLINTED off the windows of the cabin when he returned, making it difficult to see inside.

Rhett still hadn't been able to bring himself to go in since he'd been home. His hands went numb every time he reached for the door handle. Why was it so hard? Maybe it was the fact that if he went inside, he would have to face that his grandpa was gone. He'd been a larger-than-life figure to Rhett. His grandpa had revolted against any kind of hero worship from him. He'd made it clear that he was a flawed man, but to Rhett, he was a savior who took him in when no one else wanted him.

"Yeah, I know," he said when Rebel pressed himself against his leg with a whine.

He sat on the top step of the porch and squeezed his eyes shut, trying to block out the memory of the last time he saw his grandpa.

George Colton was a man who could see the full arc of his life when Rhett sat next to him on the log at the pond for the last time.

"You've made your decision?" his grandpa asked.

"I don't know when I'll be able to see you after this," Rhett said. "You've got to make it look real."

"Don't you worry about me. I'll put on a good show for everyone. I'm sorry about your folks, though."

"It won't be that bad." Rhett shrugged. "We were just starting to reconnect, so they won't miss me that much."

"That's not true, and you know it. Your folks have settled down, and they'd like to spend more time with you."

"I don't want to be an inconvenience."

"That's not what you are, and it's not what you've ever been."

They had talked well into the night about the past and the future. Rhett walked away from that conversation believing there would still be time, that when his mission was over, he'd have a few more years to spend on that log with his grandpa. Eight months into his mission, George Colton collapsed and died with his fishing pole clutched in his hand. A massive heart attack robbed Rhett of being there for his grandpa's last moments on earth.

The funeral was on a Thursday. Rhett started the day with a bottle of whiskey and ended the day passed out in the back of his truck. Rhett had known he'd have to make sacrifices during his assignment. He'd walked in with his eyes open. It was hard enough dealing with the reality of people looking at him with fear in their eyes, thinking he was a racist. He'd made the hard decision to go undercover. The next choice they forced him to make gutted him, and he was still living with the impact of that decision when he lost his grandpa.

He was numb when he found out his grandpa had left him everything he owned. The people he was associating with were thrilled, thinking they would have another base of operations when they found out he'd inherited the cabin. The news that George Colton left his wayward grandson his fishing cabin was the talk of the town. If Colton had a newspaper, it would have made headlines if they knew about the money. Rhett was smart enough to keep that part of his inheritance quiet.

George had been part of an investment club for over thirty years. Most times, the group would buy a stock, turn around, and sell it if it went up a dollar or two. His grandpa went along with whatever the group decided most of the time, but every once in a while, he'd invest some of his own money in a stock that he thought they shouldn't be so quick to sell. It turned out his grandpa's instincts were good. He left Rhett just over four million dollars. Every penny was sitting in the bank untouched, just like the cabin. He couldn't bring himself to use it.

Rhett squinted at the fishing pond off in the distance, fighting the surge of anger that threatened to overwhelm him. Damn George for thinking he could make up for what he'd lost. He was tired, tired of being angry and tired of being lost. Rebel and Jasmine were what kept him from giving up and just walking away from Colton for good.

He looked over his shoulder at the door.

"Not today, boy," he said, digging his fingers into Rebel's fur.

Rebel rested his head on Rhett's thigh with a heavy huff.

"Yeah, I know. I'm frustrated too."

He wanted to have Jasmine come out to the cabin. Maybe spend an evening on the porch, watching lightning bugs between kissing and maybe more. Rhett needed to stop indulging in a fantasy that wasn't ever going to become reality. But he also had to put the past behind him and embrace the present. Tomorrow. Tomorrow, he would go inside and start to clean up and move in. That left him with today, a sunny spring day with nothing to do.

Rhett debated whether he wanted to go fishing or maybe on a long hike when his phone pinged with a message, bringing a smile to his face for the first time that day.

Rhett typed a quick reply and stood up. "Come on, Rebel. We have something better to do than hang out here."

Talking on the phone was nice, but Rhett hadn't been able to see Jasmine as much as he'd liked. And that was his fault. He didn't want to draw too much attention and subject Jasmine to the curious looks from people when he was around town. He'd noticed the hint of fear in Jasmine's vet tech's eyes when he came into the office. But Jasmine's smile every time he saw her made it worth it, even though he worried he was asking too much from her. He didn't want people to think poorly of Jasmine for being seen hanging out with him.

Rhett opened the door of his hunter green Jeep and stepped back to let Rebel jump in. The new car was an indulgence, but one he could afford since he'd used almost none of his salary for the past two years. There wasn't anything to spend it on. Rhett lived with the bare minimum he needed to survive. He couldn't stand driving the old truck with its gun rack and stomach-churning bumper stickers, and the first thing he'd done when he'd gotten back was trade it in.

This was the first actual date he'd gone out on in a long time. He'd almost given up on the idea until he met Jasmine. He wasn't opposed to dating; he used to go out on the weekends just like normal people. There were a few times when he'd gone out on dates while undercover. Those dates were part of the job and left him feeling disgusted with himself and the women he'd gone out with.

Jasmine was the first woman he wanted to spend time with. No, every day with. It wasn't just about sex, although he'd spent plenty of time indulging in those fantasies. Her kindness and intelligence were qualities he valued in a woman. She brought laughter back into his life. Rhett didn't realize just how much laughter had been missing from his world until he met her.

She was waiting for him on the bottom step leading to her apartment. She jumped up and came toward him with a smile, wearing a pale purple sweater that was huge on her and belted at the waist. It fell to her knees, only giving a glimpse of the slim-fit jeans that were tucked into a pair of brown suede knee-high boots. That was one of the other things that set Jasmine apart from other women he'd dated. Instead of trying to show off her figure, she covered herself up. Every time he saw her, she was wearing baggy, oversized clothes.

"What do you need our help with?" he asked once she buckled herself in.

"We're going to check out some pet stores in Greenwood."

"What for?"

"We were talking at the knitting circle, and Mae suggested I should sell a few pet toys and supplies. I have room in the lobby to add a small section with items for sale. I thought we could go check out the competition, and I can get ideas on what customers are looking for."

"What's our part in this?" Rhett jerked his thumb at Rebel.

Jasmine's smile grew even bigger. "We're posing as a couple, shopping for a new toy for our dog on a Saturday afternoon."

Rhett tried not to panic. "Are you sure that's a good idea?"

"Why wouldn't it be?"

Was there any reason he couldn't, other than his own discomfort being out in public?

"Sure, why not? Let's go for it," he said.

She reached around to give Rebel a pat on the head and turned back to Rhett. "Are you going camping?"

Shit. He'd been so excited when she called that he forgot about the sleeping bag and pillow in the back seat.

"I was thinking about it. I might head up north and spend a couple of nights in the Piney Woods," he lied.

"Sounds like fun."

Thankfully, she changed the subject and asked him about the cabin and how his restoration efforts were coming along on the drive to Greenwood. What were a few more lies to the one he'd already told? He asked her about her week. Even though they talked every night, she still came up with stories about patients he hadn't heard before. He pulled over in front of the store Jasmine pointed out to him and parked. Big cities made him itch. Greenwood didn't really qualify as a city, but it had a big enough population and bustling streets to put him on high alert as he scanned the passersby. Of course there wasn't any threat, but old habits died hard. Either that or he was hyperaware that he was with a Black woman, a beautiful Black woman. He couldn't help but wonder what she saw in a plain old country boy.

Jasmine slid her hand into his when they walked into the first store. She leaned over and whispered, "We're a couple, remember?"

Once again, Jasmine found a way to push his doubts and fears away. She pulled different toys from the display, asking Rebel what he thought. Rebel played his part perfectly, tilting his head as if he were considering the pros and cons of each toy she showed him. It didn't take long for Rhett to become caught up in the fun.

Rebel was having the time of his life as they went from store to store. Jasmine insisted on buying him whatever toy he picked out at each store, claiming it was for research. The hand-holding became second nature by the end of the day. They went to five different stores, sharing what they liked and didn't like about each one. Jasmine asked his opinion about how much stock she thought made sense to have at the clinic and what kind of displays would work. It felt good to be able to help out and voice his opinion after spending most of his time listening and observing. The best part of the day was taking Jasmine to his favorite little tamale place on the way back to Colton and introducing her to another type of Southern cuisine.

He didn't want the day to end when he pulled up to Jasmine's building. He cut the engine and got out to open her door.

"You're spoiling me," she said, taking the hand he held out to her.

"My mama raised me right. That's why I'm going to walk you to your door."

Jasmine was standing on the first step, bringing them face-to-face. The light from the pink sunset cast a rosy glow over her face. Rhett reached up and cupped her cheek. When she put her hand over his and shifted closer, he lost his last bit of self-control.

There were kisses that were fun and kisses that made you ache and burn. And then he kissed Jasmine. Her kisses were like her name, soft and sweet, curling around him, bringing him back home. He could never kiss another woman after this. No one else, just her. She was the sunlight that brought him out of darkness. He needed to let go, he should let go, but he pulled her closer instead.

For too long, he'd kept anyone from getting close to him, both physically and emotionally. The sensation of having Jasmine's arms wrapped around him was almost too much, and yet he wanted more.

She made a funny little noise at the back of her throat and tilted her head, deepening the kiss. He tugged at the belt of her sweater. When it fell away, he reveled in the chance to touch her body. Her fingers made their way into his hair, digging into his scalp. He forced himself to take his time and savor every taste, tracing the fullness of her lips with his tongue. He committed to memory the way his hand fit perfectly at the curve of her waist and the softness of her hair when it brushed against his cheek.

Jasmine stiffened in his arms at the sound of the siren from one of the sheriff's SUVs. Jasmine's head whipped around, her eyes narrowing, watching the car speed down the street. Her eyes were enormous and dark, her lips wet and pink when she looked back at him with a small smile.

She exhaled, pressing her forehead to his. "I didn't mean to ruin our moment."

"You didn't ruin anything."

"It's the only bad thing about living here. I'm kind of hyperaware when my brother is out in the field."

One more reason he needed to keep his distance. It would be too much to ask Jasmine to be with someone whose job put them at risk every day.

Jasmine took her lips away from his just long enough to reconnect them with his skin just below his ear. He grunted and sucked in his breath. When her fingers tugged at the opening of his shirt, he grabbed her face, looking into her eyes. He dropped his forehead to hers, squeezing his eyes shut.

"Stop," he ground out in a harsh whisper.

She fumbled with the top button on his shirt while she pressed her mouth to his again.

"Stop," he said again with more force.

Her eyes searched his face, looking at him with confusion mixed with want.

He took a deep, shuddering breath and reluctantly pushed her away. "I can't do this."

"What… why?" she asked.

"I've got to go," he said in a low, harsh voice.

If he walked away now, he wouldn't cause more pain later. He was too uncertain and full of risk to share it with anyone. The best thing for both of them was what he was doing right now. He got into his Jeep and drove away. Rhett's eyes flicked to Jasmine in the rearview mirror, standing at the bottom of the stairs, watching him drive away.

"Don't look at me like that. This is for the best," he growled at his companion.

Rebel whined and flopped down on the back seat.

JASMINE GRIPPED the stair rail tightly, watching Rhett drive away. Bad dates happened to everyone at least once, but she'd never had someone practically run away from her the way Rhett just did.

She lifted her hand to her lips. The skies were still gray, and rain was on the horizon, but when Rhett's lips touched hers, spring bloomed, filling her senses with color and light. Jasmine dropped her hand and sighed. Clearly, the kiss wasn't the same for Rhett.

She climbed up her staircase and stopped, coming back down again. Being alone in her apartment seemed too depressing. The evening air was cool with just a hint of lilacs in the air, providing proof that spring was here. Jasmine wrapped her sweater around herself. She retied the belt firmly around her waist and then loosened it again. Maybe that was what turned Rhett off and made him leave. She blinked back tears, remembering the comments she'd endured from her former employers.

Boy, those scrubs really show off your thighs, don't they?

Over time, she started wearing larger sizes, trying to hide her body. That led to more comments about how she should take more pride in how she looked. She was too sexy or too frumpy. It didn't matter. The point was obvious; she wasn't what they wanted.

"Hey," a voice called out.

Jasmine looked up to see Presley Beaumont waving to her from her porch.

"What are ya up to this evenin'?" she asked.

Jasmine looked around. She was so lost in her thoughts, she hadn't been paying attention to where she was going.

"Just out for a little walk."

"Do you want to come up and have a glass of somethin'?" Presley asked.

"Sure, why not."

Presley did a little jump and clapped her hands when Jasmine headed up the walk. The Beaumonts lived in an elegant Victorian on a corner lot. The white house with dark green shutters was two stories with a grand wraparound porch. An ornate mahogany front door with beveled glass panes sparkled even in the evening light. Presley pointed to a large wicker sofa on the porch, between two large urns overflowing with giant Boston ferns.

"Have a seat. Do you want sweet tea or wine?"

Jasmine nodded. "Wine would be good. Thanks."

She settled herself on the blue and green paisley-printed cushions, admiring the view while Presley went inside. The old-fashioned lampposts that lined the street flickered on, illuminating the street in a warm glow.

Presley came back out with a bottle and two glasses.

"I hope this is okay. I stole it from Ashton's stash. There'll be hell to pay when he finds out, but I didn't want to give y'all wine from a box on your first visit to my house."

"I don't want to get you in trouble with your brother. Wine from a box would be okay."

Presley shook her head, setting the bottle and glasses on the table. She pulled a wine opener out of her pocket with a determined look on her face.

"Nope, I want to make a good impression."

She looked down at the corkscrew and then at the bottle with a furrowed brow.

"Would you like me to help you with that?" Jasmine offered.

Presley plopped down and held the corkscrew out to her.

"You'd better do it. The last time I tried, there were little bits of cork in everyone's glass. Dang it, I really wanted to be elegant," she muttered.

Jasmine bowed her head, pretending to focus on opening the bottle to hide her smile. Presley Beaumont was one of those people who didn't have a filter. Presley's way of blurting out whatever was on her mind was a quality Jasmine both feared and admired.

She twisted the metal corkscrew into the pliant cork, and it came out of the bottle with a soft pop. Jasmine poured the light burgundy liquid into the glass. She looked at the label and raised her eyebrows. Brothers in Arms Pinot Noir.

"Your brother has good taste."

"Yeah, he's the classy one, or at least that's what he keeps telling me."

Jasmine laughed. "I think big brothers are born with some kind of instruction manual for teasing little sisters."

Presley looked at her, wide-eyed. "Goodness gracious, I think I'd be scared to death if I had to grow up with your brother teasin' me. It's bad enough Ash and I are still livin' under the same roof."

"Isiah is all bark and no bite."

Presley frowned. "I'm pretty sure he's all bite with me."

Jasmine's heart went out to Presley. It was clear she wanted to make a good impression on Isiah. From what her brother had told her so far, Presley wasn't successful.

"Don't let my brother intimidate you. It's good for him when someone stands up to him every once in a while."

Presley gave her a skeptical look.

"Can I ask, why do you and your brother still live at home?"

"Neither of us wants to leave Dad alone. We both feel guilty, I guess." Presley looked up at the ornate arches framing the porch columns and sighed. "This house has my heart. I can't imagine living anywhere else."

They sipped their wine, watching lightning brighten the sky far off on the horizon.

"How are ya liking living in Colton?"

Jasmine thought for a minute. "It's amazing how quickly a place can feel like home. The way you talk about this house, that's how I feel about Colton. It grabbed hold of my heart the first time I came to visit Isiah here."

"I know Isiah's happy to have you here." Presley took another sip of her wine, eyeing her over rim. She set her glass down and clasped her hands in her lap, sitting up straight with her ankles crossed.

"I was wondering… well, everyone in town is wondering, and I know you didn't want to say when Mae cornered you at the knitting club, but now it's just the two of us, so… what's going on between you and Rhett Colton?"

Jasmine looked down at the contents of her glass. "Nothing. We're just friends."

It hurt to say it. Jasmine realized just how much she wanted her relationship with Rhett to be more than just friends when she heard the words come out of her mouth.

It surprised her when Presley reached over and gave her hand a squeeze. "I understand."

She wasn't being condescending or making fun of her. When Jasmine looked up, she only saw sympathy in Presley's eyes.

"The thing is, everybody's been talkin' about how the two of you were makin' out by your apartment the other night."

"Oh no." Jasmine dropped her head in her palm. "My brother's going to interrogate me for sure."

"I shouldn't have said anything."

"No, it's okay. Isiah warned me there weren't any secrets in a small town." She eyed Presley. "Do you want to tell me what people are saying?"

Presley chewed on her lip. "Well, folks are curious. I mean, everyone knows Rhett was pretending to be racist, but some people think he's going overboard trying to show he's not by seeing you."

Jasmine sat up straighter. "Wait, what? People think he's using me?"

"Well, kind of."

The idea irked her. She jumped up and paced the porch before turning back to Presley.

"He's not." Jasmine thumped her chest. "I know what it's like to be used, I know what that feels like, and Rhett doesn't make me feel that way."

She dropped back into her seat with an exasperated sigh and then noticed Presley staring at her with wide eyes.

"I shouldn't have snapped at you like that," Jasmine muttered. "Touchy subject."

"Well, for what it's worth, I don't think that. I've seen the way he looks at you, and… I wish a man would look at me that way," Presley said.

An image of Rhett's blue eyes gazing into hers just before their mouths met filled Jasmine's mind. "It can definitely take your breath away," she admitted.

Presley looked out at the night sky wistfully.

"Whatever I thought we had between us, I think I misread the signs."

"Well, I'm rooting for you."

"Thanks, Presley. I appreciate that, I really do. I'm just not sure there's anything to root for." Jasmine smiled. "You know, I've made more friends since I moved to Colton than I've ever had before. It's another reason I enjoy living here so much. Thanks for the wine and sympathy."

Presley's eyes grew wide, and a huge grin lit up her face.

"I really wanted to be friends with Isiah's sister… I mean, you."

Jasmine fought the urge to laugh. Presley was fun, and she was happy to have her as a friend, no matter what Presley's reasons were for wanting to hang out.

Chapter Eleven

RHETT NEVER made it to the mountains. Every morning, he got up and climbed out of his Jeep and walked up to the front door of the cabin, and every day, he backed away.

He was stuck, unable to figure out how to let go of the past and move forward.

A phone call interrupted his solitude, and over an hour later, he walked into a bar two towns away and made his way straight to the back. Sliding onto a stool at the end of the bar, he pulled his hat down low over his eyes.

The bartender came over and slid a beer in front of him.

"You look like shit," he said.

"Sounds about right."

The bartender scanned the sparse patrons of the bar before he leaned in, speaking in a low tone. "There was a group of guys in here last week talking about how they were gonna make a lot of money with your cousin Larry. Those bastards also mentioned your name, talking about how you betrayed Larry. They said Larry planned on making you pay for being a traitor."

"Did they say anything else?"

"He was bragging about how he and Larry broke into a clinic over in the next town. Maybe I shouldn't have called, but I figured it might help. I know you want to get that bastard." Rhett's informant shook his head. "That man is as slippery as an eel, isn't he?"

Rhett downed his beer and slammed the empty glass on the table. "Larry's not smart, but he's always been just clever enough to make sure someone else takes the blame for his crimes."

"What can I do to help?"

"Can you keep your ears open? I need names and information. I will not let him get away this time."

The bartender nodded. Rhett threw a twenty on the bar and stood. "You've got my number."

Rebel was sleeping in the front seat of Rhett's Jeep when he came out. He lifted his head, one ear flopped over and one upright, when Rhett got in.

"Sorry to disturb your sleep," Rhett said, patting Rebel's side.

His best friend yawned and lay back down with a snort. Rhett looked at the dog with envy. It would have been nice to sleep like he didn't have any cares in the world.

A WEEK passed since he'd kissed Jasmine, and despite his best intentions, Rhett found himself back in Colton's town square, sitting against a tree in the park, looking up at Jasmine's window instead of going back to his grandpa's cabin.

For a minute, he thought she might not answer when he called. Just when he was about to hang up, her face appeared on the screen.

She didn't greet him with her usual smile, and there was a note of trepidation in her voice when she answered.

"Hi, Rhett. How was your camping trip?"

"I didn't go camping." He figured honesty would be the best approach. He knew he'd messed up, and he was going to have to make it right. "I'm sorry it took me a week to pull my head out of my ass and call you."

Jasmine's chin quivered. "What happened, Rhett? I thought we were… I thought… I guess what I was thinking wasn't what you were."

"I worry. I worry about… everything. When you were talking about how you worry about your brother, I thought it would be better if I stayed away so you wouldn't worry about me. I thought I wanted to leave the agency when my assignment ended, but I don't know anymore. My job can be dangerous. I can't ask my friends and family… I don't want to be a burden to the people around me. The reality is there are people out there who hate me for what I did. I don't want anyone to get caught in the crosshairs if someone acts out."

"Oh, Rhett." Jasmine shook her head. "It doesn't work that way."

"I know that. I just have a hard time remembering it."

"It really confused me when you left. I thought that—" She pressed her lips together. "It doesn't matter what I thought."

"Yes, it matters. I shouldn't have walked away. I hate knowing I hurt you."

"I missed our calls. Do you think we can go back to being friends?"

Rhett exhaled. "I don't think I can do that."

"Oh."

"Jasmine"—Rhett rushed, wanting to remove the pain from Jasmine's face—"I can't go back to the way things were before now that I've kissed you. I can't see you and not want to touch you, kiss you, see you… all of you."

A hint of pink spread over her cheeks, making her freckles stand out.

"Thank you," he said.

She scrunched up her nose. "For what?"

"I needed to see you smile again."

"Do you… do you want to come upstairs, or are you going to keep sitting in the park?"

He whipped his head around and looked at the light in Jasmine's window. "How did you know?"

"I'm sitting by the window. I saw you when you pulled up."

Rhett let his head fall back against the rough bark of the tree. Rebel put his paw on his leg.

"Come upstairs, Rhett."

He nodded. "Okay."

Rhett said goodbye and glanced at his clothes, running his hand through his hair. The informant at the bar was right. He looked like shit. His back ached from sleeping in his car, and a hot shower instead of scrubbing down with a hose behind the cabin would have made him more presentable. He got up, his arms hanging loosely at his sides. He shouldn't have agreed to go upstairs, but Rebel wouldn't allow him to run away. He pressed his body against Rhett's leg, pushing him toward Jasmine's apartment.

Her door opened at the top of the stairs, and he could see the outline of her figure in the warm light coming from her apartment. His footsteps were heavy as he climbed the stairs.

"I didn't think to clean up before I came," he muttered when he reached the top of the stairs.

They stood toe-to-toe on the small landing. Jasmine reached up and cupped his face, running her hand over his beard, her eyes searching his.

"I don't care about that."

She took his hand and led him inside. They were both so wrapped up in seeing each other, neither of them noticed Rebel had gone inside and made himself at home on the sofa.

Jasmine laughed and went over to greet him. "I've missed you," she said, kissing the top of his furry head.

"We missed you," Rhett said.

She turned back to him, her eyes raking him over. "I don't mean to be rude, but when was the last time you took a shower?"

"I, uh, it's been a while." Since he couldn't bring himself to use his grandfather's cabin, Rhett had been using an old outhouse on the property for a bathroom and the hose for a makeshift shower.

She reached out and placed her hand over his heart. "Rhett, whatever it is you're punishing yourself for, it's time to stop."

He grabbed her hand, pressing it against his chest close enough that she could feel his heart beat under her fingertips. This woman was the only person besides his grandfather who saw him, all of him. His eyes connected with hers for a moment, and then he dropped his head. Jasmine moved closer. Rhett's other hand shot out, grasping her shoulder, holding her away, keeping her from wrapping her arms around him, while he continued to clutch her hand against his heart. A harsh sob tore from him, and he finally let go.

Rhett release the pain and sorrow he'd been holding in for so long. Jasmine let him hold her with her own tears threatening to fall. She didn't move, waiting until he was ready to let her go. Ten minutes passed, or was it an hour? It didn't matter. Every once in a while, she'd reach down and stroke Rebel's head as he pressed up against Rhett's side. The dog would look back at her with a worried expression.

"It's okay," she whispered, trying to reassure all of them.

Eventually, Rhett drew in a heavy breath and looked at her, his eyes red and his face blotchy. He let go of her and wiped his nose with the back of his sleeve.

"I didn't mean to do that." His voice was raw and a little shaky.

"You needed to. I know that sometimes when you call me and tell me you're at your grandpa's cabin, you're sitting in the park. Why are you lying to me, Rhett?"

He squeezed his eyes shut and tried to rub away the dull ache that formed in his chest.

"I wasn't lying to hurt you. I… I can't go into the cabin, not yet."

Jasmine walked him backward until the back of his legs hit the couch. She pushed him down and sat on his lap and then grasped the sides of his face and turned his head so that she could look him in the eye.

"Where have you been sleeping?"

"In my car."

"Oh, Rhett." She wrapped her arms around him. "Why didn't you say something?"

He hugged her back, burying his face into the crook of her neck. "I didn't realize what it was going to be like when I finished my assignment. I didn't know how hard it would be to pretend like everything was normal. When I met you, it was the first time I realized I could be happy again."

He pulled away from her and looked around as if he were just waking up and noticing his surroundings.

"I shouldn't have burdened you with all of that." Rhett patted Rebel on the head. "We should go."

"You keep saying that. You're the one kicking yourself out, not me. You're not going anywhere." Jasmine gave him a gentle push toward the bathroom. "Go take a shower."

Rhett gripped the doorjamb with his back to her, hesitating.

"Take as long as you need. Rebel and I will be here when you're finished."

He hesitated for just a moment before he stepped over the threshold.

JASMINE HOVERED outside the door until she heard the shower start before she went into her room and started digging through her dresser. The good thing about wearing baggy clothes was that she had a pair of sweats that would fit Rhett.

When she heard the shower turn off, she went to the bathroom and knocked, opening the door a crack. "I have clean clothes for you. Sorry, I don't have any underwear." She bit her lip. "Um, if you just leave your other clothes in there, I'll throw them in the wash."

She closed her eyes and shoved the clothes through the door.

"Thanks," he said.

As soon as he took the clothes out of her hand, she closed the door and sighed. A minute later, the door opened again.

Rhett's hair was standing at all ends around his head where he'd toweled it off. Jasmine pointed to the kitchen table.

"Sit down. I'll be right back."

She went into the bathroom and gathered his clothes, along with a comb, a pair of scissors, another clean towel, and some hair products. Once she got the wash started, she returned to where he was sitting, watching her through exhausted eyes.

Jasmine set the comb and scissors on the table and poured some oil into her palm. She rubbed her hands together and started running her hands through his hair.

Rhett let out a low moan. "That smells good. What is it?"

"Hair oil; it's a Black thing."

He smiled slightly, keeping his eyes closed.

Once his hair was conditioned, she started combing out the tangles. His golden wheat-colored strands fell in soft waves past his shoulders. Jasmine took a deep breath and picked up the scissors.

"I'm nowhere near a professional, but if you trust me, I'll just give you a trim."

He turned to face her and opened his eyes. "I trust you."

Her heart thumped and then completely flipped over. Jasmine sucked in her breath and moved away from his cerulean-blue eyes to focus on her task. When she finished, he ran his hand over his head.

"It feels good."

"I only took off an inch, just to freshen up the ends. Do you… can I trim your beard just a bit?"

When he nodded, Jasmine picked up the oil, poured a little more into her palm, and ran her hands over his beard. Rhett tilted his head back with his eyes closed, his nostrils flared. As she worked the oil in, he continued to relax under her hands. She wanted to keep touching, stroking, staying in this moment for as long as she could. When Rhett shifted, she looked down and realized they were both getting caught up in the moment. She picked up the scissors and snipped away the weeks of neglect.

"How short do you want me to go?" she asked.

"Whatever you think is good is fine."

Jasmine decided it would be better to go shorter, not knowing when Rhett might get another trim.

"Don't move," she muttered, leaning close to trim the hair above his lip.

She rubbed a little more oil through his beard and hair before announcing, "All finished."

Rhett got up and went into the bathroom. Jasmine watched anxiously while he looked at himself in the mirror, turning his face and stroking his beard.

"Is it okay?" she asked.

Rhett turned and gave her a smile. He came over and hesitated for a moment before gathering her in his arms, hugging her.

He smelled like soap, coconut, and the lavender laundry soap she used from her sweatshirt that he was wearing.

He nodded but didn't let go right away.

Jasmine reached up to smooth away the wrinkles from his forehead. "When was the last time you had a good night's sleep?"

His voice was harsh and anguished when he answered, "Almost three years."

Taking him by the hand, she led him toward her bedroom. He jerked to a stop at her doorway.

"I can't."

"Nothing's going to… we're not going to have sex. I'll sleep on the couch. But you need a good night's rest. Just one night."

She went over to the bed and lifted the covers and plumped the pillows.

"Get in, Rhett."

With a heavy sigh, he lay down. She pulled the covers up over him and gently brushed the hair out of his eyes. She looked to the doorway where his companion waited patiently.

"Come on, Rebel. You too."

Rebel made one graceful leap onto the bed and tucked himself next to his owner. Rhett stroked the dog's thick fur. He exhaled and closed his eyes.

"I'll see you both in the morning," she whispered.

He barely nodded, already half asleep. Jasmine went back to the main room. An hour later she'd just pulled Rhett's clean clothes out of the dryer when she paused, tilting her head toward her bedroom.

Jasmine heard Rebel's whine just before Rhett's shout. She ran into her room and found Rebel standing on the bed, pawing at his owner while Rhett thrashed and shouted.

"Rebel, get down," she ordered.

Rebel jumped off the bed and sat down next to it, focused on Rhett. Jasmine sat on the edge of the bed and grasped Rhett's shoulders.

"Rhett, it's Jasmine. I need you to wake up," she said in a firm voice.

She repeated her command, and his eyes flew open, looking at her in confusion for a second before they grew wide. "Did I hurt you?"

He pulled himself up into a sitting position and grasped her hands, looking her over.

"I'm fine. You didn't hurt me."

He let go of her and leaned back against the headboard with a shudder. "I was dreaming."

"How often do you have nightmares?" Jasmine asked.

"Too many."

"Do you want to tell me about them?"

He shook his head, reached for her hand again, and gripped it tightly.

"Have you told anyone about them?" she asked.

"No."

"Maybe you should."

Rhett ran his hand through his hair. "I don't want to burden anyone else with them."

"I wouldn't feel burdened."

"I appreciate it, I really do, but I'm fine. I don't need any help. I just need… I want…."

"Do you want me to stay with you?"

Rhett squeezed his eyes shut and nodded.

"Let me change into my pajamas. I'll be right back."

Jasmine grabbed her flannel pants and a T-shirt on her way into the bathroom. She changed, used the facilities, and washed her face. Standing in front of the mirror with her scarf in her hand, she glanced over her shoulder. Was she willing to let Rhett see her like this? She reached up and twisted one of her curls. It might not be sexy, but it would be much worse to wake up with a matted mess if she didn't take proper care of her hair. She pulled it up into a top knot and secured it with a scrunchy, folded the scarf into a triangle, and wrapped it around her head, protecting her curls.

Rhett's face was relaxed, his eyes half-closed when she came out of the bathroom. She slipped under the covers and hesitated, not sure what to do.

Rhett solved the problem as he snaked his hand around her waist and pulled her close, tucking her up against his side. He rested his cheek on the top of her head and breathed deeply.

"Thank you," he murmured. Jasmine lay still in his arms. She hadn't shared a bed with anyone for a long time, and she'd forgotten how good it felt. Rhett was strong enough to show her both his strength and his vulnerabilities, and that was different from her past relationship. Jasmine snuggled closer, syncing her breathing with the rise and fall of Rhett's as it lulled her to sleep.

Chapter Twelve

Jasmine stirred the next morning, half awake and half asleep, wondering why the bed was so cold. She sat up with a start, looking around. Where were Rhett and Rebel?

They were gone. No text or note, just gone.

She threw off the covers and stomped into her kitchen to start her morning routine. Drumming her fingers on the countertop, Jasmine watched the coffee drip slowly into the carafe. This morning the life-giving elixir seemed to taunt her, going slower than molasses.

With each drip, her frustration grew. How could he just get up and walk out on her like that? Once she took a few fortifying sips of coffee, frustration turned into anger. She grabbed her phone, her fingers flying over the keyboard.

You could have left a note instead of just leaving.

She finished her coffee, watching the three dots at the bottom of her screen appear, disappear, and appear again. There was a sharp ring of her coffee mug cracking against the countertop when she saw Rhett's reply.

I didn't want to be a burden.

"What the hell is that supposed to mean?" she muttered, slamming her phone on the counter.

She'd lain awake in Rhett's arms last night, picturing what life would look like waking up in bed together, having coffee in bed on a lazy Sunday morning with Rebel taking up too much room. Jasmine was ready, and she knew, or at least she thought she knew, Rhett wanted her too. Wandering back into her room, she stared at the rumpled sheets on her bed. She thought…. Jasmine pushed her fantasy of waking up in Rhett's arms and making love out of her mind.

A shower didn't improve her mood. Spending extra time on her hair and makeup didn't help either. Jasmine even considered wearing something other than her baggy scrubs. She stared at the form-fitting jeans hanging in her closet, chewing on her lip. Who was she trying to impress? If she was dressing for Rhett, it wasn't like he was around to see it.

"This is stupid," she muttered. "You're smart enough not to dress to impress a guy."

But as she slammed her legs into her oversized scrubs, she realized she was still dressing to make an impression, just a different one.

Imani and Zach were chatting over coffee when Jasmine arrived.

"You okay, Dr. Owens?" Imani asked.

"I'm fine, just didn't sleep well last night."

Imani gave her a sympathetic nod. "I hate nights like that."

"Dr. Owens, Ms. June called about her chickens again," Zach said.

Jasmine bit back a groan. June Palmer was Colton's resident free spirit, a well-meaning soul who often entertained the knitting club with her latest ideas for town improvements, much to the mayor's chagrin. Mae just about fainted when Ms. June suggested they use goats to keep the grass in the park trimmed at their last meeting.

"Which one is it this time?" Jasmine asked.

"Mary Sue."

"Do I have any appointments this morning?"

Zach shook his head. "I hate to tell you this, but you have plenty of time. You don't have any appointments until this afternoon."

"Fine," Jasmine grumbled, going into her office to grab her medical bag.

The birds chirping in the trees were in a much better mood than she was as she trudged across the park toward Ms. June's house.

"Morning, Dr. Owens." The oldest of the three sisters known as the Jewels waved from where she was weeding under the roses planted around the gazebo in the park.

"Morning, Ms. Opal."

The middle sister, Pearl, popped her head out from the other side of the gazebo and waved.

"Morning, Ms. Pearl," Jasmine called out.

The youngest of the sisters was just going into the medical clinic when Jasmine reached the other side of the park.

Ruby narrowed her eyes. "I don't mean to be rude, honey, but you look like you've had a little more lemon than sugar in your tea this mornin'."

Jasmine's shoulders drooped, and her medical bag slid to her feet.

Ruby grasped her elbow and gently led her into the waiting room. "Doc Colton won't be here for a few more minutes. Why don't you take a minute and sit with me for a spell?"

The medical clinic that sat abandoned when the old doctor retired had reopened when Dylan Colton left his job as an ER doctor in Memphis and came home to Colton. His brother Taylor and the crew from his TV show did a complete remodel of the clinic, bringing the facility up-to-date. Ms. Ruby had retired from nursing at the small hospital in Greenwood just a year before and offered to come back to help Dr. Colton out while he got the clinic up and running again.

"I have to go look at Ms. June's chickens," Jasmine grumbled.

"Oh Lord, ain't nothin' gonna happen to those chickens that the good Lord didn't intend for them if you sit with me for ten minutes."

Jasmine bit back a smile.

Ruby sat down next to her on the black vinyl sofa in the waiting room. "Now, what's got you all twisted up inside this morning?"

"A man." Jasmine sighed.

Ruby's eyes widened slightly. "If it's the one I think it is, I don't have any words of wisdom for you, honey. Colton men are as hardheaded and stubborn as they come."

"Yeah, I'm kind of figuring that out."

Dr. Colton came in, interrupting the companionable silence they shared.

"Morning, ladies," he said with a bright smile.

He came toward them with his hand outstretched. "Dr. Owens, it's nice to see you. I've been trying to get over to your clinic since you opened up, but days always seem to get away from me."

Jasmine shook his hand. Dylan Colton shared the same blue eyes and blond hair as Rhett, and there was a distinct resemblance that reminded her they were related somewhere on the Colton family tree. Where Rhett was rough around the edges, Dylan was clean-cut, wearing khakis and a crisp blue oxford shirt, with his hair neatly trimmed. He was everything Jasmine used to find attractive in a man until she met Rhett.

"I can only imagine how busy you are, being the only medical clinic in town."

"I'll admit the picture I had in my head of being a small-town doctor and having a lot of spare time to fix up my house and hang out with my family has been shattered. If it weren't for Ms. Ruby coming out of retirement to help me out, I'd be completely underwater."

Ruby beamed under Dylan's praise. "I was bored anyway. I'd already decided retirement wasn't ready for me, and I wasn't ready for it."

"I know everyone is thrilled to have the clinic open again," Jasmine said.

Ms. Ruby nodded. "Folks are saying the same about you."

"That reminds me. I was talking to Nate over at the firehouse," Dylan said. "Since we have the only two medical offices in town, he wanted us to coordinate with Emma to come up with a plan for emergency response in case we have need for it. We got lucky with the last hurricane that came through. It just missed us, and we didn't have too much damage, but next time, we might not be as lucky."

"I think that's an excellent idea. Between the three of us, we can coordinate supplies and set up a plan for triage if we need it."

"Great. I'll stop by your clinic one day next week, and we can talk more," Dylan said. "I'll let you two finish your chat. I've got some charts to update before my first patient."

"I'll be right with you," Ruby said.

"Take your time."

Dylan waved and walked into the back. He came back a minute later with an alarmed look on his face.

"Ruby, someone tried to break in through the back door," he said.

Jasmine and Ruby followed Dylan outside, where they all clustered around, looking at the scraped and bent lock someone had tampered with. Dylan looked up and down the street behind the clinic.

"I'll check in with Dax. There are cameras installed back here for his building that cover mine as well," Dylan said.

"You need to call this into Isiah right away," Jasmine added.

"I'll take care of that," Ruby said, going back inside.

Dylan frowned at the damaged lock. "I've been wondering when this might happen."

"You make it sound like it was inevitable."

"There have been break-ins at other clinics and pharmacies around the area."

"Isiah mentioned that."

Dylan tipped his head in acknowledgment.

"I think you, Emma, and I need to have a talk about this, along with our conversation about coordinating for emergency responses," Jasmine said. "We have the three places in town that have opiates on the premises. We need to make sure we have everything secured."

"Agreed. I'll let Emma know about this now."

A sheriff's cruiser came down the block and rolled to a stop in front of them, and her brother got out.

"Ms. Ruby reported an attempted break-in," Isiah said. Dylan gestured to the damaged lock. Isiah looked closely at it. "I'll see if I can pull any prints, but chances are we won't get anything clean enough to use."

Jasmine glanced at her watch. "I should get going. I've got to get over to Ms. June's."

"No problem." Dylan gave her an understanding smile. "House calls are an unavoidable part of life around here."

"Which one of her chickens is it this time?" Isiah chuckled.

Jasmine sighed. "Mary Sue."

"Good luck with that," Isiah said.

"Gee, thanks."

It was a short walk to Ms. June's house. She was waiting for Jasmine on her front porch when she arrived.

"Oh, Dr. Owens, I'm glad you're here. I've been so worried about Mary Sue. She's just not acting like her normal self."

Jasmine unlatched the gate and let herself into the front yard that was a charming, disorganized mess of wildflowers, roses, and weeds.

"Let's look, and I'll see if I can figure out what's wrong," Jasmine said.

Mary Sue was a perfectly healthy Ameraucana hen who looked as happy as any chicken could look.

"She's a beauty, isn't she?" Jasmine stroked her beautiful white feathers spotted with black.

"Are you sure she's okay? Mary Sue hasn't been very social at all. And she doesn't want to cuddle as much as she used to."

"You know, everyone has an off day now and then, even chickens."

"And there's nothing you can give her that might make her feel better?"

"Just like I explained before, unfortunately, no one has come up with an antidepressant specifically for chickens."

Ms. June's lips flattened, and her eyes flashed with anger. "Well, someone should."

Jasmine gave her a sympathetic smile. "I'm sure someone is working on it."

Ms. June gave her precious Mary Sue one more worried look before coming over and wrapping her arm around Jasmine's shoulder. "Now, let me get you a glass of kombucha before you go. I just made a fresh batch."

It wasn't the remedy she was looking for, but a glass of kombucha and a visit with Ms. June would have to be enough to keep her mind off her troubles for a while.

Jasmine kept herself distracted all day until her phone lit up at the usual time for her nightly phone call with Rhett. Her finger hovered over the green button. Did she want to accept? With a heavy sigh, she put the phone down. She'd let herself get too wrapped up in someone before.

Chapter Thirteen

Rhett's stomach sank with each unanswered ring. He should have left a note. Hell, he shouldn't have left at all. Waking up in Jasmine's bed with her in his arms felt so good. Too good. Rhett lay there, enjoying those first few minutes of watching her sleeping next to him, before reality came crashing back. He shouldn't have spent the night. He hated that Jasmine felt like she had to take care of him.

His phone vibrated again. The spark of hope quickly died when he saw the text was from Dan.

Come to the Buckthorn 7 pm

It was an order, not a request. On his way to the Buckthorn, Rhett spent the drive swinging between self-loathing for leaving Jasmine and dread from wondering why Dan wanted to see him.

The floor of the Buckthorn was bare of peanut shells when Rhett walked in. This was only the second time he'd ever set foot in the old juke joint. He tried not to think about the first time he'd come in, when he was undercover.

Dan came out from the back room. "Have a seat and get yourself something to drink. Primus is making us some catfish."

It was the one day of the week when the floors were swept clean and the tables were bare. On Sundays just about everything was closed except for the churches that flung their doors wide open.

Reid slid a glass of whiskey toward him. "Give this a try."

Rhett took a seat at the bar and accepted the glass with a nod. His eyes darted around the room. Even though the bar was closed, he felt self-conscious. This was the first time he'd been back to the Buckthorn since he came in with the group he had been embedded with. When Rhett heard that they were planning to "remind that boy they were the ones in charge," he'd asked to go along. The idea of anyone harassing Mr. Wallace made him sick to his stomach. Primus Wallace, the proprietor of the Buckthorn, was a respected member of the community and beloved by many folks in Colton. The Wallace family started making whiskey just before WWI. Mr. Wallace was regarded as a master distiller, and not just in Colton. Folks from all over the region came to the Buckthorn wanting to learn his secrets. Mr. Wallace turned them all away until Reid Ellis moved back home.

The old man shuffled out of the back room with a platter piled high with catfish in one hand and a plate of greens in the other. Mr. Wallace set the food down before turning to go back into the other room without a word. He came right back with another plate of hot water corn bread, followed by Dan carrying plates and silverware.

Mr. Wallace took a plate and piled it high with food before setting it down in front of Rhett and leaning against the bar with his arms spread out. He locked eyes with Rhett.

"You need to eat, son. You look like shit. You don't have to worry about me—we're square."

Rhett couldn't get past the lump in his throat to respond. When he said nothing, Mr. Wallace softly pounded the bar with his fist.

"Look at me." Rhett's eyes jerked back to his at the command. "We're good. You're welcome here. Now, you shake my hand."

"Mr. Wallace, I'm—"

Rhett's hand trembled as it was engulfed in Mr. Wallace's warm, calloused one.

"Let's have none of that Mr. Wallace business. Call me Primus. You did good, Rhett. You're a good man. Thank you for your service."

Rhett could only nod.

Primus dropped his hand, and Rhett picked up his fork, forcing himself to take a bite. The food was amazing, but the guilt that still lingered took away his appetite. Dan and Reid filled their plates and sat across from him at the bar. Primus brought out a bowl of water and some catfish for Rebel.

"Can he eat greens?" Primus asked.

"He'll eat them raw if you've got them."

Primus nodded and came back with a handful of greens, adding them to the catfish.

Rebel nudged Primus's hand in gratitude and then looked at Rhett, waiting for permission to eat.

"Go ahead," Rhett said with a nod.

Primus chuckled when Rebel jumped up and gobbled down his fish dinner.

The catfish was crispy and the greens spicy. Rhett surprised himself when he looked down at his plate and saw that it was empty. Dan put another piece of catfish on his plate while Reid added a piece of corn bread, and Primus refilled his glass.

When his plate was clean again, he took a deep breath and sat back. "That was a mighty fine meal. Thank you."

"My pleasure." Primus slapped him on the back and picked up his plate. "I'll let you boys talk."

Reid watched his mentor shuffle away with an anxious gaze.

Dan reached for Reid's hand. "He'll be okay."

"What's wrong?" Rhett asked.

"Primus hasn't been doing well lately. I'm trying to get him to go to the clinic, but he's stubborn," Reid said.

"That's why we wanted to talk to you. We have a proposition for you," Dan added. "We've tried asking you to come for dinner, but you keep making up excuses." He gave Rhett a wry smile. "I took a chance that you'd come if I made it an order."

Rhett started to protest and stopped. "Yeah, okay, I've been avoiding… everyone."

"It's okay. We know you have a lot going on right now," Reid said.

"That's not a good excuse. I should have reached out. You said you have a proposition for me. What do you need?"

"Reid and I have bought the old railway station. We want to open a brewery."

"You're leaving the bureau?"

Dan nodded. "I'm going to stay for another year while we get things set up. The building will need a lot of work before we can get started."

Rhett looked at Reid. "What about you? Are you going to leave the prosecutor's office?"

"Now that all the corruption has been exposed, they're going to need help to rebuild, so I'm going to stay on for now."

"What do you need me for?"

"We were hoping you could help us out working some hours here while were getting the brewery up and running," Reid said. "It's going to be a lot to manage while we're both working full-time. I'm worried about Primus and want to make sure he has extra help."

Rhett looked at Reid and Dan in surprise. "Me?"

"Look, I don't want to make an assumption," Dan said, "but you've seemed a little… lost since we came back from DC, and we thought maybe having a project would help."

When Rhett frowned, Reid added, "We just want to help."

He wasn't angry. He appreciated what his friends were trying to do. *Friends.* Dan and Reid were friends. As much as he'd tried to keep his distance, he'd made friends. Dan, Reid, and Jasmine—they were all trying to help him.

He raised an eyebrow. "Is this an intervention? I—"

"We didn't mean to offend you," Reid interrupted.

"Honey, let him talk," Dan said.

"I thank y'all for the offer, and I'm happy to help, but I don't think I'm the right person for this. I'm not very good with people. Customer service isn't really my thing."

"That's never stopped Primus," Reid said with a wry smile.

"I heard that," Primus shouted from the back.

Rhett and Dan both laughed.

Reid bumped Dan's shoulder. "Now you've gotten me into trouble."

"You know that's not possible. Primus thinks of you as a son," Dan said.

Reid's eyes became bright for a moment, and Rhett felt a pang of longing for a closer relationship with his parents. They were just reconnecting when he went undercover. Rhett knew what he was giving up when he took his assignment, and there was no undoing the damage he'd caused. Maybe someday he'd be able to join his parents for a Sunday dinner, just like a normal family, and they could have a closer relationship, but not today.

"I still don't think I'm the guy you're looking for. Have you thought about reaching out to the trade school in Greenwood? I'm sure there's someone in the culinary program who would jump at the chance to help you guys out."

"We talked about that, but we wanted to ask you first," Dan said.

"So I'm the first choice but not the best one." Dan and Reid looked at him with twin expressions of guilt. Rhett took another sip of whiskey. "Thanks, both of you. I'm happy you've found out what you want in life, Dan." He glanced down at the two men's joined hands, ignoring the twinge of envy he felt. "For both of you. I'm going to figure out what I want too."

I want a life with Jasmine.

Reid's phone buzzed. "It's Dax. I'll be right back."

He returned a minute later with a look of concern on his face. "Someone tried to break into the medical clinic."

Dan and Rhett shared a look.

"You're on leave, Rhett," Dan quietly warned.

"Yeah, okay."

Dan stared at Rhett. For a few minutes, they were locked in a battle of wills. Both of them knew Rhett wouldn't be able to ignore any threat to his community. He cared too much about Colton and the people who lived there.

"Instead of trying to get into trouble, why don't you take Jasmine out on a date?" Reid said.

Rhett jerked his head up. "Let me guess. The Colton gossip mill is in full swing."

"Small-town life," Reid said matter-of-factly.

"I may have screwed that up."

"What did you do?" Dan asked.

Rhett studied his drink, unable to admit he'd gotten scared and run away. He was falling fast for Jasmine, even though in his heart, he knew he shouldn't.

"I don't want to talk about it."

Primus came back in and leaned on the bar. "Bring her some flowers."

Rhett grimaced. "I already did that when I screwed up the first time."

"Oh good Lord, act like you got some sense, son." Primus waved his hand in a dismissive motion as he shuffled away.

"I'll take a refill if you don't mind," Rhett said.

"Okay, flowers are out," Reid said, refilling his glass. "You're going to have to up your game."

"That's kind of hard to do when I never had game to begin with."

"When we were in DC, I watched women and a few men trying to get your attention. What do you mean you don't have any game?" Dan said.

"Did you see me take anyone up on their offer?" Dan shook his head. "I've never been one of those people who spends time on apps, swiping left and right. I told Jasmine I'd take her out to dinner when I got back, but… I don't even know where. Jasmine told me it doesn't have to be anything fancy, and we could go to the Catfish, but I want to do better than that."

"Take her on a picnic," Primus shouted from the back.

Rhett thought for a minute, and a slow smile spread over his face. "I can work with that."

"Anything we can do to help?" Dan asked.

"Nope, I've got this." Rhett paused. "If you don't mind, can I buy a bottle of whiskey?"

With a bottle of Primus's good stuff in hand, Rhett headed back to the cabin. It was warm enough with his sleeping bag to sleep out on the porch, something he didn't mind doing, but now that he'd spent a night in Jasmine's bed, he was uncomfortable as hell.

Rebel snored softly at his side. "No offense, buddy, but you aren't nearly as nice to sleep with."

Rebel snorted and tucked his tail over his nose.

Rhett had one day to plan to make up with Jasmine. "You can't keep running away," he said to himself. Even if he tried, he couldn't keep away from Jasmine.

The porch boards were rough against his back, and a twinge of discomfort resonated in his shoulder when he tried to make himself more comfortable. The physical scars were deep. He would heal emotionally, but there were some wounds that were never going away.

Chapter Fourteen

Saturday morning, Rhett took a deep breath and knocked on Jasmine's door. He knew he was taking a chance and Jasmine might refuse him, but he hoped he could convince her to say yes.

Maybe she isn't home, he thought, waiting for her to answer. He'd just assumed she'd be home. Rhett started to turn away when Jasmine opened the door.

Her mouth turned down. "What do you want, Rhett?"

"I want to apologize. I… I ran away from you, from my feelings for you." He tugged at the hair tie on his wrist. "I wasn't thinking."

Jasmine's expression softened. She leaned against the doorframe. "I was really angry, Rhett."

"And you're not now?" he asked with a lot of hopefulness in his voice.

"I haven't decided yet. You've run away twice now."

"You have every right to be mad. I thought… I said I'd take you out to dinner when I got back, and I was hoping you would give me another chance and spend the day with me today. I packed a picnic for us, and I have someplace I'd like to take you."

Jasmine bit her lip, toying with the hem of the flannel pajama top she was wearing. The wariness in her eyes when she looked back at him tightened the knot in his stomach.

"I shouldn't have come," he said, backing away.

"No, wait." She reached out and snagged his wrist, stopping him. "Can you give me an hour to get ready?"

Rhett nodded. "Take all the time you need. I'll wait."

She gave him a slight smile and said, "Wait for me," before she closed the door.

He'd wait for as long as he needed to.

Rebel was waiting patiently for him when Rhett jogged back downstairs.

"Should we take a walk while we wait?" he asked.

With a quick hand signal from him, Rebel jumped out of the Jeep and came to his side. Rhett avoided the throng of people shopping at the farmer's market. Skirting the park with Rebel at his side, he made his way toward the old train depot Reid and Dan had just purchased.

While trains still passed through town, they didn't stop in Colton and hadn't for many years. Hardly any paint remained on the long, low building, and the red shingles on the roof were barely hanging on. Rhett rounded the corner and found Dan and Reid sitting next to each other on the edge of what used to be the old loading bay.

Reid waved. "Hey, what brings you this way on a Saturday?"

"I'm waiting for Jasmine. I'm taking her on a picnic."

Dan grinned. "Glad to see you took Primus's advice."

"Yeah, well"—Rhett shrugged—"I needed to do something. Looks like y'all are having your own picnic." He pointed to the small crate of beer and what looked like a couple of sandwiches wrapped in paper.

"We just got the keys, and we're going to start cleaning out." Dan grinned.

"I know I turned down your offer, but if you need any help, let me know."

"What about you, anything we can do to help at your grandpa's place?" Reid asked.

"Nah, I'm good." Rhett cringed inside. There was a long list of things he needed to do at the cabin, but it was useless when he still couldn't bring himself to go inside. He glanced at his watch. "I've got to get going and pick Jasmine up."

"Good luck," Reid and Dan said in unison.

Rhett waved and headed back toward Jasmine's apartment. She was waiting for him, sitting at the bottom of the stairs leading to her apartment.

"Hey there, have you been waiting long?" he asked.

"No," she said, getting up. "I didn't need that much time to get ready."

Rhett gazed at her. It was crazy to miss her as much as he did after not seeing her for a week. She'd changed into an oversized denim shirt that was almost a dress on her, paired with leggings and knee-high boots.

"We match," he said, pointing to his own denim shirt.

A faint tinge of pink spread over her cheeks. "I didn't do it on purpose."

"I… why is this so awkward?" he asked.

Jasmine looked at him, her dark brown eyes searching his face. "Are you going to run away again?"

Rhett shook his head. "No, I'm not going to do that again."

She gave him a slight smile and slipped her hand into his. "Come on, let's spend the day together."

Rebel jumped into the back seat while Rhett opened the door for Jasmine. He hesitated for a moment before letting go of her hand.

As soon as he was behind the wheel and they were on their way, Rhett reached for her hand again. Jasmine's grasp was warm and firm in his, and as they made their way out of town, the tension he'd been feeling drained away. The top was down on his Jeep, and Lucas Monroe was singing about country roads and summer girls. The moment took him back to his high school days. Only now, he appreciated it much more. He'd never take moments like this for granted again. They were too precious.

Wherever I'm goin', I'll never get lost. My heart will always lead me back to you.

He glanced at Jasmine, who was tapping her foot with a big smile on her face. She'd pulled her hair into a topknot, her curls dancing in the wind. This was exactly the picture in his mind when he bought his Jeep.

He turned off the main highway onto a narrow two-lane road and, after a couple of miles, turned again, leaving the pavement behind. Jasmine's eyebrows shot up when he left the dirt road, following two faint ruts in the gravel.

Rhett gave her hand a squeeze. "Trust me."

"You know that's what the date always says right before the murderer jumps out in every scary movie," she said.

Rhett laughed.

They came around a bend, and a small lake glittered blue and silver in the sunlight.

"Wow," Jasmine breathed. "This place is beautiful."

Rhett pulled up in front of a pristine low country cottage painted white with a dark green shingled roof. An older Black man came out onto the front porch, followed by a woman who clapped her hands and beamed at them. Rhett came around to open the door for Jasmine. He grabbed the bottle of whiskey he'd bought from Primus, tucking it into his back pocket before he walked over to meet them.

Rhett always thought the man he was looking at was the definition of the term *baby face*. Even now, well into his eighties, the deep russet-brown skin on Abraham Greene's face didn't have a single wrinkle. The only signs of his age were the gray in his hair and the slight stoop of his back. A yellow Lab came streaking out of the door behind him, and with a joyful bark, Rebel jumped out of the back of the Jeep and joined his friend in a happy chase.

Mr. Greene held his hand out to Rhett. When it was in his grasp, he pulled him in for a hug, patting his back.

"Young blood, it's good to see you again. I've been waiting a mighty long time to see your face."

Rhett hugged the man back. "It's good to see you, Mr. Greene."

His wife was next, hugging Rhett so hard he thought she might break a rib.

When Mrs. Greene finally let him go, Mr. Greene turned to Jasmine, asking, "And who might this beautiful young lady be?"

"This is Jasmine Owens. She's the new vet in Colton."

"Dr. Owens"—Abraham's large hand engulfed hers—"it's a pleasure to make your acquaintance."

Mrs. Greene pulled her into her arms, beaming at Rhett over her shoulder. "We've been waitin' a long time for Rhett to bring a young lady to meet us."

"Minnie, let the girl go. You're embarrassing Rhett."

Rhett dropped his head, shaking it. He should have prepared Jasmine for the Greenes. They were some of the warmest and most affectionate people he knew.

"It's a pleasure to meet you both, Mr. and Mrs. Greene," Jasmine said.

The older man smiled. "You're both grown. You can call us Abraham and Minnie." He tucked Jasmine's arm in his and jerked his head off to one side. "You come on back. I've got everything set up in my shop."

Minnie waggled her finger at Rhett. "Don't you dare leave without saying goodbye."

Rhett gave her a kiss on the cheek. "Yes, ma'am."

They walked behind the house toward a large shed painted the same creamy white as the house.

"Derek says hi. He and the grandkids are delivering an order to North Carolina today," Abraham said.

"Next time," Rhett said.

Abraham glanced over his shoulder, giving Rhett an understanding nod. As much as he cared for the Greene family, Rhett wasn't ready to see Derek and the other Greene children he'd grown up playing with. In his heart, Rhett knew they understood what he did and didn't take any of it personally, but that didn't make it any easier to face them. When he'd called Abraham and asked if he could bring Jasmine to the lake, he'd asked if he could introduce Jasmine to just the two of them for now.

Abraham let go of Jasmine's arm and pulled back the large barn door. Jasmine peered inside and looked back at Rhett, wide-eyed.

Rhett smiled. "Abraham is one of the best rod and reel suppliers in the country. People from all over come here to get one of his masterpieces."

They went into the shed that served as Abraham's and his son's workshop. A workbench took up one wall while a lathe was on another, with a smaller workbench with chisels and other woodworking tools scattered on the surface. Abraham led Jasmine over to a stool in the corner. "Now, you just sit right here, young lady, while I get you sorted out."

The old man went over to a rack of rods. "Now, let's see, your pond is about twenty-five feet, give or take. You can do a six-and-a-half or seven-and-a-half footer."

"Grandpa and I always used a seven-and-a-half."

Abraham nodded. "I remember." He pointed to where Jasmine was sitting. "I remember you as a little boy in that very spot, waitin' quietly while your grandpa and I told fish tales. Most young'uns would wiggle and squirm, but you were as still as a statue."

The memory of those days washed over him, bringing a fresh wave of grief.

Abraham picked up a rod with a beautiful burl wood handle, the light and dark shades of wood swirling together like storm clouds.

"Abraham, this is incredible," Rhett said, taking the rod out of Abraham's hand.

"It's from a burl off an old willow tree." Abraham's voice grew thick with emotion. "Your grandad brought the burl to me after that old willow by your pond went down in a storm."

Rhett looked down at the rod he was holding that suddenly became heavy in his hands.

"Your grandad told me to wait until you were ready. I figured you finally calling after all this time was a sign."

Rhett struggled to speak. When he finally got the words out, his voice shook with emotion. "Thank you."

Abraham's heavy hand landed on his shoulder and gave it a squeeze before he went back to the rack, pulled out another rod, and handed it to Jasmine.

"This one should be just about right for you, Doctor."

The handle of Jasmine's rod was a deep, plum wood.

"That's Purple Heart," Abraham said, pointing at the handle.

"You are an artist," Jasmine said.

Abraham beamed at them, hooking his thumbs in the straps of his overalls. "I've got bait and everything else you need in the basket by the door there."

Rhett turned to Jasmine and held out his rod. "Can you hold this for me?"

"Sure."

Rhett went over and gave Abraham a hug. "Thank you," he whispered. He took the bottle out of his back pocket. "I know you won't take any money from me, and Minnie will have my hide, but I thought you might like this."

Abraham looked at the bottle, his eyes lighting up. "You get this from Primus?"

Rhett nodded. "Yes, sir."

Abraham clapped his hand on Rhett's shoulder. "It's good to have you back. Now, you two go off and enjoy yourselves. I'll see you back at the house after you've filled that basket full of trout."

"Yes, sir."

Rhett grabbed the basket on the way out the door.

"What an incredible man," Jasmine said as they walked back to the Jeep to retrieve the picnic basket. Rhett stacked the basket with bait and tackle and led Jasmine toward a path leading down to the lake.

"The Greenes are good people. I've missed them."

"I should have realized." She gave his hand a squeeze. "You made a lot of sacrifices, big and small," Jasmine said. "I'm ashamed. I thought

I knew what you went through being undercover. You haven't seen the Greenes for over two years now, have you?"

Rhett's jaw ticked. "Please, don't give me that sympathetic look. It makes it worse."

Jasmine nodded. "Okay."

They followed the path along the edge of the lake until they came around a bend, and there was a small dock with two Adirondack chairs.

The dock wobbled slightly when they stepped onto it. Rhett put down the baskets between the chairs, took the poles from Jasmine, and slid each one into pole holders that were screwed onto the dock.

"Well, what do you think?" he asked.

Jasmine looked at him with a blinding smile. "It's perfect."

"Are you sure? It's not a fancy restaurant or even the Catfish."

"Don't ever tell Tillie I said this, but this is better than any restaurant in Mississippi."

A splash in the water caught their attention.

"Come on, let's get some bait on and get these hooks in the water."

Jasmine rubbed her hands together, bouncing on her toes. "I can't believe I'm actually going to fish."

"Is this really your first time fishing?"

"Yup."

Rhett reached into the basket Abraham gave them and pulled out a small container. Opening it, he tilted it in Jasmine's direction.

"First lesson, baiting a hook."

Of course Jasmine was a pro, putting the worm on the hook with surgical precision. She watched every move while Rhett showed her the components and explained how to cast.

Her first few attempts didn't go well, but on the third try, the line sailed through the air and landed in the water with barely a ripple.

"You're a natural," he said.

"You're a good teacher."

Rhett quickly got his line in the water, and they stood side-by-side at the edge of the dock, watching the sunlight create shadows on the lake.

"I grew up coming out here with my grandpa," Rhett said quietly. "He and Abraham would sit out on this dock for hours fishing. Abraham took a chance on my grandpa. He was willing to let him prove he'd changed his ways. They were lifelong friends after that."

"Can you tell me more stories about your grandpa?"

Rhett nodded with a mischievous glint in his eye. “I can. But you just got a bite.”

Jasmine let out a yelp and gripped the pole. “What do I do?”

He slipped his pole into the holder and moved behind her. Taking her hand, he positioned it correctly on the reel, guiding her through the dance with the feisty fish. When she pulled the trout free of the water, she let out a whoop and held up her catch, grinning from ear to ear.

Caught up in the moment, Rhett swooped in and kissed her.

Her lips opened, inviting him in. *This is what happiness tastes like,* Rhett thought, losing himself in the depths of Jasmine’s soft mouth. He abandoned her lips, trailing kisses along her jaw and then the spot on her neck that brought a low throaty moan from her.

“I can’t make it through a day without wanting to kiss you,” he said before returning to the softness of her mouth.

She dropped the fishing pole and threaded her hands through his hair and around his neck, pulling him closer, molding her body against his.

He wanted to strip her right there and make love to her on the dock.

Rhett ignored the splash of the fish finding its way back to the water and the line going back out. He didn’t care about anything but having Jasmine in his arms.

The sound of the pole scraping across the dock brought him back to reality.

“Oh shit. Abraham will have my hide if I lose that pole.”

He let go of Jasmine and grabbed it just before it tipped into the water. Jasmine was laughing, the sun shining on her face, her lips pink, looking at him in a way that made him feel whole and happy.

He wanted to spend the rest of his life making her look at him like that. Now all he had to do was figure out a way to be a man who was worthy of her.

Chapter Fifteen

Jasmine didn't come back down to earth after her day at the lake with Rhett until Larry Atwood showed up at her clinic.

Once they rescued her fishing pole and caught a couple of trout, Rhett set up a picnic on the dock, and they kissed and laughed their way through supper. Rhett shared stories about fishing with his grandpa. After a day by the lake and a long goodbye with the Greenes, who made Jasmine promise to come back for a visit, Rhett drove her home. He was a perfect gentleman, walking her to her door and giving her another kiss good night that left Jasmine cursing his good manners. On Sunday, Rhett took her to on a hike and, once again, left her on her front door wanting more.

Monday arrived with Jasmine determined to take the next step in her relationship with Rhett. She breezed through her morning appointments, still glowing from the memory of the heated kisses they'd shared. Angry yelling coming from the waiting room interrupted her daydreaming. She came in and found a man whose eyes were overly bright, glittering with what her gut told her was hatred bolstered by something artificial. He held a seriously underweight Staffordshire terrier shaking in his arms. The man put the dog down, and she tried to get up but collapsed back down on the floor, unable to walk.

"What's her name?" Jasmine asked while running her hand over the dog's thin coat, feeling each rib.

"She don't need a name for what I need her to do."

"What is your name?" she asked the dog's owner.

"Larry Atwood," he spat out. "Quit askin' stupid questions and get to work."

Jasmine fought to remain professional while her anger surged. The man came into the clinic belligerent, demanding that his dog be treated right away. The dog was in distress, and her enlarged nipples showed she must have had a litter of puppies recently.

"Imani, get my bag, please." Jasmine eyed Zach sitting at the reception desk. They'd just had a meeting to review protocol in situations like this. He held up his phone for a second with a nod and got up from his desk, heading out of earshot to call Animal Control.

Imani came back with her bag. Her assistant eyed the dog's owner warily.

"I think we're going to need a calcium IV set up," Jasmine said to Imani.

"What the hell is that?" Larry demanded.

Jasmine knelt down on the floor next to the shivering animal, putting her stethoscope in her ears to listen to the dog's heartbeat. "It's treatment for when a dog has eclampsia, which I suspect this dog has."

Jasmine sat back on her heels and glared at the owner. "Mr. Atwood, you can't breed this dog anymore. She has been over-bred, she's severely malnourished, and her lack of care is clear."

Mr. Atwood's jaw clenched. "I take care of what's mine just fine."

Zach came back to the desk and gave Jasmine a thumbs-up, letting her know that Animal Control was on the way.

They needed to stall until Animal Control could get there. One frustration of living in a small town was having to wait for county services. Animal Control was based out of Hanes, some thirty miles away.

Looming closer, Mr. Atwood bared his teeth, the stench of cigarettes emitting from his breath. "What the hell do you know?" he yelled. "You're probably trying to cheat me by giving her some expensive treatment she don't really need. You people are always trying to figure out how to take advantage of decent White folks."

Jasmine ignored his comment. The dog's health was more important than its owner's racist comments.

"You can't take this dog, Mr. Atwood. She's going to die if she's not treated. She'll need to stay overnight, and you should bring her puppies in as well."

"You uppity bitch, you don't get to decide what I can do with my dog."

Jasmine lifted her chin. "You brought your dog into my clinic, and I am going to do my job. I don't care what you think I am. I know when an animal is suffering."

She stood up and braced herself when he stepped toward her with his hand fisted.

"Take one step closer, and it will be the last step you ever take."

There was a deadly calm in Rhett's voice that sent a chill down Jasmine's spine.

Larry slowly turned his head, his mouth curling into a malicious smile. "Well, well, look here. It's the traitor. You know what happens to traitors, don't you? I got a rope in the back of the car, and we got plenty of trees in the park."

Zach and Imani were hovering behind the reception desk, both visibly shaken. Jasmine mouthed *It's okay* and turned back to Larry.

"Hey"—Jasmine snapped her fingers in front of Larry's face—"you don't make threats in my office. Get the hell out."

When Larry reached for his dog, she positioned herself in front of the animal.

"No, you are not taking this dog. She is going to need an IV treatment that can't be rushed. She's going to be here for at least one night, if not longer."

The dog behind Jasmine's legs curled itself into an even tighter ball, shaking so badly Jasmine could feel the vibrations through where the animal pressed herself against her legs.

"You heard the doctor," Rhett said.

"Stop acting all high and mighty." Larry jabbed himself in the chest. "You didn't get all of us, you know. I still got plenty of friends, and we know what needs to happen to a traitor like you."

Animal Control pulled up, and Jasmine winced when she saw her brother making a beeline for the clinic from Town Hall with a thunderous expression on his face.

Larry followed her gaze, his forehead wrinkling when he saw the sheriff and Animal Control.

He looked down at the dog. "She ain't worth it, anyway. I would have used her for bait, and that ain't no big loss."

Bile rose in Jasmine's throat. Isiah came in just as Rhett started toward Larry, but before he could reach him, Isiah put his hand on Rhett's shoulder, stopping him.

"Stand down, I've got this," Isiah said.

Her brother walked over to Larry, resting his hand on his holster. "I'm sure I didn't just hear you reference dog fighting, did I?" When Larry didn't answer, Isiah said in a low, quiet voice, "You want to leave quietly, or you want to spend some time in my jail?"

Larry bared his teeth. "Y'all ain't nothing but dirt," he said as he stormed past Isiah and out of the clinic.

"You okay, sis?" Isiah asked.

Before she could answer, Rhett rushed over, grasping her by the shoulders. "Are you all right? Did he touch you?"

Jasmine pulled out of his grasp and knelt down to pick up the dog at her feet. "Come here, sweetheart." She turned to Rhett. "I'm fine. I need to get her back to a room and finish examining her."

"Yeah, okay," he said, moving back so that she could head to the back.

She smiled when she heard Isiah say, "Back off, Rhett. She can handle herself."

Imani rushed into the exam room behind her. "Holy shit, that was scary."

"You and Zach did great. Now let's see if we can save this poor girl." Leaning close to the shivering dog's face, she whispered, "Don't worry, we're going to teach you how to be brave too."

An Animal Control agent knocked on the door and stuck her head in. "Can I come in?"

"I'll take pictures as soon as I get her stabilized," Jasmine said, preparing the IV. "She's given birth recently. You need to find the puppies and bring them here so she can nurse them."

The agent nodded. "Got it. Do you know where the owner lives?"

"The sheriff or Rhett Colton will know."

The agent nodded, and Jasmine went to work trying to save the pittie.

She lost track of time, focused on slowly administering the calcium IV. If they administered the calcium quickly, it could cause the dog's heart rate to drop dangerously low.

Jasmine gently examined the dog while Imani took pictures.

Zach poked his head in. "Rhett Colton is still here waiting for you."

"Thanks."

"Keep a close eye on her," Jasmine said. "I'll be right back."

Jasmine barely set foot into the waiting room when Rhett jumped up and came over, grasping her shoulders.

"You can't let Larry back in here. That man is dangerous."

"That's my problem, not yours," she said, moving away. Rhett shook his head with a frown. "You don't get to take care of me. I've proven that I can take care of myself."

"Dr. Owens," Imani shouted.

Jasmine ran back into the exam room.

"Her heart rate is dropping," Imani said.

The next few minutes felt like hours as they worked to stabilize the dog. They got her stable enough to move into a kennel in the back room. The Animal Control agent came in holding up a small carrier. Jasmine sighed with relief.

"I'm afraid there were two that already died when we got there. There's four left."

"Okay." Jasmine blew out a shaky breath.

Hearing her puppies, the mama lifted her head and tried to wag her tail.

Jasmine took the carrier from the Animal Control agent and knelt down on the floor with it in front of the kennel. She opened the carrier door first and then opened the kennel, carefully pulling out one puppy at a time and placing them close to their mama's belly. The puppies wiggled and whined until they latched on. The mama looked up at Jasmine with gratitude in her big golden eyes.

"There you go, sweet girl," Jasmine crooned. "You're a good mama, aren't you?"

"I'll get bottles ready," Imani said.

"Thanks. These little ones aren't going to get enough nutrition from their mama when she's in this condition. A milk replacer will get them the nutrition they need."

Reuniting the puppies with their mother would comfort all of them.

"Isiah followed me out to the Atwood place." The agent grimaced. "The conditions were deplorable out there. We didn't see any signs of dog fighting. He's probably got a hideout somewhere, but we'll keep an eye on him."

"Thanks. I can't stand the idea of giving her back to him when she's healed."

The agent smiled. "The sheriff strongly suggested that it was in Mr. Atwood's best interest to surrender the dog."

Jasmine's eyebrows shot up. "Oh, he did, did he?"

"The sheriff said you'd be okay taking responsibility."

"Of course," Jasmine said.

The agent nodded. "We'll be in touch if there's anything else."

"Thank you," Jasmine said.

Jasmine followed the agent out to the waiting room and was surprised to see Rhett was still there.

"Is there anything I can do to help?" Rhett asked after the agent left.

"No, nothing right now."

"Can I come back and check in later? I hated seeing how skinny and afraid that poor dog was."

"Of course you can."

Rhett nodded and headed for the door where Rebel was waiting patiently outside. Jasmine followed him, and Rebel jumped up, wagging his tail when he saw her.

"Hey, boy, how are you?"

Rebel nuzzled her hand.

"We'll come back later. I can bring you some dinner if you'd like," Rhett offered.

"You don't have to do that."

"I don't mind. It's the least I can do after—"

Jasmine held her hand up. "Don't. It's been a really intense day already, and I don't have the bandwidth right now." She noticed a woman walking across the park headed in their direction. "I have to get ready for my next patient. We'll talk later, okay?"

"Yeah, okay."

Jasmine headed inside and grabbed the chart for her next patient.

One patient turned into two when someone came in with a beagle that had an unfortunate run-in with a porcupine.

When Jasmine finally finished for the day, she came out to the lobby to find Zach sitting at the reception desk, working on files, and Rebel sitting next to him with his head on his knee.

"It looks like you made a friend," Jasmine said.

Zach looked down at Rebel with a smile, patting his head. "He's a really friendly dog."

Rebel trotted over to Jasmine, nudging her hand for more attention.

Jasmine glanced toward the kennels.

"I assume since Rebel is here that Rhett is still back there."

Zach nodded. "He asked if he could check on the pittie, and I asked Imani, and she said it would be okay."

"Thanks."

Jasmine passed Imani on her way to the back. "How's she doing?"

"Much better." Imani smiled. "You should go back there and look. It's the sweetest thing I've ever seen." Jasmine could hear Rhett sitting on the floor next to the kennel, crooning softly to the mama dog, feeding her some wet food one spoonful at a time.

He looked up when Jasmine came in and said, "Imani said it was okay to feed her. I got her to eat a little, but I don't think it was enough." With worried eyes, he glanced at the dog.

Jasmine knelt down on the floor next to Rhett. "Thank you for staying with her."

"I'm glad I could help."

The sweet little pit bull sniffed at her hand and then licked it.

Rhett reached for her hand, weaving his fingers with hers. "I overreacted about Larry and… everything."

Jasmine looked down at where their hands were joined. "So did I."

Rhett rubbed her thumb with his, sighed, and let go of some of the tension from the day. She stroked the puppies' soft little bodies, happy to see their bellies rounded and full.

"When I finished my doctorate, I landed what I thought was my dream job," she said quietly. "It was an exciting time and a kind of victory for me. I overcame a rocky start. I wasn't the top student I started out as, but I graduated with good grades, and I thought"—she inhaled—"I would work at a large animal hospital in Ohio that I did one of my rotations with. All of my dreams came true when they offered me a position. It was a prestigious practice, and a lot of my classmates wanted to work there." Jasmine swallowed, trying to control the tremor in her voice before she continued. "But they chose me, and it felt like a victory. I was proud of myself for what I accomplished. I knew I was going to have to pay my dues and work my way up. After six months, I was still doing lab work and not treating many patients. Then the comments started. My scrubs made my ass look too big, my arms were too muscular, I didn't look feminine enough, and my hair was unprofessional."

Rhett tightened his hold on her hand.

"I don't know why I'm telling you this now. I need you to understand why I was mad at you."

"I'm listening."

She took a deep breath and continued. "One day, I overheard a couple of techs talking. They said that the only reason I got the job was that the practice needed a diversity hire. That way they would be eligible to get state funds for businesses with minority employees. They hired me as a fraud." Despite her best efforts, her voice became shaky. "And then I was working late one night, and one doctor… he… he said I should get on my knees and show him how much I really wanted my job. He didn't know that I grew up with a big brother who was in the Army and a dad who insisted his daughter learn self-defense."

Rhett's breathing was shallow, and his fists clenched when she finished.

"Hey"—she squeezed his arm—"I'm okay. Like I said, I may be a positive, upbeat person, but that doesn't mean I haven't struggled. And it doesn't make me a pushover. I can defend myself when I need to."

"But you shouldn't have had to in the first place." Rhett's hand grew tight around hers. "I wish I could have been there to kick his ass for you."

Jasmine leaned her head back and looked into his eyes. "I wish you'd been there to see me rescue myself. I don't want to be rescued. I want… I want to have someone who will appreciate my courage and be there for me when I am vulnerable and need support."

Rhett rubbed his thumb over her knuckles. "I think you said it perfectly. I'm not qualified, but I'd like to apply for the position."

She wanted to stop talking and kiss him, but Jasmine needed to explain the rest.

"That's why I wear baggy clothes. Months and months of comments made me self-conscious. I know I don't need to wear clothes like this," she said, waving her hands over her baggy scrubs, "but they've kind of become my armor."

The mama looked up at Jasmine with her big golden-brown eyes and let out a little whine.

"You don't have any armor, do you, sweetheart?" Jasmine said, letting go of Rhett's hand to stroke her head.

"When you left without saying anything, it triggered some of my insecurities. I went back to that place where I didn't think I was good enough, and I got angry."

"Thank you for telling me." He paused. "I want to tell you about my grandpa. I just need a little more time."

"I'll be here when you're ready."

"Can we start over and be friends again?" Rhett asked.

"I don't think I can do that," she said with a smile.

Rhett's eyebrows shot up. "Oh."

"I can't go back to the way things were before now that I've kissed you." She repeated the words he said to her a couple of weeks ago.

He leaned in and gently pressed his lips to hers. "I don't want to be friends either," he whispered against her lips.

The intercom came to life. "Dr. Owens, it's an hour past closing. I'd stay, but I have a date tonight."

Jasmine closed the kennel and arranged a blanket over the top, giving the mama and her pups some privacy.

"Do you want me to stay with her?" Rhett asked.

"No, you and Rebel should head home. We can talk more later, okay?"

Rhett got up and stood in front of her. He wrapped his hand around the back of her neck, pulling her in for another kiss.

"I'll call you tonight," he said, pressing his forehead against hers.

"And I'll answer when you do," she said.

Chapter Sixteen

THE LUNCH crowd was in full swing at the Catfish Café. Jasmine ran her hand over the worn linoleum tabletop. The only restaurant in town, it was the gathering spot for good food and to learn the latest news even though its owner, Tillie Reynolds, was known for her "no spreading twallop" rule in her restaurant.

"Hey, sis, how are you doing?" Isiah slid into the booth across from her. "I thought we'd get to spend more time together, living in the same place, but it seems like I never get to see you."

Jasmine knew what he was really saying was that he'd been keeping an eye on her. She appreciated her protective older brother's concern, but she didn't want him to feel like he needed to check up on her all the time.

"I'm good. I've been busy making calls to a lot of the farms around the area."

Isiah narrowed his eyes. "Anyone give you any trouble? Has Larry come around again?"

"No. It's been fine, really. A few folks are a little cautious, but that's nothing new. People assume I'm younger than I am, that I'm not qualified. You know how it is."

Her brother gave her an understanding smile. "They just can't believe you're a vet and not a supermodel."

Jasmine rolled her eyes. Her brother was always trying to build her up.

Presley walked in, rushing over to their table and scooting in next to Jasmine.

Her brother's head swiveled between Jasmine and Presley, then looked back to Jasmine again, slightly surprised.

"Sorry I'm late. Ms. June came in with a longer list of ideas for town improvements than usual."

"Oh no, what was it this week?"

"I always entertain Jasmine with stories about Ms. June showing up at the mayor's office every week with her list of ideas. That was—until she became a regular at her clinic as well."

Isiah chuckled, shaking his head. "She showed up at the jail a while ago, suggesting we do dancing videos and put them on YouTube. It seems she'd seen a video of some cop doing the Cupid Shuffle in the park at a picnic, and she got it into her head that it would be a good way to foster goodwill with the community."

"Good gracious," Presley said.

"Yeah, well, both of you are getting off easy," Jasmine said. "I've been making house calls for her chickens."

Isiah and Presley groaned in unison.

"You win," Isiah said.

"What has the two of you meeting for lunch today?"

"Friends have lunch, Isiah," Jasmine said.

Isiah's eyebrows shot up. "Friends?" he blurted out.

"Don't be rude. Presley and I are friends, and we're having lunch. You can stay, or you can go," Jasmine shot back.

Presley turned to Isiah with a hopeful look in her eyes. "You can stay and have lunch with us if you want to."

Jasmine kicked her brother under the table when he took a beat too long to respond.

"Sure, I suppose so."

You'd have thought Presley had just won the lottery from the way her face lit up.

"How are things at the clinic? I heard about the run-in with Larry Atwood the other day," Presley asked.

Tillie appeared at their table. Today, her trademark gingham shirt was a sunny yellow that made her bright red hair take on a slightly orange hue.

"What can I get y'all today?" She pointed at Isiah. "You order somethin' simple. You end up running out of here before I can have your food ready too many times."

"Now that I've got a deputy hired, it shouldn't happen as often."

Tillie patted Isiah on the shoulder. "Don't you worry, I ain't gonna jerk a knot in your tail. I know folks around here have had you runnin' over hell's half acre. I'll cook as much food as it takes to keep you fed. You're exactly what this town needed, and I aim to keep you fat and sassy."

Jasmine hid her smile behind her menu at Tillie saying she was going to make her brother fat and sassy. Isiah was such a contradiction in

Colton. He still had his stern, no-nonsense demeanor, but he was much more patient and understanding with folks in town than he was back in Chicago.

They placed their orders, and as soon as Tillie walked away, Jasmine said, "I have got to be honest. I didn't understand a word she said."

Presley laughed. "Don't worry. I'll teach you how to speak Southern."

"How's that dog doing that you rescued from Larry?" Isiah asked.

"She is such a sweetheart. I think she'll be recovered enough that I can spay her in a couple more weeks."

"What are you going to do with her?" Presley asked.

"I'm thinking about keeping her."

"I might be interested in taking one of the puppies," Isiah said.

Jasmine looked at her brother with surprise. "Wow. I never thought I'd see the day when you would want a dog."

Isiah shrugged. "What can I say? I'm settling in and ready to put down some roots."

Presley glanced at Isiah and said with a nervous laugh, "I keep expecting your brother to tire of us small-town folks and want to move back to Chicago."

"I'm not planning on going anywhere," Isiah said in a low, quiet voice.

Presley's cheeks flushed bright pink when she dropped her gaze.

Tillie reappeared with their food, setting a to-go box with Isiah's sandwich in it in front of him.

"This way, if y'all have to get goin' in a hurry, you can take it with you. I should have done that half a month of Sundays ago."

"Thank you, Tillie," Isiah said.

Just then, the mic attached to the shoulder of Isiah's uniform crackled, and the county dispatcher's voice rang out with a code. He grabbed his hat and the to-go box, scooting out of the booth.

"Sorry, folks. Duty calls."

"Be careful out there," Jasmine said.

Tillie patted him on the shoulder before she bustled back to the kitchen. "Stay safe."

Presley bit her lip, holding back whatever it was she wanted to say. Her eyes tracked Isiah out of the restaurant and across the street until he got into his patrol car.

“Do you worry about him?” Presley asked, her gaze following Isiah’s taillights as he drove away.

“Of course. But Isiah’s good at his job, and he knows when to ask for backup.”

Isiah wasn’t reluctant to ask for help, unlike Rhett.

Presley finally tore her eyes away from the street and looked at Jasmine. “It’s nice that you and your brother are so close.”

“What about you and Ashton? You two seem to get along pretty well.”

Jasmine met Presley’s older brother when she opened her business accounts at the town bank he managed, and when he joined the weekly knitting nights. Ashton Beaumont seemed like a nice, easygoing man.

“We haven’t been in the past, but I’m trying to be a better sister, and I think… we might be closer now.”

The café grew busier while Jasmine and Presley ate their lunch. As customers came in, they greeted the two of them with friendly smiles and a few curious stares.

“It’s because you’re new,” Presley said in a hushed whisper.

“What is?”

“People staring. Even though it’s been a few months, you’re new and”—Presley bit her lip—“because you’re with me.”

Jasmine gave Presley a sympathetic look. Isiah had mentioned Presley’s reputation as the town beauty queen and resident troublemaker. Some of Presley’s antics that Isiah shared made Jasmine laugh so hard, her side ached. Like the time Presley decided the mayor’s office needed some updating and showed up with a box of purple floral wallpaper and gold pillows with purple tassels. Isiah’s description of the argument Presley and Mae had about Presley’s redecorating plans made Jasmine cry with laughter. Other stories made her shake her head in disappointment that someone could act that carelessly. But lately, the anecdotes Isiah shared came with a note of admiration in his voice at Presley’s efforts to improve herself.

Tillie returned with two slices of pecan pie. “I figured you two wouldn’t mind a little dessert.”

Presley watched Tillie walk away, wide-eyed. Looking at the slice of pie, she did a double-take.

“I’ve… she’s never offered me pie before,” Presley said.

“Well, there’s a first time for everything.”

Presley looked at Jasmine, shaking her head. "No, y'all don't understand. Tillie doesn't give you a slice of pie unless she likes you." Presley's voice quivered, and her eyes were bright.

"That's a nice compliment, then."

Presley inhaled deeply, dug her fork into the gooey, sugary mass, and took a bite. "I swear, Tillie's pecan pie is a little slice of heaven."

Jasmine dug into her own piece, content to listen to Presley as she shared anecdotes about the different customers while they ate.

Presley kept up her stream of chatter through lunch and as Jasmine made her way back to the clinic. When they reached the steps of the town hall, Presley stopped.

"Well, this is me," Presley announced, tilting her head toward the elegant brick. "Hey, do you want to hang out at the Buckthorn tomorrow night?"

"Sure."

They exchanged numbers, and then Presley pulled her into a hug before she jogged up the town hall steps with a huge grin on her face. Presley may not have been who Jasmine pictured as a friend when she moved here, but this was exactly what she'd hoped for—friendships and a community that welcomed her instead of treating her with suspicion and prejudice.

THAT NIGHT, she settled into the corner of her sofa with a blanket and her phone in her hand, waiting.

Her phone vibrated with a FaceTime call at eight on the dot.

"I think I have a friend… not just a friend, but someone who could be a close friend," she announced when Rhett's face came on the screen. "Hi, Rebel." She laughed when a wet nose filled the screen at the sound of her voice.

Rebel's snout was replaced with Rhett's blue eyes.

"You have a lot of friends," Rhett said.

"Yes, but not many girlfriends."

"Who is this new friend?"

"Presley Beaumont."

Rhett had just taken a swig from a beer bottle and started choking and sputtering.

"Are you okay?" she asked.

"Yeah"—he wheezed—"I just wasn't expecting you to say that. Presley Beaumont is… well, she's somethin' else."

"I know all about her past. But I also know she helped with your investigation, telling Jacob when she heard rumors about a threat against the mayor."

Rhett sobered. "You're right. I'll admit I was worried about Presley falling in with the wrong crowd, but she's changed a lot in the last year. I see her working hard trying to become a better person, and I admire her for it. I wish more folks followed her path instead of continuing to hate and destroy people."

"Because of you, most of those people are behind bars now."

"Yeah, but not all of them, and until they are, it's hard to sleep at night."

Jasmine chewed on her lip for a minute, debating if she would overstep before deciding it was worth the risk.

"Rhett, have you ever thought about talking to someone about everything you've been through?"

"Are you talking about a therapist?"

"Yes."

He frowned. "I don't need any help."

"Oh." She couldn't keep the disappointment out of her voice. He'd turned down any offer for help since the night she'd cut his hair. It was becoming harder to deal with her dismay at his rejection of each offer of help. She was a fixer by nature. It was part of her nature to want to help anyone in need.

RHETT COULDN'T suppress the kernel of worry that was always present since Larry showed up at Jasmine's clinic. Every time Rhett relived seeing him there, standing in front of Jasmine with his fists clenched, he felt sick. Jasmine said she could defend herself, and Rhett believed her, but that didn't stop him from lying in bed at night, replaying the scene in his head, wondering what would have happened if he hadn't shown up.

"Rhett, are you okay?"

He looked at Jasmine's concerned face on the screen. "Yeah, I was just thinking."

"Penny for your thoughts?"

"Nothing important."

"I was asking when I can see you again," she said with a faint blush spreading across her cheeks.

"How about this weekend?"

"I'd like that."

"Will you call me when you get back from the Buckthorn tomorrow night?"

Jasmine nodded, her smile bringing out the slight dimple on her cheek that he'd been spending way too much time thinking about for the last few days. Jasmine was a distraction and a risk, but he welcomed both.

He heard a little whine, and the pittie came into the screen.

"How's she doing?" he asked.

"She's making a good recovery. Both the mama and her puppies have gained a lot of weight in the last week. She's such a good mama."

"Do you know what you're going to do with her?"

"That's why I brought her up to my apartment for a little while tonight. I wanted to give her a break from her puppies and spend a little time with her one-on-one. I've been thinking that I'd like to keep her."

The dog in question licked the side of Jasmine's face.

"It looks like someone approves of the idea. I suspect you already have a name picked out, don't you?"

Jasmine settled the dog into her lap. "Maisy."

The dog's tail thumped once, and she lifted her face to Jasmine's, trying to give her another kiss, making Jasmine laugh. That laugh was becoming one of Rhett's favorite sounds.

"I think she approves."

"What do you think? Would you like to make this your forever home?" Jasmine asked the dog.

I would, Rhett mentally answered. Shaking his head, he asked, "Has there been any other trouble at your place since Larry? I heard about the attempted break-in at the medical clinic."

"No, it's been quiet. Dax checked the security footage, but the person was wearing one of those hats that just has the openings for your eyes and nose," Jasmine said.

Rhett snapped the band around his wrist. "No fingerprints?"

"No, Isiah said there was nothing that was usable."

"Just make sure you're being careful," he said.

As soon as he made sure Colton was really safe and he got his life in order, he could think about making a forever home. He couldn't be with Jasmine the way he wanted to, not yet, but he'd discovered he was selfish when it came to her. Being with Jasmine made him feel whole again.

Maisy nudged Jasmine again, making Rhett chuckle. "Rebel will be happy to make a new friend."

"As soon as Maisy is a little stronger, we can introduce them."

Rebel trotted toward him and climbed into Rhett's lap when he hung up with Jasmine.

"Looks like you're going to get a new friend."

Rebel snorted and rested his head on Rhett's chest.

Rhett let his head fall back against the log wall of the cabin, watching the lightning flash in the distance. The thunder was remote, and the storm would dissolve before it made it to the cabin. He stroked Rebel's thick fur. The rhythm always brought him peace.

Even with the rain, it was mild enough for him to stay on the porch; his sleeping bag would keep him warm enough. He welcomed the downpour, for a good rain made everything smell fresh and new. A good rain brought promise with it.

"We're going to finish cleaning up and get rid of Larry," Rhett told Rebel. "Then we'll figure out how to be happy."

Rebel sighed and thumped his tail before he closed his eyes. Rhett dug his fingers into Rebel's fur and let his eyes drift closed.

Chapter Seventeen

Rhett stopped by the clinic at the end of the week, just as Jasmine was loading her medical bag into the back of her SUV. He came toward her with a warm smile, enveloping her in a hug that was interrupted when Rebel decided he needed one too. Things were going well between them. They'd resumed their ritual of nightly phone calls, and she was looking forward to going out on a proper date with Rhett—which they'd scheduled for the following weekend.

Her happiness at the surprise visit quickly turned to frustration when he learned where she was going.

Rhett looked at her with a thunderous expression. "You can't go out there."

"Rhett, this is part of my job. I know what I'm doing,"

"Then you need to let me come with you."

Jasmine shook her head. "We both know that's not a good idea. The Herberts won't let me anywhere near that horse if you're there."

Rhett's jaw ticked. "I don't care," he ground out.

"You don't, but I do. I'm trying to build a reputation here, and showing up with a bodyguard isn't going to help me."

Rhett stood in front of her car, his feet apart and his arms crossed, glowering at her.

Jasmine finished loading her supplies and slammed the back hatch closed before turning to face him.

Rhett's nostrils flared. "I know that family. They are *not* good people."

"I've dealt with difficult clients who don't trust me before."

"No."

Jasmine raised her eyebrows. "Are you serious right now?"

"It's not safe."

"There's an animal that needs my help. That's all that matters. I know how to take care of myself, and if I need help, I'll ask for it."

Jasmine emphasized the last sentence, looking Rhett in the eye as she spoke. Not that he didn't believe her, but she couldn't back down.

"I don't have time to argue about this anymore." She jerked open the driver's side door and put one foot in. "Either get out of the way or get run over."

"Jasmine"—Rhett's voice softened—"please, you have to be careful. This isn't Ohio."

"Rhett, do you think I didn't deal with difficult situations in Ohio? Racism is an infectious disease, and no one is immune. I'll be careful, but this is my job."

There hadn't been many issues with the calls she'd made so far. The few people who did give her trouble were older farmers who held strong views about gender roles and would have been suspect about any female veterinarian, no matter what color they were.

Jasmine slammed the door with a little more force than she wanted to and glanced at Rhett's scowling face in the rearview mirror as she drove away. She would deal with him later. Right now, she had a patient that needed her care.

TWO HOURS later, Jasmine returned to the clinic to find Rhett waiting in the same place she'd left him. Jasmine exhaled a shaky breath. Before she could reach for the handle, he yanked the door open.

"Are you okay?"

Jasmine's mouth turned down. "Yeah, I'm fine."

Rhett pulled her out of the car and grasped her shoulders. "No, you're not okay. What happened?"

"It's fine. They didn't need a vet. The horse needs to be re-shod by a farrier who knows what they're doing, that's all. If it had been anything major, I would have had them call in someone who specializes in equines."

As a precaution, Jasmine had taken her gun, and she was glad she did. The owners weren't outright hostile. They wanted her services, so they behaved. But it was the first time Jasmine encountered that many Confederate flags before or felt as unsafe as she did visiting that farm. The owner even had the nerve to joke about paying her in black-eyed peas and corn bread. She doubted she'd ever see a penny of that bill paid off.

"You should have asked for help."

"Why? You don't," she snapped back.

"This is different."

Jasmine put her hands on his chest and pushed herself out of his grasp. He followed her to the back of her car, hovering while she unloaded her bag.

"Here, let me take that for you," he offered.

"I've got it."

She stormed into the clinic, past a worried-looking Imani and Zach, straight into her office, slamming her bag onto her desk. Jasmine held her hand up when Rhett followed her into her office.

"I don't want you here right now. I'll talk to you later."

Rhett hesitated for a minute before he turned on his heel and stalked out. Jasmine let out a frustrated groan and dropped her head to her desk.

Imani knocked on her door.

"You've got a patient, Doc."

Jasmine nodded without lifting her head. "Just give me a minute."

It turned out it was Jacob with his cat, Petunia.

"I think she's got a sliver in her paw," Jacob said when she walked into the exam room.

He cradled Petunia in his arms, looking at her with mournful eyes.

"Let me look. Come here, sweetheart," she crooned.

Jacob watched anxiously as she examined the wiggly little cat's paw.

"Here." She handed the cat back to Jacob. "Hold her for a minute while I get some forceps."

Jacob studied her with a frown. "Hey, are you okay, Mighty Mouse?"

"Yeah, I'm fine, just a frustrating day."

She focused on pulling the small sliver of wood out of one of the pink pads on Petunia's paw.

"There, got it."

"Does she need antibiotics or anything?" Jacob asked, scooping the cat back into his arms.

"I don't think so. She's current on all of her shots, including tetanus. Keep an eye out, and if you see any swelling or discharge, bring her back in and we'll check her for infection. I'd keep her home for a day or two instead of bringing her to the store with you, just to be on the safe side."

Petunia scampered up Jacob's chest and settled herself in the crook of his neck.

Jasmine chewed on her lip for a minute before she blurted out, "Was Rhett difficult to work with when you were his handler?"

Jacob narrowed his eyes. "What's going on?"

"He's so stubborn," she said, leaning against the exam table. "Why won't he let anyone help him?"

"Ah. Look, Mouse, it takes a certain kind of person to do what Rhett did. He was out there on his own, and he had to rely on his own instincts and judgment."

"I get that, but this is something else."

"Then I think this is a conversation you're going to have to have with Rhett. It's not just you. Dan and I have both reached out, invited him for dinner or to hang out at the Buckthorn. He's turned down all of my invitations. I've known you for a long time, and I know you're a caring person, but you can't fix someone who won't admit they're broken."

Jasmine blinked back her tears. "I know."

Petunia let out a little *meow* of protest when Jacob pulled her into a big bear hug.

ONCE SHE'D seen the last patient of the day, Jasmine checked on Maisy and her pups one more time before she went upstairs to change. Her baggy sweater and tall boots almost met at her knees. A scarf would be enough to keep her warm, with the evenings growing warmer. She got into her car and entered the address Jacob gave her into her GPS. It was less than a twenty-minute drive before she turned onto a long driveway leading up to Rhett's grandpa's cabin.

Rhett was sitting on a log at the pond at the lowest point on the property, with Rebel at his side. He didn't get up or turn to look at her when she sat down next to him.

"Jacob gave me your address," she said.

Rhett nodded and then reached for her hand. "I went overboard today. I know that."

"And I got defensive. I know you meant well."

Jasmine startled when a fish jumped out of the water with a splash.

"They're busy this time of night," Rhett said.

"Have you gone fishing lately?"

He shook his head. "No, not yet."

"Any reason why not?"

Rhett shrugged and reached down for a pebble at his feet with his free hand and threw it in the water, creating a ripple of circles across the surface.

"This is a beautiful place, Rhett," she said, taking in the verdant meadow beyond the pond and the trees that were bright green with spring leaves in the distance. She turned back to Rhett. "Can I ask you a question?"

Rhett nodded.

"Why haven't you invited me to come out here before?"

"I don't know. I wanted to get it fixed up first, I guess."

There was more to his answer, but it was clear he didn't want to share, or maybe he didn't want to tell her the truth.

She rested her head on his shoulder.

"I don't feel like I'm doing anything right," he said so softly she barely heard him.

"I guess it's part of your nature to see things in terms of right and wrong. But I don't see it that way. You're doing the best you can, and that's enough."

He put his hand over hers. "Thank you for reminding me."

His eyes searched hers before dropping to her mouth. Jasmine closed the distance between them, pressing her lips against his. It was like starting over. They were both tentative… cautious, building on the trust they'd already forged between them.

He shuddered and broke away when she ran her hands over his shoulders.

"Jasmine, don't think I don't want you. I just need time. I know you don't care if I'm not perfect… good enough, but I do. And I want to be the man who deserves to be with you. Can you wait for me?"

Jasmine nodded. "You may not think you're good enough right now, Rhett, but I think you're worth waiting for."

He reached for her, holding her tight. Jasmine couldn't help wondering if there would be any hope for them to have a future together if Rhett never accepted that he didn't have to be perfect for her or anyone else.

Chapter Eighteen

For a moment, Rhett thought his grandpa had come back from the dead when he saw the older man sitting on the log by the fishing pond a few days after Jasmine came to the cabin. It wasn't his grandpa, but another patriarch of the Colton family. Robert Ellis was a living legend. Everybody in town called him Uncle Robert. He wasn't Rhett's uncle, but he could claim him as kin somewhere along the twisted and tangled Colton family tree.

Rhett parked his Jeep and made his way down to the pond.

"You didn't go home for Thanksgiving or Christmas," Uncle Robert said without taking his eyes off the water.

Rhett sat down on the log next to him. "I was working."

"Bullshit."

There was no point in trying to fool Uncle Robert. No one ever got away with it for as long as Rhett had been alive, and he was pretty sure no one ever would.

"I can't stand the way they look at me. They keep apologizing over and over, and I just"—he ran his hands through his hair—"I can't stand it. I can't carry their guilt and my own. It's too much."

Uncle Robert dropped his chin to his chest. "I've been waitin' for months, thinkin' you'd show up on my porch. I figured you'd know that you could talk to me. But you're too damn stubborn." He looked at Rhett with his jaw set. "I don't know what it is in our DNA that makes the Colton men so damn difficult. I thought your cousins Dax and Taylor were tough nuts to crack, but you"—he snorted a laugh—"you're gonna give the rest of us a run for our money."

"I'm not being stubborn. I'm just… trying to figure out what my life looks like now. I don't want to do desk work with the agency. I want to be out in the field, but how can I do that now that my cover is gone? I've never pictured myself sitting behind a desk. That's not the work I want to do." He dropped his chin to his chest. "I'm trying to move on. I just can't see the path forward right now."

Uncle Robert's eyebrows shot up. "Oh, is that what you're tryin' to do? Well, you're making a mess of it."

Rhett reared back. He knew Uncle Robert could be brutally honest and would cut to the chase. This was the first time he'd ever been on the receiving end, and he didn't like it.

"You, of all people, should understand what I'm dealing with right now. I can't just pretend like everything is okay when there are still people out there who pose a threat."

"I know it's burning a hole in your belly that Larry Atwood isn't behind bars yet."

"He's been talking, telling folks he's going to teach me a lesson for being a traitor and bragging about all the money he's gonna make. I can feel it in my gut. He's behind the break-ins that have been happening."

"That's probably a reasonable assumption, but it's not up to you to take on Larry without help."

"I can't put anyone around me at risk. What if he comes after my parents or…." Rhett pressed his lips together.

"Or Jasmine Owens? That's the real reason you've been holding your parents and everyone around you at arm's length, isn't it? You're worried that they might end up getting hurt by someone who's out to get you?"

"Part of it."

"You gonna share the other part?"

Rhett shook his head.

"Does it have anything to do with why you haven't gone into your grandpa's cabin yet?"

Rhett narrowed his eyes. "How do you know I haven't gone inside?"

"Come on, kid." Uncle Robert snorted. "I can see the cobwebs from here."

"Yeah, okay. I'm just not ready yet."

Uncle Robert's mouth turned down. "I could kill your grandfather for burdening you with his guilt. That man groomed you for your mission since you were a boy. It wasn't fair to you."

"Grandad didn't make me take my assignment. I volunteered."

"Look me in the eye and tell me you didn't put yourself up to go undercover because you thought it would bring your grandpa peace. I know George never wanted you to sacrifice your own well-being."

"That's not what I did, and it's not what I'm doing."

Uncle Robert responded with a disapproving grunt.

"You don't need to worry. I'll be fine."

"In my time with the Firm, I've seen men like you, the ones that wouldn't accept help when it was offered. One by one, they all failed, either at work or in their personal lives." Uncle Robert got up, hooking his thumbs into his overalls, his weathered face somber. "Don't do this, son. Don't think you can do it all on your own."

Rhett bowed his head. "Okay."

REBEL SHIFTED in the grass with a frustrated huff. Rhett had stayed crouched in the same position in a field some forty miles from Colton for an hour now.

What was supposed to be a quick trip to the grocery store turned into something else when Rhett overheard a couple of guys talking about how they were going to be able to "score" from a guy named Larry that night.

He followed them for the rest of the day and to a dilapidated barn that night. He'd been monitoring the place ever since.

Rhett glanced over his shoulder at Dan pushing through the overgrown grass on the other side of the road. Dan crouched down next to him, squinting at the barn.

"How long have you kept this place under surveillance, and why haven't you reported this before now?" Dan asked.

"I just found out about it a few days ago. What are you doing here?"

"I was driving by when I saw you pull off the road and duck into this field. I know someone's doing surveillance when I see it."

"I'm just checking out a hunch. I don't need any help."

Dan's mouth turned down. "How many times do I need to remind you? You're on leave."

"Yeah, I know."

"Then what are you doing?"

"I know these people better than anyone else. Larry's trying to regroup," Rhett said.

"Sooner or later, he's going to catch on that he's being watched."

"He doesn't care. There are some hardcore guys still out there that don't believe the law will ever catch up with them."

Anger flashed in Dan's eyes. "Well, they're in for a reality check, then."

"I don't give a damn about Larry, but—"

Rhett jumped, and Rebel stood, his pose tense at the sound of dogs barking.

"Dog fighting." Dan's whole body went rigid with anger.

Rhett pressed his lips together and nodded. "He's using the dogfighting to lure them in; that and drugs. I can't prove it yet, but I suspect Larry is the one behind the robberies that have been happening in the area."

"We need to let Animal Control know," Dan said.

"I want to make sure it's the right people. There are still members of law enforcement around here who will turn a blind eye, including Animal Control, who will pretend like they haven't seen anything for the right price."

"Yeah, okay, I hear you. Do you have any suggestions?"

"I'm not going to make a move until I'm sure I can get Larry this time."

Dan narrowed his eyes. "I don't want anyone dealing with these guys without backup. This isn't anything for the bureau to be involved in at this point. We'll have to share what's going on with Isiah and let him handle things." Dan grabbed Rhett's shoulder and gave him a little shake. "I mean it, Rhett. You stay out of this one."

Rhett glanced toward the sounds of men shouting and dogs barking. "You know I can't do that."

Dan stared at him for a long moment. "Let's go back to the Buckthorn and talk."

They backed away through the field until they reached Dan's SUV.

"I'll see you at the Buckthorn."

It was an order, not a request.

THERE WERE just a few cars and trucks parked in front of the weathered building when they pulled up. Rhett hesitated for just a moment before he got out of his Jeep.

"We can meet in the back. That way, we'll have some privacy," Dan said.

Rhett opened the back door, and Rebel jumped out, trotting along at his side as they went around to the back.

"You can wait on Primus's porch. I'm going to let Reid know we're here," Dan said, pointing to a small house in a hollow behind the bar that Rhett didn't even know existed.

"Come on, Rebel."

There were two old rocking chairs on the porch that looked as if they might not hold his weight. He chose the sturdier-looking of the two and sank down into it, wincing at the creaking noise it made.

"Don't worry. They been on this porch for over thirty years, and they ain't broke yet," Primus said, coming out of the house with a chuckle. "I got sweet tea, or do you want something stronger?" He held up a jar of honey-colored liquid.

"Sweet tea would be just fine, thank you, sir."

Primus waved a finger at him. "None of that *sir* business, remember?"

"Thank you, Primus."

He nodded his salt-and-pepper-covered head and went back inside. It surprised Rhett that the old man didn't seem phased to see him sitting on his front porch. He went into every situation not knowing if folks were going to be happy to see him or not. Dan came up to the porch just as Primus returned with a canning jar full of sweet tea and handed it to Rhett.

Primus rested his hands on his hips, his eyes traveling the length of the porch, up to the ceiling, and back to Rhett. "You know, Medgar and Richard Colton used to meet on this porch with the rest of us when we were startin' up the NAACP chapter in these parts. The only one in Mississippi. I ain't gonna lie. It's bittersweet seeing you boys here."

"We all owe you and the rest of those folks our gratitude," Rhett said.

"It may seem like we haven't made much progress, but look at y'all. You're meeting in the daylight while we were afraid that a firefly might give us away."

Rhett didn't have the words to respond. What Primus was sharing humbled him to his core and reminded him that his two years undercover were just a drop in the ocean of history of his home state. People like Primus carried generations of struggle. He was grateful his grandpa finally realized the hate he'd embraced would put him on the wrong side of history.

"Make yourselves at home. I'm heading in," he said, jerking his thumb toward the Buckthorn.

"That man is a whole world of stories, isn't he?" Rhett said, watching Primus move slowly toward his juke joint.

Dan sat down in the chair next to him, clasping his hands in front of him. "He's a fourth-generation distiller, maybe further back than that. He said his great-granddaddy made whiskey for General Colton at the plantation."

"That's a lot of history right there."

"Primus is a good man. He helped Reid a lot while he tried to reconcile what he thought he knew about his parents with the truth. It was hard to find out the woman who he thought was his mother wasn't his biological mother and never wanted to raise him. At least he finally had an explanation for why she treated him so terribly growing up."

"I've struggled trying to make peace with my family's faults, but I can't imagine what Reid has gone through."

Dan frowned. "As bad as it was finding out the woman he thought was his mother wasn't, finding out his parents hid his race from him hurt him more. Primus has been mentoring him while he figures out who he is as opposed to who he thought he was." Dan's voice grew thick with emotion. "He's a very special person in our lives and a father figure for both of us."

"Families are complicated. Sometimes, the family relationships we choose are more meaningful than the ones we're born with," Rhett said.

"Let's talk about yours. What's going on with Larry Atwood?"

"Larry's always been crafty. I don't know how he's avoided getting any charges made against him. It was dumb luck he wasn't there the night Mae was kidnapped, and he made sure his hands were clean when everyone else was arrested. But he's trouble, and I won't be able to sleep well at night until he's caught. He'll make sure I'll always be looking over my shoulder."

"And you're worried anyone who's around you will be a target too, aren't you?"

"Wouldn't you if you were in my shoes?"

"Of course I worry about Reid, my parents, Uncle Minh, everyone I care about. Most days, our job is pretty tame. It can be more paperwork, writing reports, and interviewing people than field work. But danger comes with the job."

"Don't you feel guilty for putting them in that position?"

Dan narrowed his eyes, shaking his head. "Is that what's going on with you? Rhett, the people around you are there because they care. We're here because we care. If folks were scared or thought they couldn't handle the risk, they would leave. You've got folks begging you to let them in."

"I can't. I can't bring myself to put anyone else at risk. What if I hadn't been there to help Mae? What happens if there's collateral damage if someone comes after me? I can't do that."

"What do you want to do?"

"I don't know yet, but whatever I decide to do, I can take care of it on my own."

"That's not okay, and you know it."

Rhett rested his arms on his thighs, clasping his hands in front of him. "If I need anything from you, I'll ask."

Dan eyed him for a minute before he said, "I wish I could believe you."

After a few more tries, Dan gave up, and the two of them parted ways.

On his way home, Rhett's contact at the bar called him.

"You're not going to like this," he said.

"What's going on?" Rhett asked.

"Larry came in here tonight, and I overheard him mention he knew you were seeing the vet that stole his dog. Each time I see him, he's more strung out. That guy's dangerous."

Rhett's blood ran cold. He'd been waiting for this—this was the fear that kept him awake at night. This was why he should have stayed away from Jasmine, from everyone he cared about.

"Thanks for letting me know," he said between clenched teeth.

He hung up with the bartender, his mind racing on his way back to the cabin. Rhett remembered his grandpa's words as they sat by the pond with their fishing poles in the water while skeeter bugs danced on the surface in the evening light. *There ain't no fish that can't be caught. You just gotta have the right bait.*

A plan formed. Rhett knew exactly what bait he could use to lure Larry in and get him to do something that would put him behind bars once and for all.

It was a simple decision to make. He was more than willing to sacrifice himself to keep the town and the people he held close to his heart safe.

He would become the bait.

Chapter Nineteen

IT WAS just warm enough to hang out on Callie and Dax's porch after dinner. Jasmine burrowed her face deeper into the funnel neck of the sweater she'd stolen from her brother when she'd come home for a visit when she was living in Ohio, something Isiah still grumbled about. Jasmine enjoyed Sunday night dinners at Dax and Callie's house. It was always nice to spend time with her surrogate family, especially when she was feeling homesick.

She smiled behind the soft wool that hid the lower half of her face, watching her brother and his friends' antics playing out. Their bets and bragging evolved from who could do more pushups to who could change a diaper faster, with Isiah as referee. Jasmine watched with Callie and Mae while they laughingly shouted encouragement to their husbands. Once the babies were diapered, it became a contest to see who could get their offspring to fall asleep faster.

Dax was gently rocking his daughter in his arms, walking in circles.

"How are things going at the clinic?" he asked as he walked by.

Jasmine pulled her knees up and wrapped her arms around them. "It's going okay. I've had a couple of difficult clients, but that comes with the territory. Today was frustrating. There was a client who wasn't too happy to have a woman, and especially a Black woman, taking care of his animals. I'm pretty sure he would have run me off except for the fact he couldn't get someone else quick enough."

Dax stopped in his tracks and turned around.

"Who was it?"

Jacob jumped up from the porch railing he'd perched on and came to stand in front of her, saying, "You shouldn't be going out to farms by yourself."

All three of them—her brother, Jacob, and Dax—started peppering her with questions and demands.

"You need to tell me when you're going to make a house call," Isiah demanded.

"I'll install a tracking device on her truck just in case," Dax said.

Jasmine laughed but stopped when she realized Dax was serious.

"I have a list of people she should avoid," Jacob added.

Her brother and his two friends formed a huddle and were strategizing as if she wasn't there. They ignored her the first two times she tried to get their attention, so she put her fingers in her mouth and gave a high shrill whistle that startled both babies and made them wail.

"I didn't mean to make the babies cry. It's the only thing that works when they get like this," Jasmine said.

Callie plucked her daughter out of her husband's arms and started bouncing her. "That's okay. They were asking for it."

"If you hadn't done something, I was about to slap all of them upside the head," Mae muttered. She had Dante over her shoulder, patting the hiccupping baby, who was glaring at Jasmine with big fat tears rolling down his cheeks. Mae frowned at Jacob. "Don't be such a chauvinistic lumberjack," she said with more affection than censure.

Jacob leaned over and kissed his wife on the cheek and his son on the top of his head. "Sorry, Pixie." He turned to Jasmine. "It's just because we love you, Mighty Mouse."

"We just want to make sure no one gives you a hard time," Isiah said.

Jasmine shot her brother a look. "You know if they do, I can handle myself." She stared down the three men. "Look, I appreciate you watching out for me. I really do. I'm lucky. When Isiah came home from boot camp for the first time, I didn't just have one brother return home. I ended up with three. But you forget that I'm a grown woman and not some wide-eyed, naïve little girl who doesn't know about the dangers in the world. Isiah, you and Dad made sure I learned self-defense and how to handle a firearm."

Isiah came over and gently grasped her arms. "I know, and I'm proud to have a sister who can kick ass if she has to. But I never want to put you in a position where you have to defend yourself again."

"I'm not going to let you do that. You can't protect me every minute of every day. You can't wrap me in bubble wrap. I have a life to live, and so do you. If I need help, I'll ask for it. I'm not stubborn like—" Jasmine bit down on her lip.

Isiah narrowed his eyes. "Like who? Me?"

"Never mind, forget I said that."

"You're talking about Rhett, aren't you?" Jacob asked.

"Are you getting serious with Rhett Colton?" Isiah asked.

He was using his interrogation voice, or at least that's what Jasmine thought of it as. It was the same tone her father used when he questioned boys who came to pick Jasmine and her sister up at the house when they were in high school. And it irked her just as much now as it did when her dad used it.

She held her hand up. "This conversation is over."

"This conversation is far from over. What were you thinking, sis?"

"If you don't back down right this minute, Isiah Owens, then we are going to talk about Presley Beaumont, Mr. Knightly," Jasmine countered.

Isiah's jaw went tight while Mae snickered.

"Fine," her brother said between clenched teeth. He let go of her arms and moved over to the porch railing, leaning against it with his arms spread wide, looking out at the yard. Bringing up Presley may not have been fair, but her brother was like a dog with a bone, and she'd endured all the testosterone she could handle for one day.

Mae came over and patted her shoulder. "You okay?"

"Yeah, I'm fine. I shouldn't have said anything. I didn't mean to make the evening all about me."

"They are wonderful, caring men, but sometimes they can be so dumb," Callie said.

"And stubborn," Mae added.

"Hey, we're standing right here," Dax said.

"Well, now you know how it feels," Jasmine retorted.

Dax wrapped his arm around her shoulder. "Fair point, Mighty Mouse."

Jasmine groaned. "Are you ever going to stop calling me that?"

"Probably not." Dax chuckled.

"I'm going to need an extra-large piece of Callie's 7UP cake to make up for it."

"I think the men should feed their sisters and wives cake to make up for behaving like Neanderthals," Mae announced.

The mood remained lighter for the rest of the evening while her brother, Dax, and Jacob shared stories from their time in the service together. For all the misadventures they shared, Jasmine knew they'd faced a lot more danger than they would ever admit.

She couldn't stop thinking about what dangerous situations Rhett had been in that he hadn't shared with her. Was he talking to anyone about what gave him nightmares? It was hard to watch him hold so much inside.

"You okay, sis?" Isiah asked on the short drive to her apartment from Dax and Callie's house.

"I'm fine"—she gave her brother a reassuring smile—"really, I am. I shouldn't have thrown Presley Beaumont in your face."

Isiah sighed. "It was a low blow, but I was asking for it."

"You know you can't fix everyone, and not everyone needs fixing," she said.

"And you can't heal everyone. Some wounds are too deep. Jasmine, you are one of the most loving and compassionate people I know. You can't blame me for worrying that you're going to give too much of yourself again."

"Don't you dare. I can't believe you would—" She clamped her mouth shut.

"Rhett's a good guy, but he walks around like he's carrying the weight of the world on his shoulders. I don't want to see you sacrifice yourself again trying to help carry it for him."

"Rhett isn't Darren," she said quietly.

"Are you sure about that?"

Jasmine gripped the door handle tightly, trying to catch her breath. "This conversation is over. We may live in this same town, but that does not mean you get to interfere in my personal life. I'm a big girl now, Isiah, and I know the risk I'm taking." She took a deep breath, willing herself not to cry in front of her brother. She got out of the car, slamming the door shut.

Isiah rolled down the window, calling out, "Jas, I didn't mean…."

His words faded away as she ran up the stairs to her apartment. Jasmine leaned against the door and finally allowed her tears to fall. She sank down to the floor and put her head in her hands.

For the first time since she moved to Colton, Jasmine questioned her decision to relocate. Living close to her brother had its advantages, but privacy wasn't one of them. Deep down, she knew Isiah meant well, but she didn't need him reminding her of her failure.

Jasmine allowed herself a minute to wallow before she pulled herself up and wrapped her arms around herself, wandering over to the window. She stared into the darkness, trying to sort through her jumbled feelings. The sound of glass shattering and an alarm going off made her jump.

Jasmine pulled out her phone and quickly dialed 911 as she ran down the stairs, worried that something had happened at the clinic. When she got to the sidewalk, she froze as she saw a figure running away from the doctor's office. She'd barely started telling the dispatcher that there was a break-in when she saw her brother tearing out of Town Hall with his deputy by his side. She called out, pointing in the direction where the man had ran off. A cool breeze swept through the park, and she shivered. She went downstairs and made sure Zach was settled in for the night shift before heading back to her apartment. There was nothing she could do other than wait for Isiah to check in. It turned out she didn't have to wait long. Isiah knocked on her door less than an hour later.

"Hey, did you catch them?"

Isiah shook his head with a scowl. "No, that's why I came by. Can you give me a description?"

"Dark sweatshirt and pants. I can't give you more than that. I heard the glass break, and then I saw someone running away while I was calling 911."

Isiah paced her living room. Every few steps, he'd glance out the window, his gaze darting around the town square.

"I think it may have been the same person who tried to break into Walker's Pharmacy last week," Isiah said. "I'll have Dax check the security cameras he's got installed on the block in the morning." he muttered, looking out the window again.

Back when Rhett had alerted Jacob to the threat against Mae, Jacob, Dan, and Isiah added extra surveillance cameras to the park for the Fourth of July celebrations. The footage from Mae's kidnapping that night was used in court to convict the kidnappers.

Isiah folded his arms and leveled her with one of his no-nonsense looks. "Are you sure you have enough security at the clinic?"

"Dax put together the system for me. I don't have a lot of medications on-site at the moment, but everything is in the safe."

"Do me a favor and double-check with Dax and make sure there aren't any upgrades you can do. We've been getting calls about break-ins around the county in the last few months. Whoever it is, they must be getting desperate, trying to break into Walker's and the doctor's office. Everyone around here knows there are security cameras in the park."

"If someone is desperate for drugs, they aren't going to use a lot of logic."

"True. And they can also be dangerous when they're desperate. I want you to be extra careful, okay?"

Even though they'd just argued about his overprotectiveness, Jasmine didn't make any objection. Isiah was right, and she planned on reviewing security protocols with Imani in the morning.

"I'm gonna head back. I want to make sure the window that was broken is secure before I head in for the night."

Jasmine went over and gave her brother a hug. "I didn't mean to snap at you."

Isiah sighed and wrapped his arms around her. "You know I was just trying to be a good big brother, right?"

"Yeah, I know."

They hugged it out, and Isiah left. Five minutes later, there was another knock on her door, and Rhett was on her doorstep with a worried look in his eyes.

"Hey, I just thought I'd stop by and check in."

"Let me guess, you heard about the break-in at the doctor's office," Jasmine said with a wry smile.

Rhett leaned against her doorjamb, his hair loose around his shoulders. "I have an app that alerts me to any 911 calls in the area."

"Is that because of your job?"

Rhett snapped the elastic around his wrist. "Not really. It's because of me. I… there are still people around who, for one reason or another, were not arrested the night they kidnapped the mayor."

"Was your Larry Atwood one of them?" Jasmine asked.

"Larry is one of my cousins." His expression became pained. "Having relatives who were already involved with the organization I went undercover with was a bonus."

"Oh, Rhett."

He gave her a brittle smile. "Don't feel bad for me. Families aren't all perfect." Rhett moved closer and grasped her arms. "Tell me the truth. Has Larry been giving you any trouble? I'm worried about him coming after you, thinking it would be a way to hurt me."

Jasmine held onto Rhett's hands and gave him a reassuring smile. "Other than going around telling a few people I stole his dog, no."

Rhett exhaled and pressed his forehead to hers.

"Hey, Callie sent some 7UP cake home with me. Would you like a piece?" she asked.

Rhett nodded. "That sounds good."

She gestured to the sofa and told him to take a seat. Rebel trotted in and made himself comfortable. She cut Rhett an extra-large slice of cake and carried their plates into the living room.

"Rhett, how many other times have you driven by the clinic checking on me?"

Rhett took a big bite of cake, and closing his eyes, he inhaled while he chewed.

"You can't hide behind cake, Rhett. Eventually, you're going to have to answer my question."

He tried to look innocent. "But it's excellent cake."

Jasmine set her plate aside and leveled Rhett with a stern look. "Are you spying on me? Because I already have an overprotective brother and his two best friends watching over me. I don't need my boy—I don't need anyone else being overprotective of me."

Rhett's eyebrows shot up, and his lips curled into a smile. "Were you about to call me your boyfriend?"

Heat flooded her cheeks. "No."

"It kind of sounded like you did."

"No, I almost did, and then I stopped because… because I'm not really sure what we are."

Rhett set his plate down and took her hands in his. Her heartbeat ticked up a notch when he lifted her hands and pressed his lips to them. Jasmine could feel his pulse through her fingertips, and she knew he was aware that hers matched his.

"I wish—" He swallowed. "—there are so many things I wish, and they all involve you."

"What's stopping you from making those wishes come true?"

"You deserve much more than I can give you."

Jasmine scooted closer until her knees bumped against his. "You may think you know what I deserve, but I know what I want."

Jasmine had told Rhett she'd be patient, and she was trying, but she wanted him, and she knew he wanted her. He pulled back for just a minute, his eyes searching hers. What was he looking for?

Chapter Twenty

RHETT JUST about lost his mind when the 911 alert showed up on his phone. He'd been on his way back from Greenwood and was still thirty miles away from Colton. He pressed his foot on the gas, and the landscape became a blur. Isiah was talking to his deputy in front of the town hall when he pulled up to Jasmine's apartment.

Now he was in her arms, tasting lemon and sugar on her lips. She pulled him down until he was lying on top of her. Her legs wrapped around his, and the heat from her body enveloped him.

Jasmine was safe. He knew she was okay, but that didn't slow his heartbeat. Climbing the stairs to her apartment, he'd told himself he just needed to check and see if she was okay, and then he'd leave. When she opened the door, he realized it wouldn't be that easy.

She reached up and unbuttoned his shirt. He grabbed her hands and pulled back. Her eyes searched his face, looking at him with a mixture of lust and confusion.

"Don't touch me." He wrenched himself out of her grasp and stood up.

Jasmine jumped up and grasped his shirt again. "It's okay. It doesn't have to be perfect, it just has to be us."

Rhett dropped his forehead to hers. "I can't."

He was selfish, and he'd have to face his guilt in the light of day, but if he could have this one moment in the dark, then he could keep all of his secrets hidden.

Rhett hovered over her face. "If I stay… I… it has to be in the dark."

"You don't want to see me?"

A shadow crossed over her face, and she backed away. Rhett felt the rejection in her voice, and it pierced his heart. He grabbed her arm and pulled her to him.

"No, I can't let you see me." He kissed her forehead, her nose, her mouth. "Please, Jasmine. Every day, I try not to want you, but I can't stop thinking about you, about having just one moment with you like this." Rhett winced, trying to find the right words.

Jasmine's eyes searched his for a moment before she lifted her hand to his face, wiping away a tear that hovered at the corner of his eye that he hadn't realized was there.

"Someday, I hope you'll let me see whatever it is you're ashamed of," she whispered. He backed away, and she followed him as she mirrored each step back with a step forward. Before he reached her door, she grasped his hand and led him to her bedroom.

He hovered on the threshold, watching her close the blinds and turn off the light on her nightstand. She returned to him, reaching past him to flip the switch on the wall next to him, plunging the room into darkness. Taking his hand again, she pulled him toward her bed.

"Thank you," he choked out.

She responded with another kiss before she began to unbutton his shirt again. This time she pushed it from his shoulders and reached for the hem of his T-shirt, pulling it over his head.

He shuddered, letting his head fall to her shoulder when her fingers made contact with his skin. The darkness heightened his other senses. Her skin felt like silk under his hands. He committed to memory every inch of her body with each piece of clothing he removed. He felt the ridge of a tiny scar on her thigh, the firmness of her breasts pressed against his chest. His own physical need for her warmth drove him to lay her on the bed.

He ran his finger down the valley between her breasts and indulged in examining every curve, dip, and dimple of Jasmine's body with his hands and mouth.

Her fingers brushed over his shoulder, and he hissed. It wasn't fresh pain he felt, but the memory of the physical pain that caused his emotional turmoil. His blood thrummed in his ears. Sadness and lust were a cocktail that made for a strange intoxication.

He moaned when her hands drifted down the length of his back. Jasmine brought her hands back up and tangled her fingers in his hair, pulling him to her, capturing his lips in a kiss. She parted her lips, inviting him to explore the sweetness of her mouth. He groaned. No matter how deeply he delved into her wetness, he was still dying of thirst. He needed more.

"Rhett," she panted, "you can take your time on the next round. Right now, I need you."

She thrust her pelvis against him while she blindly reached for the nightstand drawer, fumbling through the contents until she pulled out a foil packet and pressed it into his hand. Rhett inhaled, taking in the lavender scent of the oil she'd used on his beard. Lavender was supposed to be calming, but the scent mingled with the natural perfume radiating from her skin only heightened his arousal.

"Are you sure?" he asked.

She moaned. "Yes." She reached up, cupping his cheek, and he fought the urge to turn on the light so he could look in her eyes. He knew he would see his own desire reflected in them. He'd made a lot of sacrifices; not being able to see Jasmine's face at this moment would be added to the list.

Jasmine lifted her lips to his, pulling him into another deep kiss. Her hands roamed over his back, moving lower, urging him toward her entrance.

He left a trail of kisses down her neck and over her breasts. Rhett didn't remember how he sheathed himself. All he knew was that when he sank into her warmth, he'd found his way home.

THE WINDOWS were open, allowing sunlight to stream through, illuminating the room. Jasmine turned on her side and rested her head on her hands. Rhett's blue eyes were staring back at her, his fingers toying with one of her curls.

"Oh no." She groaned, reaching up to pat the top of her head. "This is going to be a mess."

Rhett's forehead wrinkled. "What's going to be a mess?"

"My hair."

"It doesn't look messy to me. It looks beautiful."

His voice had a low, husky tone that brought back memories of the night they'd just spent together. Even though Rhett was the one who asked to make love in the dark, the truth was it helped ease some of her own insecurities. She hadn't been intimate with anyone in a long time. The months of criticism and comments about her body at her old job had stripped away her confidence. Last night she felt safe and able to embrace her sexuality again.

She sat up and noticed that, at some point in the night, Rhett had put on a T-shirt and boxer briefs. It was strange knowing that underneath the thin cotton knit was a toned body. He didn't have a six-pack or overly large muscles, but his body fit against hers perfectly.

"Stop thinking like that," he said.

"Then stop looking at me like that," she teased.

The surrounding air heated, and desire shimmered around them like the spring sunlight before Rhett jumped out of her bed.

"I'll make us some coffee and get the dogs fed," he muttered.

Jasmine clutched the sheets to her chest, looking at the empty doorway Rhett just walked through. What was it about his body he was ashamed of? She showered and set to work untangling her curls.

"Can I help?"

Jasmine looked at Rhett's reflection in the bathroom mirror. He leaned against the doorway with a cup of coffee in his hands.

"You want to help with my hair?"

He nodded. Coming forward, he set the cup on the bathroom counter. "That's for you," he said, gesturing to the cup. He picked up a bottle of hair oil from the counter and sniffed it. "Is this the stuff you used on my beard?"

"No, it's this one."

Jasmine reached for a different bottle and handed it to him. Rhett sniffed it and closed his eyes, his face relaxing. "That's the one," he said, nodding.

She'd just shared her bed with this man, and yet this was oddly a more intimate moment. He opened his eyes and asked if he could help again.

"I... there's not really much to do. I put product in it and then comb out the tangles."

He gestured to the toilet seat. "You sit, and you can tell me what to do."

Jasmine pulled her robe tightly around her and sat down. She'd never shared her hair routine with a partner before. No one ever asked. In some ways, what they were doing now was more intimate than having sex.

Rhett squeezed some of the conditioner in his hand and ran it through her curls the way she directed him to. He held the wide-tooth comb over her head and hesitated.

"You start at the ends and work your way up," she instructed.

He took a handful of hair and ran the comb through the ends. "Like this?"

Jasmine nodded, eyeing Rhett's face in the mirror. It was cute the way he chewed on his lip with his eyes narrowed, focused on combing out the tangles. When he finished combing, he asked what was next.

She pointed to a bottle of hair oil and explained how to put the product in her hair. Step by step, she led him through the process until he'd put the last product in and twisted the strands.

"Do you do this every day?" he asked.

"No, just on wash day or if I forgot to wear a scarf because a sexy man made me lose my good sense."

She was teasing, but a flash of pain crossed Rhett's expression.

"I don't want you to have any regrets about last night," he said.

Jasmine stood up and wrapped her arms around Rhett's neck. "I don't have any regrets. As a matter of fact, I'd be happy if you wanted to take me back to bed right now."

When he stiffened in her arms, she placed a soft kiss on his mouth. "It's okay."

"I… just can't, not yet."

She grabbed his arm, refusing to allow him to pull away. "One day at a time, Rhett. This is new for both of us. We'll figure it out together."

He exhaled and dropped his forehead to hers. "Thank you."

"Can I ask you a question?"

Rhett nodded.

"Why did you want to help with my hair?"

His head jerked up. "It's not some kind of fetish thing. I don't want you to think that. I would never—"

"Rhett, stop. I know you don't feel that way."

"But I did spend a lot of time with people who held racist beliefs. I need you to know that stuff they spewed never touched my heart. I wanted to help with your hair because… it's a part of you, and I wanted to take care of you."

Jasmine's stomach did a little flip-flop. She pulled him into another kiss, this one leaving them both breathless when they drew apart.

"Come on. I have to check in at the clinic, and then we can get some breakfast," she said.

They got dressed and headed downstairs. Once she checked in with Zach and sent him home, they went into the back.

She opened the first kennel. “Hi, Maisy,” she said to the dog wiggling with happiness.

Rhett smiled. “So you’ve decided to keep her?”

Jasmine returned his smile and scratched Maisy between the ears. “Yeah, this sweetheart is going to stay with me. My brother is thinking about taking one of the puppies when they’ve been weaned.”

“I can’t believe this is the same dog. She’s transformed, and her pups have gotten so big in such a short amount of time.”

“It’s amazing what a proper diet and lots of kindness can do,” Jasmine said.

Rhett smiled and kissed the top of her nose. “I’m happy to help. Put me to work.”

“Hey, mama. Would you like a break from your little ones today?” Jasmine asked, kneeling next to Maisy’s kennel.

Besides Maisy and her puppies, there was another dog and a cat being boarded while their owners were out of town. Adding boarding to the services she offered provided another income source while she continued to build her practice.

Rhett knelt down next to the enclosure where a golden retriever named Roxy was looking up at him, her whole body shaking with happiness.

“Can we take her for a walk too?” Rhett asked.

“Sure, I think Roxy would like that.”

Rebel trotted to Rhett’s side. He’d positioned himself between Maisy and Roxy, clearly appointing himself their guardian.

Rhett was laughing at the golden retriever, who insisted on stopping to smell every flower and blade of grass.

Ms. June was standing at her garden gate when they went by. “Oh, my goodness, you have an entire pack today, and a helper, I see,” she said with a twinkle in her eye.

“Good morning, ma’am.” Rhett nodded.

Ms. June pulled Rhett into a hug. “Don’t you dare call me *ma’am*. You….” Her voice broke, and she buried her face into a startled Rhett’s shoulder.

Ms. June had been with Mae when she was kidnapped. The kidnappers used her to get to Mae, and one kidnapper hit Ms. June during the kidnapping.

He looked at Jasmine with panic in his eyes. She handed him Maisy's and the other dogs' leashes and gently pried Ms. June away from him.

"Oh, I didn't mean to do that," she said, wiping her eyes. "I'm thankful for everything you did for all of us. I think about what would have happened, not just to the mayor but to all of us, our community, if you hadn't stayed with those people. I'm so grateful."

Ms. June said every word with gratitude, but Jasmine could see the discomfort in Rhett's eyes.

"Thank you, ma'am… Ms. June."

After politely but firmly turning down Ms. June's latest batch of kombucha but accepting a dozen eggs instead, they were able to extract themselves from their impromptu visit and continue on their way. Rhett was quiet the rest of the way down the block.

He finally broke his silence. "I hate it when people do that."

"People appreciate you. They're grateful for what you did."

"I don't want people to feel like they have to thank me."

Jasmine stopped and looked at him. "People don't feel obligated to thank you. They *want* to."

The only acknowledgment he gave to her statement was the firm set of his jaw. "There are over eight hundred hate groups in this country. I spent two years of my life, I sacrificed… everything, and I was only able to get rid of one. I failed."

Jasmine reached up and cupped his cheek, making sure he looked her in the eye. "You did not fail. It wasn't just one group. You provided the FBI with information that's uncovered a whole network. They're still making arrests, Rhett. It takes time. But what's more important is that you brought an entire community together."

Rhett shook his head and tried to pull away, but Jasmine wouldn't let him. She dropped her hand to his arm and held him in place, giving him a little shake.

"You're a good man, Rhett Colton. Why is it hard for you to believe people care about you?"

He leaned down and gave her a toe-curling kiss.

"The only thing I'll ever need is to know you care about me," he whispered against her lips.

Jasmine couldn't dismiss the voice in her heart that wondered if it would be enough.

CHAPTER TWENTY-ONE

RHETT GRIPPED the phone tightly, listening to the curt voice on the other end of the line. "I made sure he got the message."

"Thanks."

"You should have seen the way his eyes lit up when I mentioned your grandpa left a stash of guns and cash in the cabin. You'd have thought it was Christmas. It made me want to punch that bastard in the face."

"I figured he would. I'll take it from here," Rhett said.

There was another armed robbery at a pharmacy in the next town over a few days ago. The cashier and the pharmacist were just getting ready to close when they were held up. He still didn't have any proof, but in his gut, Rhett knew Larry and whoever he had working with him were escalating. When he heard about this latest robbery, Rhett knew he needed to take action. It was only a matter of time before someone was going to get hurt.

When he went over to Jasmine's that night, Rhett found her exhausted and teary after a long day of work that ended with her having to help a family say goodbye to a beloved pet.

He made her a cup of tea and held her close while she cried. Eventually, she got up and went to the bathroom. Jasmine came back with her tears washed away and a faint smile on her lips.

"Thank you," she said, sitting back down next to him.

Rhett pulled her into his lap. "I'm glad I could help. You've been working a lot of long days this week."

Jasmine brushed her thumb under his eye. "And you haven't been sleeping well."

He'd been spending almost every night at Jasmine's for the last two weeks after that first night he'd stayed. Guilt churned in his belly. Rhett cherished every moment he spent making love to Jasmine. He wanted to turn on the lights, but he couldn't bring himself to tell Jasmine why he'd asked her to turn them off in the first place. He was ashamed and scared. What would happen when he revealed himself to her? Would he repulse her? Would he be able to live without her touch if she walked away from him? It was impossible to sleep wrestling with all of those questions night after night.

"Have I been keeping you up?" he asked. "I don't want you to lose sleep with me here. I can—"

She stopped him with a kiss that made him forget everything but how good Jasmine felt in his arms. When they broke apart, she ran her hand over his beard. Jasmine leaned in and sniffed. "Have you been using my hair oil?"

"It feels nice, and I like being surrounded by you, by your scent, wherever I am."

She nuzzled his cheek. "I like it. It smells different on you."

"What does it smell like?"

Jasmine looked at him with a twinkle in her eye. "Like lavender and lemon, sunshine and meadow grass."

What was her secret? How was Jasmine able to make him feel whole again? No one else could soothe his wounds and, when it was just the two of them in the dark, make him forget they were there.

Jasmine pressed her hand to her mouth, trying to suppress a yawn. "It's been a long day."

"It's okay, baby."

Rhett kissed the top of her head, her curls tickling his nose. She drew her feet up under her and tucked herself closer. A few minutes later, her body relaxed and sank into his side. Rebel and Maisy were curled up together on the oversized dog bed in the corner. It was a moment like this that he'd always wanted, the same sense of calm and belonging he had the first time he sat on the log, fishing with his grandpa. He wanted to share a moment like this with Jasmine at the cabin. It was finally time to open the door and let himself in.

He woke up to some kisses on his nose and mouth. Jasmine's hand snaked under his T-shirt, sending a shot of lust straight to his groin. He was thinking with his dick and not his head. That was the only explanation he could give for almost giving into the moment, forgetting the room was bathed in morning light.

He jerked away. "Stop," he said with more force than he intended.

Jasmine got out of bed and wrapped her arms around herself. Disappointment replaced the look of desire he'd seen in her eyes just a moment before.

"Jasmine, I didn't mean to push you away."

"Don't." She held her hands up, backing away another step. "I can't keep doing this with you. Whatever is keeping you from showing yourself to me, whatever it is, I can help you."

"I don't need any help." Rhett pulled the elastic off his wrist and drew his hair up while he got out of bed.

"LISTEN, I just—"

Jasmine shook her head, ignoring the note of desperation in Rhett's voice. There wasn't anything he could say that would salvage the moment. She knew in her heart that he wasn't going to be able to.

"No, I can't keep doing this. I won't. I'm finally at a point in my life where I'm not going to let a terrible experience from the past determine my future." Jasmine took a deep breath and forged ahead, knowing her next words might end their relationship. "But… you haven't. I can't imagine what it was like for you when you were undercover. You're still there, Rhett, living in the past, and it's keeping you from having a future and being happy. Every day, there are people trying to help you, and you turn them down, turn us down."

She couldn't go on without telling him the truth, all of it. He needed to know, and she needed to say it out loud.

"I had a boyfriend. Darren was—" She smiled faintly at the memory of the man she'd met her first year of grad school. "He was nothing like you except for one thing. He always thought he could do everything on his own. For anyone who didn't really know, he came across as confident and self-assured." Jasmine wrapped her arms around herself, grabbing the sides of her sweater, trying to ward off the icy chill threatening to encase her heart once again.

"Did you know that the suicide rate for veterinarians is almost three times higher than the general public?"

"I didn't know that."

"Veterinarians are compassionate people. It's our empathetic nature that draws us to want to help animals. But that same trait makes it hard not to take on the pain and suffering of our patients… or the world. In school, they taught us to be aware of depression and suicidal thoughts and lectured that there was no shame in asking for help. I don't remember when I first noticed that Darren was sleeping more than usual." She took a breath. "He wouldn't ask for help. I thought if I stayed with him, if I loved him enough, I could help him get better. It wasn't enough. I was trying to take care of Darren and keep up with my classes. But I couldn't.

"I had a test that I couldn't miss one day, and after it, I checked my phone and saw a message from one of his friends. Da… Darren had—" Jasmine covered her eyes. "I was… I thought I didn't try hard enough, that I didn't do enough. My grades slipped, my friends drifted away, I almost lost… me, mourning and punishing myself. Pulling myself out of that depression took everything I had in me. That's why it was such a big deal to graduate with honors and get my dream job."

Rhett was a watercolor figure through her sheen of tears. So she didn't wipe them away. She was afraid to see a look of pity in his eyes. She fought not to slip back into the dark depression that consumed her after she lost Darren.

"You only let me help with Rebel because you were desperate and you didn't have any other option," she said.

When Rhett objected, she interrupted, "I'm not finished. I care about you, Rhett, but I know I can't help you or save you unless you're willing to help yourself. I'm not going to sacrifice my life again. That's not what's best for you, and it's not what's best for me."

"I don't want you to worry about me," Rhett said. "I never wanted you to worry about me."

"But I do worry about you. I've been waiting for you to invite me over to see your grandpa's cabin, and every time I offer to help, you turn me down. I can't keep making love to you in the dark, Rhett. I can't keep waiting for you to open your heart and trust me. Why is it okay for you to worry about me, but I can't do the same for you?"

Rhett turned away, his jaw rigid, his hands clenched.

Jasmine had experienced heartbreak before, but this time, the pain came with a strange sense of acceptance.

Rhett looked as if she'd slapped him in the face. "I do trust you, I just—"

"I need you to leave, Rhett. I think we need to spend some time apart while you figure your life out."

He stood there, staring at her for a minute, before he backed out to the living room. Maisy came into the bedroom and pressed herself against Jasmine's side. She didn't drop to her knees and bury her face in Maisy's soft fur until she heard the click of the door. Time didn't care about grief or breakups, and she had a clinic to run. After a few minutes, Jasmine picked herself up and went into the bathroom to wash her face. She didn't have any eye drops. No matter how much makeup she put on, her red eyes couldn't be disguised.

Imani gave her a worried look when she came through the door of the clinic. "Dr. Owens?"

"I don't want to talk about it," Jasmine muttered, heading toward her office.

She managed to keep a smile on her face through the only appointment she had on the schedule that morning. As soon as her patient and their owner left, she went back to her office and tried to focus on the paperwork that she'd been putting off. She'd just sent off a supply order when her brother walked in with two coffees.

"What's this for?" she asked, taking it from his hand.

"Imani thought you might need an extra cup this morning."

Jasmine took off the lid and blew on the hot liquid with a frown.

"Anything you want to tell me?" Isiah asked.

"No."

"Are you okay, sis?"

"You don't have to worry. This isn't like last time," she said quietly.

There was a knock on her door, and Presley popped her head in. "I was just wonderin' if y'all wanted to—" She saw Isiah and stopped. "Oh, never mind."

"That's okay, Presley. What were you going to ask?" Jasmine said.

"I was just checking to see if you wanted to have lunch."

"Thanks, but I don't think I'd be good company."

Presley gave her a worried look. Her eyes flicked to Isiah before she looked at Jasmine again. "Well, if y'all need anything, you know you can stop by anytime and—" She glanced at Isiah again. "I'm not just sayin' that to make myself look good. I really mean it."

Jasmine found her smile for the first time that day. "Thanks, I appreciate that."

The door closed, and Isiah gave her a perplexed look. "What in the world was that about?"

"It wasn't about anything but Presley being a good friend."

"She isn't the type of person you'd normally hang out with," Isiah scoffed.

Jasmine gave her brother a sharp look. “Maybe you shouldn’t be so judgmental.” She stood up, pressing her palms against her desk. “Thanks for the coffee, Isiah, but I’m not in the mood to defend my friendships with you today.”

Isiah’s eyes widened for a second. “Jas, I didn’t mean to upset you.”

“I know.” She took a deep breath. “It’s been a really shitty morning. I didn’t mean to snap at you. I’m just a little raw right now.”

“Can you just tell me if I need to go kick Rhett’s ass for breaking my baby sister’s heart?”

“My heart isn’t broken. I’m just… sad.” Jasmine’s voice trembled just a little.

“Aw, sis. I hate seeing you like this.”

Jasmine tried to give her brother a reassuring smile, but it didn’t have the desired effect when a tear escaped. Isiah came around her desk and pulled her into a brotherly hug.

“I’ll be okay,” she said.

“I know you will, but that doesn’t mean I can’t give you a hug.”

“Please don’t say anything to Mom and Dad.” She sniffed. “They’ll start calling nonstop.”

“Yeah, okay.”

RHETT WAS numb as he stood on the porch of his grandpa’s cabin. He turned away without even trying to go in. He snapped the band on his wrist until it broke. With a heavy sigh, he dug through his Jeep until he found another one. Rebel gave him a mournful look.

“Sorry, buddy. I haven’t been a very good friend, have I?”

Rebel let out a short bark.

“How about you and I head into Greenwood to get some supplies, and I’ll get you a new Frisbee?”

Rebel jumped into the front seat of the Jeep.

“I’ll take that as a yes.”

He rested his hand on the scruff around Rebel’s neck as he headed down the road. Once again, Rebel was saving him from himself. He spoiled Rebel at the pet store with a couple of extra chew toys and the biggest bully stick he could find. Rebel was trotting at his side, carrying the bully stick proudly in his mouth, while Rhett balanced a large bag of dog food on his shoulder. His phone vibrated just as he threw it in the back of the Jeep.

Larry took the bait.

His gut clenched. This was what he wanted and what he needed to do, but that didn't mean he wasn't worried his plan might not work. But it was better for everyone if he took that risk.

IT DIDN'T take long for Larry to show up. His beat-up truck was parked in front when Rhett arrived back at the cabin. Rebel whined, lifting his nose to sniff the air, his ears pricked forward. Rhett went around to the passenger side and opened the door. He glanced toward the cabin and then used hand signals. Rebel took off like a shot, with tiny puffs of dirt coming up where his paws kicked it up on his way into the woods. Rhett bowed his head, allowing himself a moment of relief. When he was undercover, he'd trained Rebel to go to a hiding spot on the property, an old shack that was barely standing in the woods. Rebel wouldn't come out until Rhett gave the whistle that would signal the all-clear. It was a precaution to keep Rebel safe. It was where he'd sent Rebel the night they kidnapped Mae. Knowing that it worked that night reassured him it would work again.

He stood up and pulled his hair back. With a deep breath, Rhett walked toward the cabin.

"THERE YOU go, little one. That was the last one. You've got all your shots," Jasmine said to the little brown-and-white spotted puppy looking up at her with doleful eyes.

"Is Fluffy gonna be okay?" The little girl's voice quivered as she held her father's hand in a tight grip.

"Fluffy is going to be just fine. I promise it didn't hurt him too much, and now he's going to stay healthy and happy." Jasmine smiled down at the short-haired male puppy named Fluffy and gave the poor little guy a treat.

There was a knock on the door, and Imani came in with a worried expression. "Dr. Owens, Rebel is here."

Jasmine's stomach clenched in nervous knots. "Will you tell them I'll be out in just a minute? I'm just about done."

Imani gave a slight shake of her head. "Rhett isn't with him."

Jasmine froze for a minute and said, "Can you finish up here?" She tried to keep her voice as calm as possible.

"Sure."

Jasmine quickly left the exam room and found Rebel in the lobby, panting. She knelt down, and he whined and licked the side of her face before trotting back over to the door and looking at her over his shoulder. She opened the door, thinking he wanted water from the bowl she kept outside for any furry friends that might need a drink. Rebel followed her but didn't go outside. Staying by her side, he pawed at her leg and looked out the door again.

Imani was just coming out of the room with Fluffy and his owners.

"I've got to go," Jasmine said.

"Don't worry, I'll take care of things here."

Jasmine nodded and ran into her office to grab her keys. In the car, Rebel kept his eyes focused on the road as she sped toward Rhett's cabin. Rebel started barking when she turned into the driveway. Jasmine recognized the beat-up truck with the Confederate flag sticker. It was the truck Larry Atwood got into after their confrontation at her clinic. She gripped the steering wheel and backed out, pulling off to the side by a stand of trees that blocked the view of the cabin. She looked at Rebel.

"I know you don't want to, but I need you to wait here," she said.

She got out and ran to the back of her truck. There was no chance she would approach the cabin without being armed. She opened the lockbox she kept in the back and pulled out her pistol, holstering it at her side.

She called her brother as she walked down the driveway to the cabin. "Isiah, I need you at Rhett's cabin as quickly as you can get here."

"What's going on?"

Jasmine heard a raised voice at the cabin. She hung up and started running.

Chapter Twenty-Two

When Rhett arrived at the cabin, he drew up short when he saw the door was open. He only hesitated for a second before he stepped across the threshold. The furnishings were all still there, only in chaos. The room was a mess. Half the drawers of his grandpa's desk were strewn across the floor, along with their contents. Small feathers were still floating through the air from the sofa where the cushions and pillows were ripped apart.

Larry was in his grandpa's favorite spot by the fireplace with a view of the pond and the valley beyond. There was a creak of protest from the chair when Larry sat forward, his hand clutching a pistol against the armrest. His eyes glittered with whatever drug he was high on and were ringed with dark circles.

"Where is it?" he demanded.

Rhett moved slowly into the room. "Where is what?"

"Don't pretend like you don't know. Where's the money your granddad left behind?"

"I don't know what you're talking about."

"Don't you lie to me, traitor," Larry shrieked.

Rhett kept his tone calm and indifferent. "I'm not lying."

Larry rocketed out of the chair and held the gun to Rhett's chest.

Rhett didn't flinch. "What you do now will determine if you spend a decade in jail or the rest of your life."

A shadow of doubt passed over Larry's face. "You took away my friends. I can't make any money. My wife left and took the kids."

"I didn't do that. You did."

Larry's jaw ticked. "You don't deserve all this. You betrayed George and everything he stood for."

"Exactly what do you think Grandpa believed in?"

"That our people need to stay together, that we're better."

"Better than what, Larry?"

"The White race is the superior race. Deep in your heart, you know that."

"There was a time when Grandpa believed that. You're everything Grandpa used to be, angry and bitter. Just like you, he believed that somehow he was being cheated in life. That if Black people were getting ahead in life, that must mean he was being denied whatever they gained. That version of Grandpa hasn't existed for a very long time. The person you're describing hasn't existed for a long time."

"What's that supposed to mean? I know what your grandfather stood for. You betrayed his memory, his race, and the movement."

"You're wrong. I did everything I could to honor his memory. I've done everything I can to be the man George wanted to be. He never believed he could redeem himself, and I've tried to do it for him. You're a drug dealer who uses dogs to fight his battles, and you're a racist. You're going to go to jail, Larry, but you aren't a murderer—George was."

Larry pulled back, and the pressure of the gun on Rhett's chest eased. "What the hell are you talking about?"

"Grandpa was one of a group of men who made a list of who they considered troublemakers that needed to be taken care of. Medgar Evers was on that list. Callie Colton's grandfather was on the list as well. There were nine men altogether. They killed Medgar Evers and four others. Some left Mississippi, and a few stayed, living in fear for their lives and the lives of their families."

"I don't believe you. He didn't have nothing to do with that."

"Wait here, follow me, or shoot me, I don't care."

Larry shoved past Rhett when he entered the back bedroom, where Rhett reached up to the top shelf of the closet and pulled out a manila envelope. Larry's drug-filled rage hadn't made his search very thorough.

"Sit down," Rhett ordered.

The springs on the old box spring creaked under Larry's weight. He was still holding his gun, but his finger was no longer on the trigger.

"You think you're tough, but some pictures you're gonna see might turn your stomach," Rhett said.

Larry's hand shook as he opened the envelope and pulled out a sheaf of papers and photographs. His eyes grew wide when he shuffled through them.

"That's from Grandpa's FBI file. By the time he worked up the courage to confess to his involvement in the murders, they weren't interested in an old man full of regrets. His finger wasn't directly on the trigger. Not speaking up isn't a crime. But he knew he had blood on his hands. He spent the first half of his life full of hate and the second half trying to make up for it.

"Is that what you want your legacy to be, Larry? You've demonized an entire race of people you don't even know. Nate Colton, the fire chief, is an Army veteran. He fought in Iraq. Joseph and Ella Colton have volunteered in this community for their whole lives. Hank at the barbershop has offered free haircuts to every veteran in town. These are all Black people who have given something. What have you ever done that makes you superior to these folks? While you were out spewing garbage and bringing drugs and guns into our community, the Jewels were making sure your children were fed."

Larry's face paled.

"Yeah, that's right. The Jewels were sneaking food over to your house because you were putting all of your money up your nose or in your veins and didn't think to leave enough for your family to have a decent meal. Tell me again how that makes you the master race?"

Larry's finger twitched on the gun.

"Look at yourself, Larry. You're strung out, and I know you're the one behind the break-ins at clinics and pharmacies around the county. I lured you here to convince you to turn yourself in before you make a mistake and someone gets hurt. One way or another, I'm going to make sure you end up in jail where you belong. Shooting me will only get you there sooner, and if that's what it takes, then I'm willing to make that sacrifice."

"The hell you will."

Rhett froze at the sound of Jasmine's voice. His heart seized when he saw the muzzle of a gun trained on Larry and Jasmine's finger on the trigger. "Don't even think about it," Jasmine said when Larry's hand wrapped around his gun.

He kept his eyes trained on Larry as he moved forward and prayed that, for the first time in his life, Larry did the right thing. He didn't move when Rhett approached him. They locked eyes for a moment before Larry let go of his weapon and held his hands up. Rhett took the gun and trained it on Larry as he backed away.

"Jas—"

"Shut up," Jasmine cut him off. "We'll talk about this later. Have you got him?"

"Yeah, it's okay now. He's not going anywhere."

"Fine," she said in a curt voice.

Jasmine lowered her gun at the same time they heard sirens in the distance coming closer.

Rhett's gut clenched with shame at putting Jasmine in this position. How did she know to come here?

When Larry shifted on the bed, Jasmine trained her gun on him again.

"Jasmine, I've got him. You don't—"

"Shut up," she ordered again.

He could feel the waves of anger radiating off her. They weren't directed at Larry—it was aimed at him.

It was only a few minutes before the sound of the sirens filled the air.

"Jas? Rhett?" Isiah called out, and Jasmine let him know they were in the back bedroom. Isiah ran in with a deputy in tow, their guns drawn. A second later, Dan showed up.

"Get him out of here," Isiah said to his deputy.

"What are the charges?" the deputy asked.

Isiah glanced at Rhett. "I'm assuming this was breaking and entering?"

When Rhett nodded, the deputy reached for his handcuffs.

"I ain't gonna resist," Larry said as the deputy pulled him off the bed and started reading him his rights while he put the handcuffs on.

Isiah jerked his head toward the door. "Take him out to the car."

Rhett handed Isiah the gun. "This is Larry's."

Isiah secured the weapon and looked at the two of them. "Who's going to explain to me what happened here?"

Jasmine lowered her gun. She didn't make eye contact with Rhett. "He can tell you what happened before I got here. All I know is that this asshole decided he'd rather sacrifice himself than ask for help."

Her voice was flat. Each word left a bruise.

"Let me know if you need anything else from me," she said to her brother before she turned and walked out the door.

Dan stayed behind after Rhett gave his statement to Isiah.

"What the hell were you thinking?" Dan asked. "You know better than to pull a stunt like this without asking for backup. Hell, you didn't even tell me—" Dan pressed his lips together and looked away.

"You have Reid now. I didn't want to put you in danger."

"I… what does that mean? Yes, I have a person in my life that I care deeply about, and he feels the same way about me, and because we want to grow together and build a life together, we talk about my job and the risks that are involved. It's not your burden to protect me. I'm too angry with you right now to have this conversation, but you know there are going to be repercussions from this stunt you've pulled." Dan frowned at him. "You need to think about if this is the right job for you. The agency doesn't need a lone wolf. We need people who know how to be a part of a team."

"Dan, I—"

Whatever he was going to say was met with silence because Dan had already walked away. Rhett stared at the empty doorway for a long time. What had he done? He was trying to protect the people he cared about, the people he loved. And now he was alone. The past two years came crashing back.

Isolation.

Fear.

Worry.

He needed to explain to Jasmine why he did what he did.

CHAPTER TWENTY-THREE

JASMINE DROVE back into town on autopilot. She intended to go home but somehow found herself pulling up to the Beaumonts' grand Victorian instead.

Presley took one look at her when she answered the door and enveloped her in a hug.

"Oh, honey, whatever is wrong, I'm sure we can make it right," Presley said.

Jasmine could only nod while tears streamed down her face.

"Come on, I'll fix you some tea."

"Could you put some whiskey in it or, better yet, leave out the tea altogether?" Jasmine said in a shaky voice.

Presley wrapped her arm around Jasmine's, leading her into the kitchen. "Nobody throws a better pity party than I do," she said with a sympathetic smile.

"I can't stay very long. I've got to go to the clinic and check on Maisy."

Presley paused, pulling a bottle of whiskey off the shelf. "You wait just a minute."

She went into the pantry and returned with a large picnic basket. "Take a seat, I'll be quick." Jasmine sat down on one of the leather barstools at the kitchen island and watched Presley fill the basket with roast beef, leftover mashed potatoes, and an enormous slice of chocolate cake, along with enough snacks to keep an entire movie theater happy. The bottle of whiskey she'd pulled off the shelf went in along with a bottle of wine.

"Ashton will kill me for stealing from his stash again, but this is an emergency," Presley said, shoving the bottle into the overflowing basket. "All right, let's take this pity party to your house."

Jasmine gave her a grateful smile. "Thank you, Presley. You didn't have to do this."

"We're friends, and friends take care of each other."

Why couldn't Rhett understand that?

They'd just reached the front door when Ashton came in. He took one look at the picnic basket, his eyes narrowing.

"Exactly what do you think you're doing with that bottle of wine?" he asked.

"We're commiseratin'," Presley said, straightening her shoulders and giving her brother a defiant look.

"What do you mean you're commiserating?"

Presley put the basket down and wrapped her arm around Jasmine's shoulder. "Jasmine needs a girls' night."

Ashton's eyebrow shot up. "And she wants to have it with you?"

"Ashton Theodore Beaumont, don't you dare ruin this for me. I've finally got friends who are worth knowing. You better act right, or I swear I'll cream your corn."

"We can leave the wine. We've got whiskey," Jasmine offered.

Maybe it was the slight warble in her voice, but something made Ashton stop his banter with his sister and look at her. His teasing smile fell.

"Take the bottle. As a matter of fact"—he held up his finger and dashed into the kitchen, returning with a slim bottle—"here, take this too. It's a nice port that will go well with all that chocolate you've got in there." He gestured to the basket.

"Thank you, Ash," Presley said.

Jasmine fought past the lump in her throat. "Thank you."

Ashton patted her on the shoulder on the way out the door. "You let me know if there's anything you need, ya hear?"

Jasmine didn't trust herself to speak, so she just nodded with a grateful smile. It only took a couple of minutes to drive from Presley's house to her apartment. In less than ten minutes, they were upstairs with Presley on her knees, showering Jasmine's new roommate with kisses.

"Oh, isn't she just the sweetest thing?" she exclaimed. "What are y'all gonna call her?"

"I named her Maisy."

Presley proceeded to coo and pet Maisy, who soaked up the attention. After a few minutes, she stood up and turned her attention back to Jasmine with a stern look. "You get comfortable while I unpack the snacks."

Jasmine gave her friend a mock salute. "Yes, ma'am."

When she came back out in her favorite flannel pajamas, Jasmine was given a glass of wine with bits of cork floating around in it.

"Do you want to tell me what happened?" Presley asked.

Jasmine took a deep breath. "It's not what happened with Rhett, it's about what happened when I was in grad school."

She told Presley about Darren and what she'd said to Rhett when she left him.

"Lordy, I don't know what to say." Presley drew in a shaky breath. "I thought y'all got to have fun playin' with animals. I didn't realize…." She bit down on her lip.

"Many people see my profession the way you do. The thing that makes us good at our job, our empathy and compassion, is also what makes us vulnerable."

Presley reached across Maisy and grabbed Jasmine's hand. "If you're ever struggling, you say something to me, ya hear? I know we haven't known each other that long, but I like spending time with you, and I want to be your friend. I don't want anything to happen to you, because I care about you."

"We are friends. I didn't realize how much I was missing having girlfriends in my life until I came to Colton. Living in the same town as my brother is nice, but you're much more fun to hang out with."

"Good." Maisy nudged her nose under Presley's hand.

Jasmine laughed. "Someone's greedy for more attention."

"I wish Rhett wasn't being so stubborn. I know Mae and Emma have talked to a therapist after what happened the night Mae was kidnapped and he saved them. That was just one night. Rhett's spent years havin' to pretend to be like those people." Presley's face fell. "I hung out with some of those folks too, but it was because I didn't know any better." She shook her head. "No, that's not right. I just didn't want to know. I was lazy."

"I don't think you were lazy. Sometimes we pretend we don't see or know things because it's easier than to face reality or things we don't want to know about ourselves. It's human nature, I guess. All I know is that I can't go on pretending everything is okay when it's not. It's not fair to me or the person I lo—" Jasmine cleared her throat. "The people I care about."

"I know you don't need to hear this from me, but I think you did the right thing. I just hope Rhett figures it out one day."

Jasmine swallowed past the lump in her throat. "So do I."

Presley refilled their glasses.

"I'm so… mad at him for saying he was willing to sacrifice himself," Jasmine said.

"I can't believe he did that. What in the world was he thinking?"

"Whatever it was, he didn't ask anyone for help. He should have talked to Dan or Isiah… or me. He could have trusted me."

"Maybe you can make him see—"

Jasmine put her hand up. "You can't force someone who doesn't want to change or want help."

"You're right. I shouldn't have said that. I stood around watchin' Dax's mama try to bend people to her will. All it did was make her a bitter, lonely woman who thought no one was ever good enough if they didn't do what she wanted. Did you hear? She died in jail a couple of weeks ago. I don't want to end up like that, thinkin' I have all the answers when all I really have is a bunch of opinions based on lies."

Jasmine wrapped her arms around herself and nodded.

"What are you going to do now?" Presley asked.

"Move on, I guess. I'll be sad for a while, but I'll get over him eventually."

Her words tasted sour. Right now her heart was calling her a liar, but she needed to pretend it was true for her own sake.

Presley studied her for a minute with her forehead wrinkled. "Can I ask y'all somethin'?"

"You don't have to ask first," Jasmine said. "You can just ask your question."

"I tried to warn you." Presley made a face, watching Jasmine fish a piece of cork out of her glass of wine.

"That's okay." Jasmine took a big sip. "What's your question?"

"Oh, why do you wear baggy clothes?"

Jasmine set her glass down on the coffee table and ran her hands along the frayed hem of her top. "They didn't like the way I dressed at my old job. Some of the other doctors would make comments about my body that made me feel uncomfortable, so I started wearing baggy clothes, and I guess I just… got used to hiding."

"And I'm trying not to stand out so much." Presley frowned. "I don't think it's fair. Men complain if our clothes are too tight and if they're too loose. How are we supposed to know how to dress for them?"

"Maybe we're supposed to just dress for ourselves."

Presley looked at her thoughtfully for a minute. "Mae's always reminding me I should do things for myself, not for some guy's approval. I'm still workin' on breaking that habit. Maybe my idea wasn't a good one."

"I can't tell you if it was a good idea or not if I don't know what it is."

"I was gonna suggest we do some shopping therapy. It always makes me feel better. Well, sometimes it does, for a little while."

Jasmine put her finger through the hole in the knee of her pajama pants as she thought about their conversation so far. She wasn't going to ask Rhett to change, but that didn't mean she couldn't push herself.

"You know what, I think a little shopping therapy would be a good thing."

Presley's eyes lit up, and she reached for her phone. "Do you have any clients tomorrow? I'll text Mae and let her know I'll be late." She sent her text and turned to Jasmine. "Are you ready for chocolate?"

Jasmine looked down at her empty glass. "Definitely, and more wine, please."

Once they refilled their glasses and laid out all the food from the picnic basket on the coffee table, they settled in with Maisy snuggled between them.

Presley stroked Maisy's smooth brown fur while the dog looked up at her with an adoring gaze. After focusing her attention on Maisy for a few minutes, Presley asked, "Hey, Jasmine. I know we're not dressing to impress a man, but… I've been wondering. What's your brother's favorite color?"

Jasmine laughed, and they spent the rest of the evening swapping embarrassing stories about their brothers and gorging themselves on all the food Presley brought.

Her heart still hurt, but Jasmine knew that, with time, her wounds would heal. It was too bad she couldn't say the same for Rhett.

Chapter Twenty-Four

Rhett stood paralyzed, waiting on the porch, willing Jasmine to come back. He'd given Isiah his statement and gotten chewed out by Dan, which he deserved. None of it mattered. The look on Jasmine's face when she walked away would haunt him for the rest of his life. When the shadow of the moon stretched across the pond and reached for the cabin, he gave up.

He got into his Jeep, started the ignition, and turned it off again. Rebel cocked his head.

"Where am I going?" he asked.

Rebel barked and put his paw on Rhett's leg. He dropped his forehead to the steering wheel and fought to get air into his lungs. Each breath was harder to take, and the pain in his chest grew. He gasped, frantically fumbling to get the engine started. His foot was heavy on the gas, making the Jeep fishtail as he drove down the dirt road. He drove blindly. How he made it to his destination, Rhett would never know, but eventually he pulled into the yard and cut the engine.

Uncle Robert came running toward him when his knees hit the ground, and he let out a low, guttural yell.

"I got you, son," Uncle Robert said.

Rhett gasped. "I can't breathe."

Rebel pressed himself to his side, wedging his head under Rhett's hand.

"That's okay. I'm gonna breathe for both of us."

He nodded when Uncle Robert told him to sync his breathing with his. They sat like that for a long time, with Rhett sitting between Uncle Robert's legs with his back against his chest, while Uncle Robert inhaled deeply until Rhett could breathe on his own again.

Eventually he managed to sit up, resting his arms on his knees with his chin on his chest, taking a few deep breaths before he made it to his feet. There was a firm grasp on his elbow and Rebel on his other side, guiding him to the porch.

"I'll get you some water," Uncle Robert said, pushing him toward one of the rocking chairs that lined the porch that ran the length of the cabin.

Rhett sank down into the rocking chair and leaned back, closing his eyes.

Uncle Robert returned with a glass of ice water and a bowl. He pressed the glass into Rhett's hand and set the bowl of water at Rebel's feet, giving the dog a pat on the head. The rocking chair next to Rhett creaked when he sat down.

"I'm proud of you, son. I know it wasn't easy to come here. Whatever happened to bring you to my doorstep, I'm here to listen and offer whatever support I can."

"Jasmine broke up with me."

Uncle Robert's mouth turned down. "I can't say I'm surprised. Trust me on this, no woman wants to be kept at arm's length. They want to be able to help, to contribute equally in the relationship, and you weren't letting her do that."

"There's more." Rhett went on to tell Uncle Robert what happened with Larry.

"Jasmine… I shouldn't be upset. She did the right thing. I never should have started anything with her, but I couldn't help myself," Rhett said.

"Stop it." Uncle Robert slapped his knee.

Rhett jerked his head up and cringed at the angry look he saw on Uncle Robert's face.

"Damn it, boy, you're just like I was, willing to sacrifice yourself when you don't have to." His voice softened. "You've had the same look about you since the first time I met you, when you were barely as tall as your grandpa's knee. I wondered then how someone so young could carry themselves like they have the weight of the world on their shoulders. Why do you have such a hard time accepting affection and help from people?"

Rhett opened and closed his mouth, trying to come up with an answer. "I guess I figured since no one wanted me, I wasn't… I don't know, lovable, I guess."

"Why do you think no one wanted you?"

"I always felt guilty that Grandpa had to come and get me. He shouldn't have had to take on raising another kid just because my parents couldn't handle the responsibility."

"Lord, what a mess George made." Uncle Robert shook his head. He angled his chair to face Rhett. "Your momma's family wanted you, but your grandpa fought like the devil to keep you."

"What?"

He barely remembered his other grandparents or any relatives on his mother's side of the family. He hadn't seen them since he was a little boy.

"Those folks tried to take you when you first came to stay with your grandpa. But he wouldn't let you go. Your grandpa could see the hate in their hearts. They were living in a White supremacist compound up in Idaho and wanted to take you to live there with them. George wouldn't stand for it and ran them off."

Rhett's body went numb as he realized the fate his grandpa saved him from. He'd wondered from time to time why his mother never really talked about her family. He'd never considered how conflicted his parents must have felt by letting him stay with his grandpa. They must have thought he was the lesser of two racist evils.

"Your grandpa was a complicated man, but don't ever think you weren't wanted."

"I'm having a hard time remembering that and moving on," Rhett confessed.

"You remember the movie *Shawshank Redemption?*"

Rhett nodded.

"You've got a decision to make, son. Just like Red says in the movie, you can get busy livin' or get busy dyin'. There's a whole lot of people who want to see you live your life, want to be a part of it, and want to help you just as much as you've helped them.

"I—" Rhett cleared his throat. "I'm ready to start living."

Robert leaned forward, looking at Rhett with narrowed eyes. "When was the last time you ate?"

He thought about it for a minute and confessed, "I'm not sure."

"Come on, I've got some stew I can warm up."

They moved into the cabin, where Rebel immediately curled up on the braided rug in front of the fireplace.

"Take a seat while I get us set up," Robert said.

Rhett settled himself in one of the large leather chairs next to the fireplace. Both the physical and mental energy he'd used finally caught up with him. Staring at the flames, he tried to process what he'd just learned about his family dynamic.

"Rhett? Come on, son," Uncle Robert said, shaking Rhett's shoulder. "Let's get some food in your belly, and then you can go to bed."

The smell of beef, vegetables, and biscuits filled the air. Rhett's stomach grumbled in anticipation of a good meal that it had been denied for far too long.

The table was set with two bowls filled to the brim with stew and a plate of drop biscuits in between them.

Rhett took a bite and closed his eyes, taking a moment to appreciate the savory broth. Suddenly he remembered his companion and looked to the empty spot in front of the fire where Rebel fell asleep.

"I don't have any kibble, but I warmed up some leftover chicken and rice for him." Robert pointed to the corner of the kitchen where Rebel was licking an empty plate.

Rhett's voice was raw from the emotional release. "Thank you."

Uncle Robert put his spoon down and rested his forearms on the table. "You know, when all those boys came back from WWII, there wasn't any such thing as PTSD. Some of the ones who had a hard time settling back into their lives just… drifted away, ended up homeless, or in an institution, or dead. And then there were some who seemed just fine on the outside while they were slowly tearing themselves apart on the inside. When I first came back to Colton, there was a man." He smiled slightly. "Half of the folks around here called him Nate, and the other half called him Joe. It was a long time before I learned his real name was Jonathan. We met at Turtle Pond, where we were both looking for a little solitude and maybe a fish for supper. Jonathan was a Montfort Point Marine. Do you know what that is?"

Rhett shook his head.

"The Marine Corps recruited a hundred and fifty engineering students from Tuskegee during the war," Uncle Robert began. "Back then, the corps was still segregated, but Truman ordered them to desegregate. They trained at Camp Lejeune. Only they weren't allowed on the base unless a White officer escorted them. They built a separate camp, Montfort Point. Those men served in the Pacific, dropped off on hellhole islands to build roads and landing ramps for the other troops, other White troops that were given all the credit and the glory.

"Jonathan and I would fish and talk. One day, I got a bite. It was a big son of a gun who put on a real fight. I was in the water almost up to my waist. I called out to Jonathan to help me. When I looked over at him, he was standing only ankle deep, but his whole body was rigid, and I realized he was holding his breath. We'd gone fishing together many times, and Jonathan went into the water but never more than to let the edge of the pond lick the toe of his boots. I'd watched him lose more than a fish or two because he didn't go in deep enough to fight it. He never asked for help, and I figured since he didn't ask, that meant he was all right."

Uncle Robert looked at him with a sheen in his eyes. "Rhett"—he cleared this throat when his voice broke—"that was the day I learned Jonathan served in the Pacific without knowing how to swim." Uncle Robert swiped his hand over his eyes. "PTSD is a powerful thing. It's not enough to admit that you have it and just go on with your life as if nothing is wrong. You have got to learn how to ask for help when you need it. Son, you need help, and I'm here to give it to you. So are Jacob, Dan, Jasmine, your parents. All you have to do is ask. People will not stop loving you just because you asked for help. You aren't a burden, Rhett."

By the time Uncle Robert finished talking, Rhett's head was bowed, and his tears flowed freely. He couldn't hide the part of him that always feared being a burden, that was afraid his needs would push anyone who cared about him away. Now that his wounds were exposed, he couldn't hide in the dark anymore.

He stayed at Uncle Robert's that night and the next few days after that. It had been a long time since he'd done that much talking. It wasn't easy, but it did get easier, and the band of tightness that Rhett had learned to live with started to ease. He felt unbalanced as it began to loosen its grip. It wasn't just Uncle Robert who Rhett spent time with on his porch. Nate, the captain of Colton's fire department, showed up one night, and he shared his experience from when he'd come back from his tour of duty in Iraq. One of Uncle Robert's buddies from the CIA joined Nate. In the days that followed, men and women showed up on Uncle Robert's porch to talk, or listen, and sometimes to just sit in the silence of understanding.

As the days passed, Jasmine's heartache didn't disappear altogether, but each day it hurt a little less to breathe.

Jacob and Dax kept making up excuses to come by the clinic or her apartment to check in on her. It got so bad, she put a sign on the clinic door saying they could only come in if they had an animal that needed help. She knew they meant well, but they were making her crazy.

When Reid told them that Larry had requested drug counseling, Dan looked at him skeptically and said, "I have a hard time believing that."

Jasmine was at the Buckthorn with Isiah, sitting at the bar with Dan while Reid chatted with them between customers.

She didn't really feel like going out, but she was trying to give her brother an olive branch. Isiah was furious with her for being so reckless. Jasmine apologized, and she knew her brother would forgive her eventually. She'd put herself in danger, and he had every right to be angry with her. She'd acted on instinct and… love.

She bowed her head, blinking back a sudden wave of tears.

Dan nudged her shoulder and gave her a sympathetic smile. He picked up his glass and clinked it against hers.

"Here's to better days."

Jasmine took a deep breath and picked up her glass.

"Larry couldn't make bail. He's going to have plenty of time to attend counseling in jail," Reid added.

Isiah scowled. "He can do all the counseling he wants. I don't want him back on the streets anytime soon."

"He's no upstanding citizen, but he gave up some names of other folks he was running with. There have been four more arrests from the information he gave the prosecutor's office."

Isiah tipped his head in acknowledgment.

Jasmine had received a call from Animal Control the other day, asking if she could take dogs that were rescued from a backyard breeding operation they'd discovered as part of a raid that took place based on information Larry had given them.

"Maybe things will finally calm down around here. I swear, this town has more drama than I saw back in Chicago," Isiah said.

"I think Colton is on the right track for a good future. A lot of people around here are invested in making this a good place to live. It's one reason I wanted to move here," Dan said.

Reid leaned across the bar with a raised eyebrow. "One reason? Babe, I thought I was the only reason."

Dan laughed, grabbed Reid's arm, and pulled him across the bar for a quick kiss.

"Hey, what'd I tell you two about canoodling in my bar?" Primus shouted.

Reid's face turned beet red while Dan's attempt at looking guilty failed when he couldn't stop laughing.

Jasmine watched the two men with envy. That was what she wanted, a relationship that was a partnership. Dan and Reid trusted each other, and they shared their successes and failures. They didn't worry about being a burden to one another.

"Sis, you're moping again," Isiah observed.

"Sorry."

Her brother looked at her thoughtfully for a moment. "You're not going to get over him, are you?"

"You can fall in love quickly, but it can take a lot longer to fall out of it," she said.

"Listen, I'm just as pissed off at Rhett as the two of you are, but I'm not ready to give up hope yet. When he's finally ready to ask for help, I'll be here," Dan said.

Reid rested his hand on Dan's forearm. "I'm going to remind you you said that when the time comes."

Jasmine took a sip of her beer and thought about what Dan said. Was she willing to wait for Rhett and give him another chance? She couldn't stop her heart from hoping that he would ask.

Rhett wasn't ready to face Jasmine yet. He wanted to, and he would. First, he needed to talk to Dan. He'd start with that, and if he was successful there, his idea for how he could apologize to Jasmine just might work. When he finally worked up the nerve to call, he wondered if Dan would pick up or if he was still too pissed off.

"I'm sorry," Rhett said before Dan could say hello.

There was a beat of silence. "Is that why you called, to apologize?"

"No, an apology won't count until I look you in the eye when I'm giving it. I hope you'll give me that chance. I'd like to meet with you, if that's okay."

There were hushed voices in the background for a minute before Dan sighed. "Reid and I are at the Buckthorn."

The place was quiet, with just a few customers scattered around the dimly lit room. Rhett braced himself for stares and whispers, but most folks were caught up in their own lives and didn't pay attention to him. He slid onto a stool at the end of the bar next to Dan, who was talking quietly with Reid, holding hands across the bar.

"Can I get you something to drink?" Reid asked.

"Whiskey would be good, thanks."

Dan still hadn't acknowledged his presence as Reid nodded and poured the drink.

"I'm gonna let you guys talk it out," Reid said, "but if you don't, I'll be back to knock your heads together until you do."

Dan watched his boyfriend walk away and then turned to Rhett. "You asked me to meet you, and I'm here, but only because Primus and Reid wouldn't let me say no. What do you want?"

Rhett downed the rest of the contents in his glass and wheezed a cough. Reid poured him the good stuff.

When he caught his breath, Rhett said, "I came to tell you I put in my paperwork at the bureau. What I did was reckless, and you're right, the agency doesn't need a lone wolf. I owe you an apology. I also came because I… I came to ask for your help."

"I have to say I'm disappointed that you're leaving the bureau, but I understand and think you've made the right decision. There are still ways you can help the agency if you're open to talking about it."

"I am." Rhett glanced at Reid walking up to the bar and back to Dan. "I'd like to talk to both of you… I mean, I'd like for us to hang out more. The two of you offered me your friendship, and I didn't accept it the way I should have, but if you'd give me a chance, I'd like to now."

Dan's expression relaxed a bit. "You didn't reject our friendship. You were holding yourself back."

"We knew you just needed time to heal. Believe me, after what I've been through with my family, I understand," Reid said.

Rhett rested his elbows on the bar. "Thanks."

Primus came in from the back. "Good to see you again, Rhett."

"I'm happy to be here," he said and realized he meant it.

"You said you came because you need help. What is it you need help with?" Dan asked.

Rhett explained his plan. When he finished, Dan and Reid were both grinning at him.

"Well, what do you think?" Rhett asked.

"I think that might be the most romantic thing I've ever heard." Reid looked at Dan. "You're going to have to up your game, babe."

Dan's face lit up. "Challenge accepted."

Presley walked into the bar with her brother Ashton. They exchanged a surprised look when Rhett waved them over to where he was sitting at the bar.

"Their drinks are on me," Rhett told Reid.

Presley crossed her arms, giving him a stern look. "You hurt my friend."

"You're right, I did. I hurt a lot of people, and I'm trying to make things right. I'm glad you came in tonight. I was going to come and talk to you tomorrow. I'm hoping you'll help me apologize to Jasmine."

"It depends. Are you gonna be a jackass again?"

Ashton choked on the whiskey Reid just served him. "Good Lord, Presley, you've been hanging out with Mae too much. You could give direct directions."

Presley lifted her chin. "I'm standing up for my friend."

"You're a good friend, Presley," Rhett said, "and I'm glad Jasmine has you for a friend."

"Just remember"—Presley waggled her finger at him—"if I help you, you can be her boyfriend, but I still get to be her best friend. She's the first one I've ever had, and I'm not willing to give her up just yet."

Rhett laughed and then tried to cover it what a cough at the fierce glare Presley gave him.

Presley put her hand on her hip and cocked her head. "Now, what do y'all need me to do?"

Chapter Twenty-Five

THE SOFT clacking of knitting needles filled the air of the coffee shop, replacing the usual chatter that accompanied the knitting club on their Tuesday night meetings.

Jasmine kept her focus on her new project. She'd finished the hat she'd made for Rhett but didn't have a chance to give it to him before they broke up. It was a known rule in the knitting world that if you started a project for the person you were dating, you'd break up before you finished it. The superstition was right; she never should have made something for him. She bit the inside of her cheek and focused on the rhythmic seed stitch pattern. It was a simple pattern. She couldn't focus on anything more intricate.

"You okay, honey?" Ms. Ruby asked.

Jasmine let the brown cashmere yarn she'd been trying to turn into a scarf fall into her lap. "Yes… no… I don't know."

"He's going to come around, wait and see," Presley said, setting a plate of cookies and a pot of tea on the table.

"But I can't put my life on hold waiting for him to," Jasmine said.

Presley sat back down next to Ms. June and picked up the pink yarn she'd been working with. Under Ms. June's sharp eye and patient tutelage, it was starting to look like the scarf it was supposed to be.

Jasmine gave her friend a grateful smile. Presley's insistence on a positive outlook on life could be both annoying and helpful. It was at Presley's insistence that she was at knitting club tonight.

"Here, have some tea," Callie said.

"I think we need something a little stronger," Ms. June said, pulling out a jar filled with a dark honey-colored liquid. "I've been experimenting with making some bourbon-infused kombucha."

Mae made a gagging sound that she tried to cover with a cough.

Ashton reached into his knitting basket. "Great minds think alike, Ms. June."

He set a bottle of wine on the table.

Mae gave him a grateful look and jumped up. "I'll get us some glasses."

Jasmine looked at her friends around the table. "Thanks, everyone. I appreciate y'all so much."

Presley's eyes lit up. "I think that was y'all's first *y'all*. It's official—you're one of us now."

Jasmine laughed and then burst into tears.

Presley got up and came around the table to put her arm around her. "I'm sorry. I didn't mean to upset you."

"I'm not upset. I'm happy. Coming to Colton was the best decision I could have made, and it really feels like home. I have family and friends here, but I'm also…." She pressed her lips together.

"Heartbroken?" Ms. Ruby asked.

Jasmine nodded.

Ms. Ruby set her knitting down and slowly stood up. "Come on, honey. Let's you and I have a talk."

Jasmine followed the older woman outside. Ms. Ruby stopped and took a deep breath before guiding them to the steps of the gazebo.

Jasmine pulled the sleeves of her sweater over her hands as they made themselves comfortable on the top step.

Ms. Ruby blinked up at the star-filled sky for a minute before she spoke. "I don't know exactly what happened to you before." Her lips curled into a slight smile. "Of course, Presley has let enough things slip here and there that I've been able to piece a few things together."

She turned to Jasmine and took one of her hands in hers. "I'm sorry you couldn't save the person you loved and you almost lost yourself trying to. But Rhett isn't the same person. Colton men are too pigheaded." She snorted a laugh. "Sometimes they're too damn stubborn to admit they are better, stronger, with us by their side rather than trying to protect us and… well, that don't matter anymore. My time has passed, but that doesn't mean you can't have your future with Rhett."

The bitterness and regret in Ruby's voice brought fresh tears to Jasmine's eyes. "What do I do?" she asked.

"Give him a little more time, but if you really care about that man, you don't put up with his foolishness for too much longer. You go get him and make sure he knows come hell or high water, you're gonna stand by his side. That you're gonna stand with him through the good and the bad."

Jasmine sighed. "I don't know if I can do that. Can't beg him to let me help him."

Ms. Ruby looked at her thoughtfully. "Maybe he is asking for help in his own way. Did you ever consider that he can't bring himself to say the words, but he's still asking? He's doing it in other ways, and that boy doesn't even realize it."

Had Rhett asked for help? He did ask her to be patient with him. She thought about the way he'd asked if she wouldn't mind picking up some hair ties for him the next time she bought some for herself. And the time he'd asked if he could borrow one of hers, and how he didn't put it in his hair but slipped it on his wrist and started snapping it. She hadn't realized that maybe there was more to why he called every night and was always seeking her out.

Jasmine gasped and looked at Ruby with wide eyes while the older woman nodded.

"He just hasn't figured out how to ask the right way, how to say the words out loud."

Jasmine gave Ms. Ruby a hug. When they pulled apart, she asked, "Are you sure it's too late for you?"

"I'm an old woman now. What man is gonna want me?"

"I've always wanted you," a gruff voice said.

Jasmine and Ms. Ruby jumped up when Uncle Robert appeared from the other side of the gazebo.

Uncle Robert pulled off his worn Biloxi Shuckers baseball cap and clutched it in front of him. "Ruby Colton, I've waited too many years to say things that I should have said a long time ago."

Jasmine's eyes flicked between Uncle Robert and Ms. Ruby.

"Robert Ellis, what do you think you're doing lurking in the park, eavesdropping?" Ms. Ruby put her hand over her heart. "Good Lord, you just about gave me a heart attack."

Jasmine saw the determined glint in Uncle Robert's eyes and decided she needed to make a quick exit.

"I'll just leave you two to talk," she said, making her way down the gazebo steps.

Uncle Robert's deep Southern drawl drifted through the night air, following Jasmine as she hurried back to the coffee shop with a worried glance over her shoulder.

"What in the world is going on? You look like you've been chased by a ghost," Mae exclaimed when Jasmine burst through the door.

"You'll never believe what just happened."

Before Jasmine could finish her story, everyone in the room clustered around the window.

"Oh dear," Ms. June said.

"It's about damn time," Mae murmured.

"I don't know, y'all. Ms. Ruby looks like she's fixin' to turn him to a haint," Ashton said, watching the scene with a frown.

The ongoing commentary continued while they watched the back-and-forth between the two of them. Ms. Ruby threw her hands up and started to walk away when Uncle Robert grabbed her by the shoulders, said something, and crushed his lips to her.

Presley gasped. "Well, I'll be."

They all looked at each other, wide-eyed.

"I feel like we should do something, but I'm not sure what," Ms. June said.

"Well, we can't all tumble out of here while they're neckin' in the park. We might as well have another glass of wine," Mae said.

Callie cleared her throat. "Mae has a good point. We should give them a little privacy."

Jasmine went back and retrieved Presley, who practically had her face plastered against the glass, and dragged her back to their table.

No one was really interested in picking up their projects again. They all kept sneaking glances out of the window while they dropped stitches.

"What were you and Ms. Ruby talking about, anyway?" Presley asked.

"That's none of your business, Pres," Ashton admonished.

"Sorry," Presley said.

"It's okay. We were talking about the different ways people ask for help," Jasmine explained.

"I'm not sure I understand," Mae said.

Presley's hand shot into the air. "I know the answer to this one." She turned to Mae. "It's like when you're havin' a bad day, and you ask me to get you one of Tillie's meat loaf sandwiches and some sweet tea. That's your favorite comfort food. It's your way of saying you need help."

Mae put down her knitting and put her hand over Presley's. "Thank you."

Jasmine nodded with approval. "That's exactly what I meant. We all ask for help in different ways. For some people, it's hard to say those three words out loud. 'I need help.' Rhett's been asking for help. We just haven't been listening."

"So, what do we do now?" Callie asked.

"Wait," Uncle Robert said from the doorway, hand in hand with Ruby.

Ms. Ruby's lips were swollen and her cheeks pink. She didn't make eye contact with anyone as she started gathering her things.

"Some people"—Robert's eyes darted toward Ruby—"some folks dig their heels in. The more you try to help, the more they're going to try to do it all on their own. Rhett and I have been talking, and he's been doing some hard thinking."

Uncle Robert turned to Jasmine. "Give him another week, and if Rhett hasn't come around by then, you have my blessing to go out there and"—his eyes flicked toward Ruby—"kiss some sense into him."

Presley grinned and nodded while the color in Ruby's cheeks went from the delicate pink of a peach to the deep red of a turnip.

"Now if y'all excuse us, I'm going to escort Ms. Ruby home." He took Ruby's arm and paused as they headed to the door and looked back at the table. "My home."

"Lord have mercy." Mae fanned her face. "He has got a serious Sam Elliot vibe going on. I had no idea Uncle Robert could dickmatize someone like that. I hope Ms. Ruby is wearing some lacy underwear tonight."

"Oh, Mae!" Callie and Emma both admonished at the same time.

"I think she's got a point." Ashton waggled his eyebrows.

Ms. June's eyes were bright with unshed tears. "Think of it. They waited all these years. I treasure every minute with my husband. I'm so sad for all the minutes they missed."

Presley went over and put her arm around Ms. June's shoulder.

Jasmine looked down at her watch. How many minutes had gone by since she'd last seen Rhett? What if those minutes stretched into years?

She couldn't help looking for him and hoping Rhett was waiting for her when she left the coffee shop. But the only thing in the park was the long shadows from the moonbeams.

Jasmine replayed her conversation with Ms. Ruby over and over in her head until she'd gotten so worked up, she'd twisted herself into knots. She was tired of debating with herself how much longer she should wait to try and see Rhett again. By Friday, when Presley called, insisting that she join her and spend the day picnicking and sunbathing at Turtle Pond, all Jasmine wanted to do was spend the weekend under the covers with Maisy to keep her company. But Presley refused to take no for an answer and, after threatening to come over and drag her out of the house in her pajamas if she didn't come out with her, Jasmine reluctantly agreed.

Maisy huffed and laid her head between her paws, looking up at Jasmine.

"I know. I don't want to go either."

A honk announced Presley's arrival.

Jasmine did one more quick check in the mirror and shrugged, patting her leg.

"Come on, girl. This is as good as we're going to get."

Maisy's puppies were weaned. Three of them had found their forever homes. The fourth puppy, a silvery-gray little boy, was still at her kennel, but Jasmine suspected he would be going home with her brother any day now.

She clipped the pink leash onto Maisy's matching collar and headed downstairs to Presley waiting for them in her convertible.

"I promise you, y'all are gonna have a good time," Presley said, peeling away from the curb.

Jasmine grabbed the armrest and held on for dear life.

Chapter Twenty-Six

A DRAGONFLY raced alongside Presley's convertible, dancing on the wind filled with the sweet smells of summer. Jasmine lifted her face and tried to enjoy the warmth of the sun.

"So, what do y'all think?"

"Think about what?" Jasmine blinked at Presley. "I'm not sure I'm going to be very good company. Maybe I shouldn't have come."

Presley wouldn't stop pestering her for a day at the pond. Jasmine wasn't feeling very social these days, but moping around wasn't going to do her any good. She hadn't seen or heard from Rhett since she'd walked away from him. It was what she wanted, a clean break. At least that's what she kept telling herself. Jasmine tried to go on and pretend like there wasn't a hollow hole where her heart used to be. She managed to keep her mind off of her troubled heart during the day. It was after the clinic was closed and she climbed the stairs to her apartment, when she didn't have to hide anymore, that she let herself cry.

She rubbed her hands on the pair of jeans she wore. These weren't the baggy ones she'd been wearing. This pair hugged her curves all the way down to the tapered ankle. With a nod to the warmer weather, she'd picked out a blouse with flowers scattered over a dark lavender background. Maisy plopped her head on her shoulder from the back seat, giving Jasmine a quick doggy kiss before sticking her head back into the wind, clearly enjoying her first experience in a convertible.

"I know you may not feel like it, but I promise this is going to be fun, and y'all look really pretty."

Jasmine picked at the sleeve of her blouse. She didn't really care about looking nice; she just wanted to see Rhett again. She missed him, and no matter what she wore, it wouldn't cover up her longing to see him again.

Jasmine looked around, for the first time paying attention to her surroundings. Her eyes widened when she saw the large Help Wanted sign.

When Presley turned past the sign at the end of Rhett's driveway, Jasmine gasped. "What are you doing?"

Presley's lips curled into a smile, but she kept her eyes on the road. "Didn't you see the sign? I thought we'd just stop for a minute and see if there's anything we can do."

Jasmine's mouth dropped open when she saw the large group of people in front of Rhett's cabin.

Dan and Jacob were putting the finishing touches on a new roof. Mae and Reid were brushing a fresh coat of paint on the front door and around the trim of the brand-new plate-glass window. Tillie and Callie were bringing trays of food from Tillie's station wagon over to a row of tables that were set up in front of the cabin. The Jewels were arguing about where to put the lavender plants that were scattered around the front of the cabin while Uncle Robert leaned on his shovel, waiting patiently for direction. Mr. and Mrs. Greene were down by the pond with a few others that Jasmine assumed were their children and grandchildren.

Maisy jumped out of the car with a happy bark when she saw Rebel, and the two of them took off in a game of chase. Presley got out of the car while Jasmine sat motionless, trying to process what she was seeing.

Wait, she thought, doing a double-take. *Is that my brother on the roof too?* She got out of the car and took in the scene playing out in front of her before seeking out Rhett.

"Come on, there's a lot of work to do before we can sit down for supper." Presley came back over and linked her arm through Jasmine's.

"What in the world is going on here?" Jasmine asked.

"You saw the sign," Presley said with a mischievous smile.

Jasmine dug her heels in. "Presley, I am not taking one more step until you explain what the hell is going on."

"I asked for help, and these good folks were kind enough to come out and spend the day lending me a hand."

Rhett's low drawl washed over her heart like sweet wildflower honey. She spun around, and there he was. His face had more color in it, and the circles under his eyes were almost gone. The sun was behind him, creating streaks of gold and light brown in his hair that fell around his shoulders and his beard that was neatly trimmed.

He gave her a slight smile and nodded to Presley. "Thank you for coming out today."

Presley let go of Jasmine's arm and started backing away. "I'm gonna see what I can to do to help Tillie."

Rhett shoved his hands in his pockets. "I was wondering, can I show you what I'm working on? I know what I want to do with this place, but I'd really like your opinion and"—there was a spark of hope in his eyes—"and your help."

Help. Rhett was asking for help.

Jasmine fought to keep her voice light and from throwing herself into his arms. She took a deep breath and nodded. "Okay."

He pulled his hand out of his pocket and reached for hers and then dropped it to his side, pressing it against his leg.

They walked around the other side of the cabin, where there was a grassy hill with a stand of trees behind it. When they reached the top of the rise, Rhett pointed down to the cabin and the pond below.

"I want to build a barn over to the side and three small cabins on the other side of the pond. I've been talking to Taylor, and he wants to take on the project for his show." He took a breath and turned to Jasmine. "I was thinking I'd like to use this place as a retreat for first responders and veterans with PTSD. I reached out to a place in Montana that specializes in animal therapy. I'm going to go out in a few weeks and take a look at their facility. If it works out, they might be willing to partner with me, sharing resources and helping me make sure I get my retreat set up with all the right accreditations. While I'm there, they're going to help me get Rebel certified as a therapy dog, and he'll be able to work with folks who come here."

Jasmine listened while Rhett laid out his plan. His voice was tinged with excitement and hope.

"I'm going to name it Kingfisher Ranch," Rhett said.

"That's wonderful, Rhett."

He looked down at where her hand rested at her side. His fingers brushed against hers, testing. When she didn't pull away, he grasped her hand and looked Jasmine in the eye. "Will you please stay after everyone leaves? There's more that I want to say, to… tell you, but I'd like to do it when everyone else has left."

"I'd like that." She smiled faintly. "I've missed you."

Rhett squeezed her hand. "I missed you too. I should have reached out. I wanted to, but I needed to figure out… well, myself."

"How's that going?"

"Good, I think." He let go and swept his arm over all the activity below them. "So many people came out to help. It wasn't easy to ask, but I'm glad I did."

Jasmine was so overwhelmed with pride, she didn't know if she could contain it. Walking away from Rhett on the day she found him with Larry wasn't easy. She'd questioned her decision every day since, but she knew it was up to Rhett to decide when he was ready, and now here he was asking for help and, more importantly, doing what he needed to help himself.

"Will you tell me more about your idea of turning this into a retreat?" she asked.

His expression brightened. "Taylor and his crew are measuring for the barn foundation. He's contacted another show that features barn building, and that crew is coming out next week to do the build." He watched the men pounding stakes tied with red ribbon into the ground with a slight smile. "I didn't know what I was getting into when I invited him over. I wasn't sure Taylor would answer my call."

"Why wouldn't he?" Jasmine asked.

"I…." Rhett ran his hand through his hair. "There were things I believed about my family that weren't accurate. I got it into my head that I wasn't wanted. I thought if I was a burden to people, that they wouldn't want me or care about me."

She reached for his hand. "I'm sorry that you thought you weren't worthy of being loved."

He looked down at their joined hands and at her. "Thank goodness for Uncle Robert setting me straight. I've been staying with him for the last two weeks, and we've been talking a lot. Our talks helped me realize what I wanted to do with my inheritance."

"Does this mean you're leaving the FBI?"

Rhett nodded as they started walking back toward the cabin.

"I'm going to stay on as a consultant, and I'm volunteering with a group of retired agents who are working on cold case files, civil rights cases."

"That's great, Rhett. I have to admit, I was worried. You're passionate about your job, and that's a wonderful thing, but I hated seeing the toll it took on you."

"I know, and I didn't do anything to make it easy. Uncle Robert is right: Colton men are stubborn. Sometimes, it takes a while for us to pull our heads out of our asses."

Jasmine bit her lip, trying to keep from smiling. "Ms. Ruby said the same thing."

Rhett chuckled. "I bet she did."

"Hey, are y'all gonna get to work, or are you just going to enjoy the view?" Tillie called out.

Jasmine looked down at her outfit. "I'm afraid I'm not dressed for painting or carpentry."

"You're here, and that helps more than you'll ever know."

Jasmine looked around the property, picturing the cabins and barn that Rhett described. It was a beautiful piece of land and would provide a calm and peaceful place where people could heal their troubled souls. Rhett was good with animals and, combined with his own personal experiences, she believed the retreat would be a success.

Her brother was climbing down from the roof when they reached the cabin. He slung his arm around her shoulder and kissed the top of her head.

"Good to see you, Mighty Mouse," he said with a twinkle in his eye.

She pulled herself out from under his arm. "Gross, Isiah. You're all sweaty."

"Well, if you two would stop making moon eyes at each other and get to work, you'd be sweaty too. I brought some work clothes for you," he said, jerking his head toward the inside of the cabin. "Get changed. Rhett needs help to get this place fixed up."

Jasmine glanced at Rhett, who suddenly became interested in his shoes. His hair hid his face, but she could guess by the color of his neck that it must be beet red.

She leaned toward her brother and murmured, "You've been keeping secrets from me."

Isiah whispered back, "We agreed to stay out of each other's personal lives, remember?"

Jasmine shot him a look that let him know he'd be getting a stern talking-to for this later. Isiah responded to her silent admonishment by throwing his head back and laughing. He slapped Rhett on the shoulder.

"Come on, we're almost finished up on the roof. You'd better work with us, Rhett. Otherwise you'll just be flirting with my sister, and neither one of you will get anything done."

It was Jasmine's turn to blush. Her brother's teasing didn't really bother her. In his own way, he was letting them both know that he was giving them his support.

Isiah dragged Rhett off, and Jasmine went into the cabin to change. Presley was already changed and measuring out shelf paper for the cabinets, which were sporting a fresh coat of soft white paint. She looked at Jasmine, scrunching up her nose.

"It's an awfully plain color, don't you think? I would have picked something brighter, but Ashton always says I want to make everything look like a bordello. There's somethin' for you to change into in my bag by the door."

Jasmine paused and glanced around the cabin, getting a good look for the first time since she was there with Rhett and Larry. She'd been so focused on protecting Rhett that she hadn't paid any attention to her surroundings. The place wasn't big, but the windows let in lots of light, and the vaulted ceiling in the main room made the space feel bigger than it was. Memories of Rhett telling Larry he was willing to sacrifice himself washed over her as she walked down the hallway to the bedroom. There were no footprints in the dust or cobwebs overhead this time. The bathroom across from the bedroom was dated but spotless, and there was a faint scent of furniture polish lingering in the bedroom, the shining dresser along one wall proof of its use. New sage-green sheets and a green plaid blanket covered the bed. A braided rug and a small bedside table with a lamp were the only other decoration in the room. She leaned against the doorway, taking it all in, replacing the memory of her time here before with hope of a better future.

She came back out and grabbed the clothes Presley brought and went to change in the bathroom.

"Quit daydreaming in there," Presley shouted.

Jasmine smiled at her reflection in the mirror as she pulled her hair into a poof on top of her head.

"Rhett's done so much to help all of us. I'm glad he finally gave us a chance to do somethin' for him," Presley said when she came back out.

"So am I."

"Mae and I picked out some new kitchen stuff we can put away as soon as we get these shelves papered," Presley said, pointing to a stack of boxes in the corner.

It didn't take long to get the cabinets ready, and they started unpacking boxes, putting new dishes and glassware away.

"Don't you think wallpaper with big flowers would have looked nice?" Presley said.

Jasmine stood back to admire the pretty blueish-green color on the kitchen walls. The only thing the room needed were some barstools for the island and maybe a patterned roman shade for the window that looked out toward the hilltop she'd been standing on with Rhett.

"You're doing it again," Presley said.

"What?" She blinked at her friend.

Presley laughed. "You're all daydreamy."

"I'm just a little distracted by"—she waved her brush around—"all of this."

"You could have knocked me over with a feather when Rhett called last week," Presley said.

Jasmine looked at her friend in surprise. Anyone who knew her well knew Presley wasn't great at keeping secrets.

"I still can't believe he did this."

Presley started sorting the silverware into a new holder, keeping her eyes on her task as she spoke. "Some people can change if you give them a chance. Not everyone will take it, but if someone does, shouldn't you… I don't know, welcome them back with open arms or somethin'? Or at least give them another chance? That's why when Rhett called, I was happy to help."

Jasmine swallowed past the lump in her throat and said softly, "You're right."

She stopped what she was doing and gave Presley a hug. "Thanks for bringing me here. You've been a good friend, and I appreciate you being a shoulder for me to cry on these last couple of weeks."

"Thanks for letting me. Maybe"—Presley bit her lip—"maybe you can tell your brother I can do somethin' right once in a while?"

Jasmine gave her friend a sympathetic look. "He may not show it, but he notices. And you know what? If he doesn't, that's his loss. You just keep doing you, okay?"

Presley's eyes were bright when she nodded. "I'll try."

"Queens fix each other's crowns. I've got your back."

Presley started to laugh. "Oh Lord, I was Miss Pickled Pigs Feet at the county fair one year. You should see the crown."

By the time Presley finished sharing all the various pageants she'd been in and the crowns in her collection, they were both crying from laughing so hard.

When they were done in the kitchen, Jasmine went to look for Rhett. He was just coming down from the finished roof when she came out. She shaded her eyes, looking up at the new hunter green metal panels.

"It looks good," she said.

Rhett stood next to her with his hands on his hips, following her gaze to the roof. "It really does. With the fresh paint on the doors and window trim, it looks"—his voice cracked—"it looks just like it did when I first came out here."

"I'm glad you made this your home. You love it here. It's where you should be."

Rhett turned to look at her. "I know that now."

He put his hand over hers, and the two of them became lost in each other's gaze, with many unspoken words hovering between them. Tillie called out that supper was ready, breaking the spell. It was a wonderful thing to see all the folks who came out to help Rhett. Jasmine sat next to him. Her body tingled with awareness every time his arm brushed against hers. As much as she loved being surrounded by family and friends, she couldn't wait for everyone to leave so they could be alone.

The sun was lower in the sky when people started to leave. Tillie filled Rhett's refrigerator and freezer with leftovers. She gave them both a kiss on the cheek, announcing with a wink that they had enough food to stay in the cabin all weekend.

Her brother and Presley said goodbye, and Rhett was off to one side talking to Uncle Robert. Taylor was wrapping up with his film crew. He'd reworked his production schedule so they could start working on Rhett's project next week.

One by one, people left with hugs, kisses, and promises to come back and help when Rhett needed them. Rebel and Maisy were curled up on the porch, exhausted from playing all day.

"Do you want to sit by the pond for a bit?" Rhett asked.

Jasmine held her hand out for his. "Sure."

Chapter Twenty-Seven

Jasmine was here. Rhett kept seeking her out throughout the afternoon, worried that he'd been dreaming and she hadn't really come. There had never been this many people at his grandpa's cabin before. Re-entry was hard. He still felt uncomfortable asking for help and believing that people weren't there out of obligation or because they felt bad for him, but because they genuinely cared.

The past two weeks leading up to today were a strange mixture of healing and grief. With Uncle Robert's help, he was finally letting go of the last two years and the feeling of being a burden. He was humbled by the response he got from everyone he asked to help with his vision. For the past few days, Taylor Colton and his building crew started coming by with ideas for how he could make his vision a reality. Their enthusiasm for his project boosted his confidence. And then Dax, Isiah, and Dan came over and started helping him rehab the cabin. Together, they worked on replacing the old metal roof with a new one. With their help, the cabin was looking the way he remembered. For the first time, he could look around him and believe that his grandpa really was proud of him.

At the pond, he and Jasmine sat on the log. A slight breeze made ripples on the water, bringing the scent of fresh spring grass and spring flowers, reminding Rhett that this was a time of renewal.

Rhett's chest tightened. He took a deep breath and reached for Jasmine's hand, threading her fingers with his, thankful to have her at his side. She didn't make him whole again. That wasn't her job, but having Jasmine in his life made him want to be the best partner, lover, and, he hoped, husband he could be. That meant sharing everything, exposing everything he was to the woman he loved.

"Thank you for staying," he said. "I have something I want to tell you."

Jasmine looked up at him. "Okay."

"I was so confident when I started my assignment. I'm used to being independent and taking care of myself." He rested his cheek on her head, taking the comfort her closeness offered. "To me, asking for help meant I was being a burden."

He felt her stiffen and kissed the top of her head. "I know that's not true, but it's something I had in my head and my heart for a long time."

Reluctantly, Rhett left Jasmine's side to stand in front of her. He needed to look her in the eye when he told her.

"During my assignment, I made a choice. I did something that I… I hate myself for doing."

Jasmine was looking up at him with trust in her gaze that made him struggle to find the words to explain. Before he lost his nerve, Rhett reached behind his head and pulled off his shirt. His jaw was set when he turned his back to her.

He heard the quick intake of her breath when she saw the words carved into his shoulder in thick, dark ink.

"I had to prove my loyalty," Rhett said.

He heard her stand up. He pulled away when her touch grazed the black ink that spelled out *White Power* under an iron cross.

"It's okay," she said.

Rhett tried to move farther away from her reach. "No, it's not."

"Stop," she ordered.

Rhett froze. At the first faint touch of her fingers, he hissed. She gently ran her hand over the tattoo. When she finished, Jasmine wrapped her arms around him from behind.

Her lips burned against his skin. "This isn't who you are. They may have marked your body, but they didn't mark your soul."

He didn't respond but grasped her hands and held on tightly.

"Is this why you wouldn't make love to me with the lights on?" she whispered against his back.

He nodded.

She circled around him, keeping him encircled in her arms until she could press her cheek against his chest.

"I didn't want to be with you when I'm like this. I was going to have it removed, but the laser specialist said… the ink is deep. And then I just… it didn't matter anymore. Then I met you and I…." He tightened his hold on her, resting his chin on the top of her head.

"I hated you, thought I didn't want you." Jasmine sniffed

Rhett cupped her chin and lifted her face to his. "Never think I don't want you. When you look at me, the way you see me—if I'd known you when it started, I would have done it all for you, to make sure this is a place where you would feel welcome, somewhere that you'd always feel safe, and it would have been worth it."

"Oh, Rhett, you have to stop offering to sacrifice yourself."

"You're right. I'm going to work on that. I'm figuring out that I can serve without sacrifice. I can give to others and still save a part of myself for me… for you. And when I forget—"

Jasmine put her fingers over his lips. "The people who care about you will remind you."

He leaned his forehead against hers. "I understand why you walked away, and I'm willing to wait and to work on being a better man. Just, please… will you leave the door to your heart open just a little for me?"

Jasmine grasped his face and brought his mouth to hers. "The door is open, Rhett," she whispered against his lips.

Her lips parted just before he claimed her mouth. Thinking about how close he came to losing Jasmine and moments like this brought tears to his eyes.

Jasmine was back in his arms. No matter what happened in the future, he'd carry this moment with him for the rest of his life. The last glimmer of daylight faded away while they stood in each other's embrace. They walked back to the cabin under a canopy of stars.

Rhett hesitated when they went inside. "I can sleep on the sofa."

Jasmine shook her head with a sensual light in her eyes. She took his hand and led him down the hallway.

She pulled off her boots and turned off the overhead light, bathing the room in moonglow before moving over to the bedside table and switching on a small lamp, casting the room on a low, warm light.

Turning back to him, she asked, "Is this okay?"

He nodded, watching her come toward him. She reached behind him and tugged off the band that held his hair up, letting it fall loose around his shoulders. He sucked in his breath and forced himself to stand still when her fingers trailed beneath his collar and brushed against his shoulder.

"Kiss me," she whispered, her eyes searching his.

He leaned down and pressed his lips to hers. Jasmine pulled back and gave him a sharp look.

"Kiss me," she ordered.

This time, he didn't hold back. He captured her lips and poured all of his emotion into the kiss. When he pulled away, he brushed his thumb over the freckles that were scattered across the bridge on her nose.

"I can't believe I almost missed this," he murmured.

"Missed what?" she asked with a bemused smile.

"Seeing you like this, in the darkness and the light." He looked around the room. "I wish I'd thought of candles. I want to be able to see you. Candlelight would have made it more romantic."

"Next time," she said, tracing the neckline of his shirt with her fingertips.

Jasmine grasped the hem of her shirt and pulled it over her head, revealing a lacy black bra. She reached for the hem of his shirt and gave it a tug.

"Your turn."

He exhaled, his hands shaking. His heart hammered in his chest when he revealed his bare torso to Jasmine.

They stood face-to-face. Her hands mirrored his tracing a path across her chest, caressing the skin just above the top of her bra. Jasmine's fingers traveled lower in synch with his. Her breath hitched when he undid the button on her jeans. Rhett slid his hands down her hips, mesmerized by the little shimmy she did to remove her jeans. They quickly stripped down until there was nothing more between them. He'd been naked in front of Jasmine before, but he never felt exposed the way he did now.

"This is what I wanted every night I've been with you. To see you, all of you," he said.

He grasped her hips and guided her back until her knees hit the edge of the bed.

She tried to pull him down on top of her, but he braced himself above her.

"I don't want to rush. I want to take my time and see every inch of you," he said.

Jasmine looked at him with a shy smile. "I'm not—"

Rhett silenced her with a quick kiss. "Don't you dare say you're anything but perfect."

He traced his fingertips over her lips, watching the heat flare in her eyes. Now Rhett could see every contour of Jasmine's body he'd memorized in the dark. When he found a freckle on the inside of her thigh, he worshipped it with his mouth until Jasmine squirmed beneath him.

He tensed when her fingers brushed against his tattoo and then dug into his marked skin.

"This isn't who you are. Stay with me, right here, right now. Nothing else matters but us," she said, grabbing his hand and pressing it to her breast. Tremors ran through Rhett's body as he fought for control. She lifted herself just enough to allow him entrance; he filled her completely.

"Hold still," she commanded when he tried to move. She held his face in her hands.

"I love you, Rhett Colton, and you will never offer to sacrifice your life ever again. You belong to me. Do you hear me? You. Belong. To. Me."

"I'm yours."

"Say it again," she ordered.

"I love you, Jasmine, and I'm yours."

Rhett kissed her, putting all of his heart and soul into making sure Jasmine knew how much he treasured her. He would never put his life at risk again, not when there was a lifetime of moments like this to look forward to.

Eventually Jasmine summoned the strength to prop her chin on his chest, smiling at him with a sated look on her face.

"Baby, are you okay?" she asked.

Rhett grunted, wrapping her tightly in his arms.

Jasmine smiled and pressed a kiss over his heart.

"I'm having a hard time finding the right words. There's so much I want to say. So much I'm thankful for," he whispered. Rhett lifted her chin and pressed a soft kiss to her lips. "I have never felt as complete as I do with you. From now on, I only want to make love to you when I can see your face and look into your eyes." He grabbed her hand and pressed it against his heart. "I'm going to spend every day appreciating every moment, big and small."

Jasmine lifted herself until her face was level with his. "I meant what I said, Rhett. I love you, you are my heart, and I don't give you permission to give your life to anyone else."

He pulled her on top of him, reveling in being able to see the look of desire in her eye. "Yes, ma'am," he drawled, taking her lips in another long, drugging kiss. The light by the side of the bed stayed on through the night.

Chapter Twenty-Eight

RHETT PACED the front porch of the cabin all morning. He'd snapped the hair tie on his wrist so many times, he broke it, and then he freaked out, rummaging through the cabin looking for a new one. All of Jasmine's attempts to distract him had failed, so she let him pace while she sat on the top step, sipping her coffee, waiting for their guest to arrive. His head whipped toward the driveway when the roar of a motorcycle echoed in the distance.

After Rhett had shared his tattoo, he told Jasmine about the letter that was included in his grandfather's will. George had contacted a tattoo artist, a guy named Paul who George believed could ink a cover-up of the ugliness marked on his skin. Rhett had reached out to Paul, who'd be arriving any minute now.

Jasmine got up and stood with him, watching the figure on a large dark crimson and chrome motorcycle headed toward them down the driveway. The driver pulled up to the house and cut the engine.

"You must be Rhett. I'd know you anywhere from the pictures George showed me," a muffled voice said beneath the helmet.

The rider pulled off the helmet to reveal a woman with a wide-open smile.

"You're Paul?" Jasmine asked.

The woman's lips quirked. "Short for Paulina, but if you want to be friends, you'll call me Paul."

The intricate flowers and birds that covered Paul's arms fascinated Jasmine. The woman looked to be about the same age as Jasmine. She was tall, with creamy brown skin and a short spiky hairstyle with purple tips. Her light hazel eyes looked around the cabin's porch with curiosity.

"Where can I set up?" Paul asked.

"Is the porch okay?"

Paul squinted at the porch. "That can work. We'll need a comfortable chair for you. I need a table for my equipment, and if there's not an outlet, then I'll need an extension cord."

Rhett ran his hand through his hair. His eyes sought Jasmine's with a hint of anxiety. "Yeah, I can take care of all that." Rhett reached for her hand and held on tightly. "Will you help me?"

"Always," she said with a smile.

Some of the tension eased from Rhett's face, and together, they gathered what they needed. Once Paul sterilized the area and had all of her equipment set up, she went back to one saddlebag on her motorcycle and pulled out a sketch pad.

"Do you want to see the design?"

Rhett hesitated, looking to Jasmine for reassurance. She nodded.

"Go ahead," Rhett said.

Paul flipped open her pad and held it out to Rhett. His hand trembled as he took it from her.

"It's pretty close to what your grandfather originally asked for. I had to make a few modifications once I saw the picture you sent me."

"It—" Rhett cleared his throat. "—it looks really good." He turned the pad toward Jasmine so she could see the design.

The drawing was a scene of the pond with two figures silhouetted against a twilight sky. A man and a boy sat on a log with their fishing poles in the water.

"It's beautiful," Jasmine said, reaching out to trace the outline of the two figures with her finger.

"The outline of the two figures should help cover the original design," Paul said, turning to Rhett. "Are you ready?"

Rhett took a deep breath and nodded.

"Here, let me," Jasmine said when Rhett fumbled with the buttons on his shirt.

She unbuttoned his shirt and slid it from his shoulders. She set the shirt over the porch railing and pressed her hands to Rhett's chest, feeling his heart pounding against her palms.

"It's going to be okay."

He lifted one of her hands to his mouth, kissing her palm. "I know it is, I'm just… nervous, I guess."

He pressed a gentle kiss to her forehead before he pulled his hair into a topknot, straddled the chair, and rested his arms on the back of it. The buzz of the tattoo gun competed with the buzz of the bees that had discovered the lavender plants the Jewels had planted in front of the porch.

Rhett didn't show any sign of being in pain. Instead, he looked at her with a trance-like smile.

"It happens sometimes," Paul said, wiping the blood away from his skin. "Some people sort of sink into the pain, and it begins to feel good."

With each layer of color and detail that Paul applied, Jasmine could see Rhett letting go of the last two years of his life. While she worked, Paul shared the story of how she met Rhett's grandpa. Apparently George had been doing his research and asking around to find someone who specialized in cover-ups.

Paul laughed softly as she worked the ink into Rhett's skin. "That old man must have spent a hundred hours in the shop, peppering me with questions and watching me work. At first it annoyed the hell out of me. I thought he didn't trust me because I'm a woman, a minority. It happens all the time." She changed ink. "It didn't take long to figure out why he was being so darn particular. He really loved you, Rhett."

Rhett turned his face into his folded arms. A wet spot appeared on the weathered floorboard. Rebel came over and leaned against his side. Rhett let his hand drop, digging his fingers into his soft fur. Jasmine's heart ached at the scene playing out in front of her. She wanted to help, to relieve his pain, but that wasn't what Rhett needed. He needed to feel his pain, to release it and replace the pain with the love his grandpa gave him.

Paul started applying the next color. "Like I said, at first he kind of pissed me off, but then I started listening to him, like really listening. Your grandpa shared a lot of history with me, some good, some bad. I appreciated he was honest about what he'd done wrong and how he tried to fix it." She wiped Rhett's shoulder again and sat back to examine her work. "He sure was right about this tattoo. It's going to look real nice when it's finished, and you'll never know anything else was there."

Jasmine put her hand over her heart and took a deep breath. She hadn't realized how worried she'd been that the cover-up wouldn't work. Rhett visibly relaxed as well.

She didn't know how long the three of them were out on the porch before Paul finally announced that she was finished. Jasmine ran inside and grabbed the mirror off the bathroom wall while Paul applied antiseptic soap one last time to Rhett's new tattoo.

She held up the mirror while Rhett craned his neck to see the intricate piece of artwork that covered the ugliness he'd lived with for too long.

His eyes filled with tears that he didn't try to blink away. "Thank you," he said in a hoarse whisper.

Paul gently applied a piece of clear protective film over the fresh ink. "You're welcome." Resting her hands on her hips, Paul looked around the farm again. "You've got a nice place here. I drove through town on my way here. The town square sure is pretty."

"I hope it wasn't too long of a drive for you."

"It's just two hours of open road from Memphis, and there's nothing better than starting my day with a good ride."

"Can we get you anything to eat or drink?" Jasmine offered.

"Nah. If you don't mind, I'll get my stuff cleaned up, make use of your bathroom, and then I think I'll head back into town and checkout that Catfish Café I saw when I passed by."

"You're in for a treat. Nobody makes better food than Tillie, and her pies are a religious experience."

Paul rubbed her hands together, grinning. "Now you're talking."

Rhett pulled out his phone and called the café while Paul was in the bathroom and asked Tillie to make sure he got the bill for Paul's lunch.

"That was a nice idea," Jasmine said when he hung up.

"It's the least I can do. When I asked her how much this was going to cost, she refused to take any money."

"I suspect your grandad took care of it."

Rhett nodded, his eyes shining. "I miss him," he blurted out.

She put her arm around his waist and her hand on his chest. "I know you do, but he's right here with you," she said, patting his heart.

Paul came back out and reviewed the aftercare instructions one more time. When she said goodbye, she handed Rhett a picture. He looked down at it as Paul got on her motorcycle and rode away. The image was faded, and the edges were worn. He couldn't remember if it was his mother or father, or maybe it was someone else who stood behind him and his grandpa that first summer he came to Colton to visit him. Rhett was only five years old, and it was his first time sitting on the log, fishing next to his grandpa at the pond. Their bodies were silhouetted against the water, grass, and sky, the image that was now a permanent part of his body.

"I don't know what to do now," Rhett said.

"What do you mean? Did you have something else that needed to be done at the cabin?"

"No… I mean, I—" A single tear hovered at the corner of his eye. "I didn't realize just how much that tattoo was holding me down. Now that it's gone, I feel like I can breathe again. I asked for help and made all of these plans to transform this place, but there was a part of me that… I don't know, didn't believe it was really possible." Rhett shook his head. "No, that's not it. I couldn't see a future where I could run this as a therapy ranch and… to be the man I wanted to be for you."

Jasmine pressed her lips to one cheek and then the other, kissing away his tears.

"Somewhere along the way, you lost hope." She wrapped her arms around his neck and placed a soft kiss on his lips. "This is what it feels like to hope again."

He pulled her closer and whispered against her lips, "It feels good."

THAT NIGHT, Rhett looked down at the woman sleeping next to him. He would never get enough of seeing her, all of her with the lights on. Feeling the softness of her skin in the dark was a gift he didn't think he deserved. He was propped up against his headboard with a pillow protecting his shoulder. There was a slight tinge of tenderness, one that he welcomed. Rhett sought out the mirror in the bathroom, time and time again, to look at his new tattoo, marveling at what Paul created. He appreciated his grandpa for leaving him the cabin and money, but this was the part of his inheritance that meant the most to him. He picked up the picture that was propped up against the lamp on the nightstand. He flipped the picture over to read the words his grandpa had written on the back again.

"Of all the gifts I ever received, you were the greatest. When your assignment is over, it's time to live your life. Please don't sacrifice yourself for hate again; you are too valued and too loved."

Jasmine stirred at his side, her legs intertwined with his. He kissed her curls, and she gave him a sleepy smile.

"Why aren't you sleeping?" she asked.

"I'm too happy to sleep."

"It's okay to go to sleep. It will still be there in the morning."

He wrapped his arm around her and pulled her until she was lying half on top of him. She shivered and snuggled closer when he ran his fingers down her spine.

The skin on his shoulder pricked at her words, letting him know the ink was still there.

"It may take me a day or two to believe it."

Jasmine reached up and trailed her fingers along his jaw. "I'll remind you every day for as long as you need me to."

RHETT WOKE up to soft kisses that quickly became heated. He winced when they broke apart and he tried to sit up.

"Are you okay?" she asked.

"I'm a little sore." He tried to look over his shoulder. "How does it look?"

"There's some dried blood under the tape. Right now, the image isn't clear, but it's going to look wonderful when it heals."

Rhett cradled her face in his hands. "Thank you."

"You don't have anything to thank me for."

"Yes, I do. Thank you for being patient with me so that we could be here now. Thank you for waiting for me to find my way out of the dark, for being here when the sun rises… so I can make love to you again when I can see the light in your eyes."

Rhett lifted his head, fusing their mouths. And with the sun casting shadows across the bed, they welcomed a new day.

Epilogue

SPRING RETURNED to Colton. Water glittered like sapphires in the sunlight. A slight breeze created ripples across the pond. A bright blue kingfisher took off from its perch on a cattail, swooping over the water, enjoying the warm day. The trees that ringed it morphed into a quilt of dark green, gold, and orange. The mare in the corral by the barn whinnied, tossing its mane in the breeze. She wouldn't be alone for much longer; soon the other stalls in the barn were going to be filled with more horses for the equine therapy program that would be starting at the ranch.

Kingfisher Ranch had just welcomed their first group of clients. The cabins were booked through the rest of the year, and they were making plans to add a bunkhouse and more cabins in the spring.

Rhett looked down at his wife, standing next to him on the hilltop overlooking his grandpa's cabin that they now called home. Jasmine smiled up at him.

"I love you." She leaned up and kissed him.

"I love you too."

They'd said their vows under the gazebo in a small ceremony with just family and a few friends. They held the reception in the newly built barn, decorated with barrels planted with dahlias and marigolds in orange, yellow, and purple courtesy of the Colton Garden Club. Twinkle lights created a canopy of starlight for them to have their first dance as husband and wife. Jasmine's parents came down from Chicago. Rhett was scared to death her parents wouldn't give their blessing, but they welcomed him into their family with open arms and, to his surprise, hit it off with his folks. He'd gone from feeling alone to being surrounded by family. His relationship with his parents was growing stronger every day. They started family counseling and working toward having the relationship Rhett always longed for. His parents spent so much time volunteering at the ranch, they were talking about moving to Colton, something Rhett found himself really excited about.

He looked down at his new tattoo. The words Jasmine repeated to him at their wedding were written on his forearm in beautiful script, surrounded by kudzu and laurel vines shaped into a heart. *Helping someone is loving someone. I will always be by your side, helping and loving you forever.* There were moments when he'd lost sight of his future and lost hope. Having Jasmine come into his life made him hope again and find his way to a fulfilling life beyond his wildest dreams.

JASMINE LOOKED up at her husband, the sun casting a warm glow over his features. The dark circles and haunted look in Rhett's eyes were gone. There were still some nights when the nightmares returned, but they didn't come very often now. He'd gone from being isolated and alone to being surrounded by friends and family.

Kingfisher Ranch was the success she knew it would be. Along with helping veterans and first responders, in a few weeks they were going to host their first group of veterinarians who were seeking a place to process and heal from the stress of their job. On Tuesday nights, while Jasmine went to her knitting group, Rhett started meeting with Uncle Robert and a group of ex-agents and veterans. Jasmine was doing some healing of her own, meeting with a support group for veterinarians to talk about her experience with Darren and the clinic in Ohio.

Jasmine came to Colton hoping for a fresh start and found much more—community, family, and love.

She reached for Rhett's hand and gazed up at him, her lips curling into a smile. "You know, it's a good thing you've become a pro at asking for help."

Rhett raised a brow and replied, "Why is that?"

"Because you're going to need a lot of help in a few months."

"What am I going to need help with?"

She pressed his hand to her stomach. "You're going to need to ask someone to help at the ranch so you can spend time with your new son or daughter."

His eyes grew wide, and his face broke into a huge smile before he cupped his mouth and shouted, "Help, I need help!" Jasmine giggled as Rhett swept her up into his arms and kissed her—a kiss infused with joy and hope.

AUTHOR'S NOTE

SOMETIMES IT'S easier to offer help than to receive it. But we are at our best when we can both give and receive.

Please, if you or someone you know is struggling with depression, please ask for help.

National Suicide Prevention Line 1-800-273-8255 or 988

Keep Reading for an excerpt from
Be the Match
An Emerald Hearts Novel
by Eliana West

AN EMERALD  HEARTS NOVEL

BE THE *Match*

ELIANA WEST

An Emerald Hearts Novel

A senseless accident leaves Ryan Blackstone a single father. His son, Leo, survives, only for the hospital to discover he has leukemia. Ryan's only hope to save him is a bone marrow donor.

A donor registry reveals a perfect match for Leo but unearths an unsettling family secret: Ryan's wife's brother isn't dead. Then they meet, and Ryan realizes Dylan could save him as well.

Dylan McKenzie stopped thinking about his family's betrayal when they kicked him out twelve years ago. They would rather say he is dead than gay. So the news of his sister's death comes as a shock. Dylan is afraid being pulled back into the family will hurt him again, but meeting Ryan *and Leo upends his plan to keep his heart closed.*

Ryan almost lost everything. Now he must decide if he can gamble losing his family to have everything he's ever wanted. Together, he and Dylan could be the perfect match.

Chapter One

"I'M SORRY, Mr. Blackstone, I know this is hard to hear so soon after losing your wife," the pediatric oncologist said in a sympathetic and yet emotionless tone. Ryan figured when you'd given the news enough times, it became easier to say—but not easier to hear. "I concur with my colleagues that have reviewed your son's case. Leo has leukemia."

What was it about that word that sounded like a snake wrapping itself around his son's tiny body? Ryan gripped the arms of the chair and tried to slow his heartbeat.

"What happens now?"

The doctor steepled his hands. "We'll begin a course of chemotherapy. The first round will be aggressive. You need to be prepared for that."

"When will we know if it's working?"

"Months. Or longer. We can't predict how a body will respond."

Ryan walked out of the doctor's office in a daze. His wife's passing in a car accident three weeks ago was terrible. Now the same accident that spared his son led to a horrible diagnosis. It was an unspeakable thought, but it was a slight consolation that he could give up the role of grieving husband and focus on Leo.

A widower for three weeks and he was already sick of the sad looks and words of comfort everyone around him wanted to offer. He couldn't stand another person telling him how perfect he and Lindsay were together and what a wonderful life they'd shared. Ryan didn't know what wonderful was supposed to be, but it wasn't what he shared with Lindsay. His sister Stephanie had introduced them. Lindsay and Stephanie were sorority sisters at Florida A&M. Lindsay McKenzie was vivacious and driven. His parents thought she was the perfect partner for him. His sister insisted they were right for each other. He proposed to get people to stop asking him when he was going to rather than as a declaration of love. At first it was convenient that Lindsay took over their homelife so he could manage the rapid success and growth of Blackstone Financial

Technologies. As time went on, her insistence on living a lifestyle that matched her vision and goals strained their relationship.

Seattle Children's Hospital was only three miles from his home but separated by Lake Washington. Thankfully, the traffic on the 405 bridge wasn't heavy in the late morning, and he pulled up to his home on the other side of the lake in less than twenty minutes. He looked up at the white façade, and the usual feeling of gloom settled over him. Ryan hated the house Lindsay insisted they had to have. The white stucco exterior with massive columns, arched windows, and terra-cotta roof belonged in California, not in the Pacific Northwest. He'd wanted a midcentury home or maybe a classic Craftsman. Lindsay insisted they needed something grander where they could entertain clients and her society friends. The right home, the right friends, belonging to the right country club, those were the things that mattered to Lindsay. It made her a better fit with his family than he was. His parents and sister adored Lindsay, their values all aligning: money, social status, and conservative views.

Ryan parked in the three-car garage next to the house, his gaze flickering to the empty spot where Lindsay's Mercedes had been. She had insisted a $150,000 SUV was necessary when she became pregnant. Not because it was supposed to be safer, but because it's what her friends with kids drove. That car still sat at the far end of the garage. No, it was her other Mercedes, the one she insisted she needed for her "fun" car, that couldn't withstand a head-on collision with a street racer who lost control.

His sister pounced on him as soon as he walked in the door. "What did the doctor say?"

He took a moment to steady his voice. "He confirmed the diagnosis. Leo will need to start chemotherapy. We have an intake appointment with oncology at Children's tomorrow."

Blue eyes the color of the lake outside the window, a match to his own, became bright with unshed tears. "Oh no. Have you told Mom and Dad yet? Lindsay's parents?"

"No, I'm still trying to process the diagnosis myself. Where's Leo?"

"He's upstairs in his room with Mrs. Lieu." Stephanie's mouth turned down. "I think now it's even more important to hire a proper nanny for him. Mrs. Lieu is hardly qualified for the special care Leo is going to need."

"Stephanie, I'm not going to have this argument with you again. Mrs. Lieu has worked for me since before I married Lindsay. She's a part of this family and an excellent caregiver for Leo."

Stephanie's mouth pressed into a thin line. This wasn't over. He could see the fight in her eyes. Most of the time it was easier to give in than argue, but Mrs. Lieu's presence in his life was nonnegotiable.

His sister never warmed up to the Vietnamese woman he'd hired as a housekeeper. When he first started his company, he bought a building in Seattle's Belltown neighborhood and used the lower floors for office space. Ryan turned the top floor into an apartment. Mrs. Lieu kept him fed and the condo from turning into a pigsty while he worked a grueling schedule at his financial tech company. It was the one thing he put his foot down with Lindsay. Whatever home they moved to, Mrs. Lieu came with it. Lindsay realized with Mrs. Lieu around she had more time for her friends and hobbies, so she let go of any complaints. The two women weren't friends, but as long as Lindsay stayed out of Mrs. Lieu's way, and as long as Mrs. Lieu kept the refrigerator stocked with salads, there was peace in the land.

Ryan ran his hand through his hair and heaved a sigh. "Look, Steph, I have a lot to take care of before tomorrow. I've got to rearrange my schedule, and I'll be working remotely from now on."

"I've got it. I'll take care of work for you. Don't worry about that."

"I didn't mean to snap at you before. It would be good for Leo to have a nurse. I can't ask Mrs. Lieu to care for Leo and manage the house. That would be too much for her."

Ryan never intended for Mrs. Lieu to help care for Leo and handle everything else she did: cooking, cleaning, and managing scheduling for the gardener and other services. He knew she would if he asked. Mrs. Lieu was more of a grandmother figure to Leo than Ryan's own mother was. She loved Leo as if he were her own grandchild, and Ryan loved her for it, but it was too much to ask of her. He'd been putting off hiring a nanny. At first he thought he could manage everything on his own, but he was already overwhelmed trying to keep up with work and Leo's care. His sister was right; as usual she was looking out for him, and he needed to remember to appreciate it.

His sister's expression brightened. "I'll call an agency tomorrow."

He should take care of it himself, but he already had so much to deal with, it would make it easier to let Stephanie take care of it.

"Thanks, sis."

Between Mrs. Lieu and his sister, Ryan could focus on what he loved, writing algorithms and studying numbers. He'd always had a natural affinity for math. He happily spent hours analyzing data. Before he received his degree in data science and his master's in business and technology, he sold the first banking program he'd written. A year after college he created an investment algorithm that every investment firm in the country was clamoring to buy. Instead of selling the program, his parents encouraged him to start his own firm, and Blackstone Financial Technologies was born. With his family's involvement and Stephanie's leadership in sales, they grew the company to nearly a billion dollars in revenue last year. He started life in a well-to-do family; now they had wealth that meant anything they wanted or needed was always within reach. Ryan didn't care about the money, but he enjoyed the convenience it brought to his life and happily shared it with his family and Lindsay's parents. Being able to use work he enjoyed to take care of his loved ones reassured Ryan he was fulfilling his role in the family. Oldest son, big brother, responsible husband and father. All the roles he'd been taught a man was supposed to fulfill. For a long time, he'd believed it was enough to make him happy. Since Lindsay's death and Leo's diagnosis, he'd started questioning what brought him happiness and a sense of fulfillment.

"We'll talk tomorrow. Don't worry, Ryan, everything's going to be okay." Stephanie gave him a quick peck on the cheek and said goodbye. Thankfully, she didn't mention prayer, as Lindsay's parents constantly preached. Their answer to everything was faith, sometimes putting prayer before common sense.

Ryan went upstairs to Leo's room. His heart stuttered the same way it had every day since the accident. The dark shadows under Leo's eyes, against his pale skin, seemed to get worse with each passing day. He was going to lose his light brown curls, the fine strands a mixture of his parents'. Every day Ryan got to look at bright blue eyes that matched his own and brought him more joy than he'd ever thought possible.

"Daddy!" Leo pushed himself out of Mrs. Lieu's arms and threw himself into Ryan's arms.

Ryan's little boy wasn't as energetic as he used to be, and the bruises he'd gotten in the accident still stood out against his skin. Ryan picked him up, Leo's small body clinging to him like a spider monkey.

"Did you have a good day, buddy?"

Leo's face fell. "I didn't get to go to school again, Daddy."

Ryan rubbed his back, sharing a worried look with Mrs. Lieu over Leo's shoulder. "I know. But you know what? Summer is almost here. What do you think about starting summer early and not going back to school?"

"Because I'm sick?"

"Yeah." Ryan's voice became thick. "You're going to have to spend some time at the hospital, but I'll be there with you the whole time."

"But Mommy won't be there, will she? Because she's still dead."

A child's wisdom could bring great joy or break your heart. There wasn't a parenting book in the world that could prepare you for that. Ryan decided early on that honesty was best when it came to what happened to Lindsay. Her parents could weave fairy tales about how she was an angel in heaven, but Ryan didn't want to create a narrative that would give his son false hope.

"You're right. Mommy won't be there. But I'll be there, and Mrs. Lieu will be there, and your Aunt Stephanie. Maybe Grandma and Grandpa McKenzie will come for a visit, and grandma and grandpa Blackstone too."

"Grandpa McKenzie only wants to talk about football." Leo pouted while he fastened and unfastened the top button on Ryan's shirt.

"I think Grandpa McKenzie likes to share about his job with you."

"I don't want to play football or be a football coach."

"And you don't have to. You can be whatever you want to be when you grow up."

Leo wiggled out of his arms. Ryan put him down gently, and he went to play with his Legos.

Mrs. Lieu gestured for Ryan to follow her out to the hall.

"What did the doctor say?"

"The same as all the others: leukemia. He's going to have to start chemo right away."

The diminutive woman's face fell. After a few moments, she nodded. "Okay, then. I'm going to cancel my trip home."

"I can't ask you to do that. You've been looking forward to visiting your family in Vietnam for months."

"You aren't asking. I'm telling. You send me every six months. Missing one trip won't be a sacrifice. Besides—" She tilted her head, gazing up at him, her dark eyes beginning to brim with tears. "—you are my family too. You were there for me when I lost my beloved Danh nine years ago, and I'm going to be here for you now."

He'd argue, but once Mrs. Lieu made up her mind about something, she became a heavy stone that would not be moved without a significant amount of effort. It was a different kind of stubbornness than his sister's. Mrs. Lieu always listened, and her determination came with motherly love. Knowing she would be with them for the tough days ahead was a relief.

"Thank you, Su." He rarely used her first name. Calling her Mrs. Lieu seemed to fit. It might have seemed more formal, but it was always said with genuine affection.

She patted his cheek. "We'll get through this one day at a time. It's not going to be easy, Ryan, but I'll be here."

SLEEP ELUDED him again that night. Sleepless nights had become a constant after Leo's diagnosis. Ryan would need every moment of rest he could get to make it through the tough days ahead. Fear kept his eyes open. Staring at the ceiling, Ryan couldn't stop replaying the meeting with the doctor in his head. At the first signs of the sky lightening to a dull purple-blue, Ryan left his bed. It would be another rainy spring day in Seattle. The gray reflected his mood. He walked into his home office and sat down at his desk with a heavy sigh as he made preparations for what was to come. As weary and heavy as he felt now, Ryan wasn't prepared for the brutal days, weeks, and months ahead fighting to keep his son alive.

ELIANA WEST, the recipient of the 2022 Nancy Pearl Award for genre fiction, is committed to embracing diversity in her writing. That means she doesn't limit herself to a single genre. Instead, Eliana welcomes every story that comes her way with open arms. She aims to create characters that reflect the diversity of her community, with a range of social backgrounds, ethnicities, genders, and sexual orientations. Eliana loves to weave in historical elements whenever she can. She believes everyone deserves a happy ending.

From small towns to close-knit communities, Eliana West loves stories that bring people from different backgrounds together through the common language of unconditional love and acceptance. Eliana is a passionate advocate for diversity within the writing community. She is the founder of Writers for Diversity and teaches classes and workshops, encouraging writers to create diverse characters and worlds with an empathetic approach.

When Eliana isn't plotting her characters' happy endings, she can be found embarking on adventures with her husband, traversing winding country roads in their beloved vintage Volkswagen Westfalia, affectionately named Bianca. Whether it's traveling abroad or exploring locally, Eliana and her husband are always willing to get lost and see where the adventure takes them.

Eliana loves connecting with readers through her website: www.elianawest.com.

Follow me on BookBub

THE WAY Forward

BOOK ONE

Mockingbird Bridge Book One

The small town he couldn't wait to leave is calling him home....

Dax Ellis returns to Colton, Mississippi, a changed man. He traveled the world, earned a fortune, and made a lifetime of memories, but now he longs to put down roots. Time hasn't been kind to his hometown, and Dax wants to help—if only he can convince everyone he's not the same petulant boy he used to be. Especially the one woman who has every reason not to trust him.

Librarian Callie Colton cherished summers with her grandparents, in the town her ancestors helped build, in spite of the boy who called her names. Now that Colton is her home, life is quiet until Dax returns... and, along with him, threatening letters on her doorstep. He may still have the power to hurt her, but she's not the same scared little girl she used to be.

But as the danger escalates, Dax will have to face his past to find a way forward for the relationship they were cheated of once before.

THE WAY *Home*

ELIANA WEST

Mockingbird Bridge Book Two

A letter from the past will transform their future...

Taylor Colton always loved the crumbling plantation house passed down through his family for generations. Now he's bringing his popular renovation reality show to the small town of Colton, Mississippi, so he can bring the plantation house known as Halcyon back to life for the cameras.

After an ugly breakup, Josephine Martin needs a new start to heal her broken heart in peace. A hidden letter reveals a family secret that leads her to Colton to protect her family's history and honor a promise made before the Civil War… and to a house she didn't know was hers.

Suddenly, Josephine must decide if she's ready for the challenge of restoring a rundown mansion and its history, and Taylor's facing a challenge he can't charm away. Together, they must untangle a tragic history, a rocky relationship, and risk everything they love. Can they overcome the past to find their way home?

Scan the QR code below to order

THE WAY *Beyond*

ELIANA WEST

Mockingbird Bridge Book Three

When she finds out his secret, will he lose her for good?

Jacob Winters has a secret: he's come to Colton undercover as an FBI handler. He didn't plan to stay, but the small town has charmed him with a sense of community that he hasn't felt in a long time. And his attraction to the beautiful Mae Colton complicates things even more. Jacob doesn't do relationships—he won't risk making memories he might regret.

Mae Colton loves her little town of Colton, Mississippi, and doesn't want to leave. In fact, instead of moving on to bigger things—namely a political career in D.C.-like she'd planned, she wants to run for a second term as mayor of Colton. But not everyone in town supports this choice, including the commitment-phobic Jacob Winters.

Mae is ready to make their secret relationship official and go public, but that would break Jacob's one rule. When a threat against Mae's life forces him to admit the truth of his feelings, he has to race to save the woman he loves before it's too late.

Scan the QR code below to order

Four
Holly
Dates
ELIANA WEST

An Emerald Hearts Novel

Four dates
A chance to reconnect
A different way to embrace the magic of the holiday season

Soccer star Nick Anderson is new to Seattle. He's thrilled to see the shy girl he remembered from high school when he visits the local Children's Hospital. Unfortunately, his excitement is one sided. With the help of her friends, he's got four chances to show Holly another way to celebrate the holiday season.

Holly Williams had worked hard to become a pediatric nurse at Seattle Children's Hospital. The only problem is she hasn't taken the time to enjoy it. Now the popular guy she secretly crushed on in high school is asking her out not just for one date but for four.

As Holly and Nick get to know each other again, they each learn what the holidays are really all about.

Summer of Noelle

ELIANA WEST

An Emerald Hearts Novel

Star midfielder for the Seattle Emeralds, Hugh Donavan looks forward to his visits to Children's Hospital and spending time with the young patients. What he looks forward to the most is seeing one nurse who's captured his attention.

Noelle Williams is ready to open her heart again, but she isn't interested in dating a professional athlete after a disastrous marriage to one, no matter how kind and charming Hugh is.

With encouragement from friends and one special little patient to live her life to the fullest, Noelle agrees to one date with Hugh.

Will the magic of summer in Seattle lead to love?

Scan the QR code below to order